Relativity Returning Home
BOOK II

ARCHER A. GRANT

This is a work of fiction. Character names and descriptions are the product of the author's imagination. Any resemblance to actual persons, living or dead, is entirely coincidental.

Copyright © 2025 Archer A. Grant
All rights reserved. No part of this book may be reproduced in any form without permission from the author, except as permitted by U.S. copyright law. The author expressly prohibits anyone from using this work in any manner for purposes of training artificial intelligence technologies to generate text, including without limitation technologies that are capable of generating works in the same style or genre as this work.

Proofreading provided by the Hyper-Speller at
https://www.wordrefiner.com
Cover by Chris Era

ISBN: 979-8-9912908-3-8

DISCLAIMER

Because of my roles working for the United States Government and security clearances I hold; this manuscript is subject to a thorough security review by the Defense Office of Prepublication and Security Review. It has passed all reviews and any requested changes have been made.

I am required to add the following disclaimer: "The views expressed in this publication are those of the author and do not necessarily reflect the official policy or position of the Department of Defense or the U.S. government. The public release clearance of this publication by the Department of Defense does not imply Department of Defense endorsement or factual accuracy of the material."

DEDICATION

This book is once again dedicated to my amazing wife and children. Without them, this wouldn't be possible, or nearly as fun as it has been. In addition, this book is dedicated to the memory of both of my grandfathers, who either directly or indirectly have woven their legacy into these stories.
Grandpa Dave – 1933 ~ 2022
Grandpa Jim – 1934 ~ 2024

For a more in-depth look and visualizations of the characters, ships, and worlds, visit my website at:

www.archergrantbooks.com

For a glossary of terms, visit the website or jump to the end of the book. Be sure not to spoil the ending!

If you would like additional information about upcoming books, such as Relativity: Returning Home, and The Breaker Series, visit the website and join the mailing list. I'd love to go on this journey with you.

ACKNOWLEDGMENTS

I would first like to thank my wife again. This might sound like the last book but she played a much different role this go around. Not only did she support and encourage me, but she took the extra step of reading early drafts and providing important feedback. The last book she cheered me on from afar, this one she was right there with me. She talked to me about where I was at in different stages and what was going on with the characters. She helped to add another element to each of the characters and the story that I hope is reflected in this book.

My kids played another pivotal role in this book. There excitement at seeing the first book made them even more interested in this one. That excitement helped drive me to finish this one much quicker than I thought I could and certainly faster than the first one.

I would like to thank the professional team that provided my proofreading. The suggestions and improvements made a real impact on everything going forward and a much smoother read for you, the reader.

To the graphic designer, who, building off of our previous work, helped to design a cover that pairs well with this series. Thank you.

One more thank you to the reader. Whether it's one (just myself) or many, thank all of you. For anyone that is considering writing something themselves, the hardest part is starting. Please start.

FORWARD

I never had aspirations to really write a story growing up, and here I am on my second with many more planned. The first book in this series started off as a stand along, one-time deal. I had many ideas in my head but this one captured my attention. As I wrote the first book, everything that followed formed. At the start, the amount of effort and work it took to get that first book complete didn't afford me time to think about whether or not I wanted to do more books. As I finished up the first book, I looked back at the journey, and realized how much fun and fulfilling it was. From that point on I knew I had to get all the other stories out. This is just the beginning!

PROLOGUE

Maggie–Unknown

Captain Maggie 'Face' Lorrent felt herself slip in and out of consciousness. Was it an hour, a day, a week? Longer? She couldn't tell. The lights wherever she lay faded in and out. She wasn't sure if the lights were the ones fading, her eyes, or her mind. Not only did she not care, but she also didn't even know she should care. Time held no meaning, yet it was somehow the most important thing to her. If she could only remember why. She remained awake for only minutes at a time. The time in between, unmeasurable. Each time she woke up, she had only passing memories of the previous time. A fog passed between her and her thoughts.

From time to time, she caught glimpses of a strange yet familiar shape. Not human, but something she had seen before. She couldn't quite place it. The initial thought when she saw it didn't give her fear. She wasn't sure why. Not only could she not place the creature, but she also couldn't place herself. The thought that she had seen no humans for this same amount of time still hadn't dawned on her. Her brain had not yet fully processed her predicament.

Each time she awoke, her concentration scattered. She wasn't sure why she couldn't focus, even on her name. What was her name? Fear and panic took over as she struggled to move, but couldn't. Her hands and legs were locked in place with some type of strap. The same material stretched across her forehead, pinning it back. Something pressed against her forehead. Sleep replaced her panicked struggle.

And then she felt fully awake. As if startled out of a bad dream. But only this time, she awoke from a bad dream into a nightmare. Her surroundings seemed different. The cold hard bed, no longer beneath her, was replaced by the cold hard floor in a small room. Fear replaced the physical and mental restraints. She no longer felt like she awoke in a hospital, or worse, a mental hospital on a lockdown protocol. She recognized the small room as a jail cell. Not exactly, but close enough.

Her clothes were gone, but she didn't shiver. Small beads of sweat formed along her body. Her lips and mouth were dry, much like the air in the room. Her skin felt rough and cracked. She noticed what looked like a floating platform in one corner. The cloth identified it as a bed, but no one had placed her on it. At first glance, even she couldn't fit on it. It had pristine white sheets partially covered by a dark brown blanket. The blanket looked rough to the touch, like some type of wool. Maggie quickly went over to it and wrapped herself up, confirming the roughness, but it also had a slight earthy scent to it. She didn't cover herself for warmth, but because of a natural human instinct. Maggie assumed there were eyes on her, either through a camera or a two-way mirror. She didn't want to give whoever, or whatever, the satisfaction of seeing her like that.

Then she remembered that in all of her bouts of

conciseness, she never saw a human. All she remembered seeing looked like the Razuuds she thought she fought with. But why had they captured her? She only had questions at this point. She assumed now she was awake and alert, someone would come to see her.

Maggie waited and waited, but nothing happened. She stayed awake as long as she could, but finally sleep overtook her. When she awoke, she spotted a cup against one wall opposite her bed. The cup contained what looked like a green and brown sludge, but it didn't smell too terrible. She thought it must be some sort of food, but erring on the side of caution, she did nothing with it.

As time crept on, her eyelids became heavy once again and she slipped off to sleep. No dreams came.

She woke up to a low grumble sound. Startled, she looked around the room. The sound came once again, but this time, now awake and alert, she realized it came from her stomach. She looked back at the door; the cup remained. Or maybe they, whoever they were, replaced it. Either way, a cup of the sludge sat there on the floor.

This time, she weighed her options. She could either die of poison or die of hunger. Either way, she would die. She would rather die on a full stomach. Time to get it over with and find out the answer, Maggie thought to herself. She deliberately walked to the cup, lifted it to her lips, and took several small drinks. Maggie initially tried to avoid the taste, but it turned out to taste better than it smelled. She drank a little more but waited a while before having anything else, just in case it made her sick. Once she thought she would be fine, she returned and finished the cup. She thought it strange to have to use her basic wilderness survival training in a situation like this. When in a space battle, would she ever need to learn how to forage for food and test new foods to determine if they are edible or not? It turns out that it has paid off now.

This process went on for several more cycles. She could only assume that they were days, and since she had nothing else to go off of, she began counting them as such. From her count, she had been in this cell for at least fifteen days, not counting the time span she had limited recollection of. But it could have been more. There was no way to keep track. No actual point either, other than to try to keep some semblance of sanity.

As time passed, she noticed more and more. There were no windows in the cube-shaped room. She didn't expect actual windows, but even the brig on her ship had vid screens that showed some type of view. Prisoners would go crazy otherwise. It felt like a similar size to the jail cells she had been to in the past. She could only assume this was their version. The walls, floor and ceiling were some type of light-gray rough ceramic. She brushed her hands across the abrasive concrete-like edges. Instead of roughing up her skin, though, it felt smooth and weirdly glassy. A single light in the center of the room looked like a glowing section, flush in the ceiling. She could almost reach it because of the abnormally low ceilings. But what good would that do her?

She assumed the slits in the floor near a corner were some type of drain. Now that she saw them, it felt as though the floor slanted in that direction. Maggie didn't see a vent of any type, but knew there had to be one somewhere. She felt a slight breeze disturb the tangled hair dangling from her head. The thought of her hair and how gross she felt made her cringe. Decidedly, there were more important things to worry about right now. She could also hear sounds. Not voices, but loud banging, almost like an active construction site.

She let her mind wander for a moment. Taking in the unfamiliar sights and sounds of her prison overwhelmed her, and she needed to think of something else. Anything outside of this room. What could that noise be? She focused on it more. When she visualized the sounds, she naturally felt like it would be the noise if someone had been beating on and cutting up her fighter or whatever remained of it.

That realization hit her, and it hit hard. A flash back, or more, a rush of emotions, the same emotions she now realized that she felt when these creatures were trying to pull her from her ship. That's the last thing she remembered. She got knocked out right after seeing her ship being torn open for them to extract her. And now she felt just like she did then. Fear and panic mixed with rage. She sat on her bed and brought her knees to her chest. She remained like this for what felt like the rest of the day.

With heavy eyes, she just about dozed off when she thought she heard someone calling her name. That woke her up. She hadn't heard her own name since being here. She listened for it again. *"Maggie."* Almost like a whisper. Distant, yet very near. She tried to focus. *"Maggie."* The voice said again, a little louder this time. Unmistakable. Someone called her name. She still got the feeling of it being both far away and close.

"Maggie!" She could no longer remain silent.

"Who's there? What do you want?" Maggie responded, trying to match the volume and tone.

"It's no time to be afraid. You're stronger than this, or at least I thought you were." The voice returned, ignoring her questions.

"Where am I?" Maggie returned with a slight trembling voice, trying to get some information from whoever spoke.

"Have you gone soft on me? People used to fear you." The harsh tone of the voice seemed vaguely familiar but distant.

She couldn't quite make out the source. Maggie looked around but couldn't see any speakers or anything that could make that sound.

"Where are you?" Maggie asked, hoping one last time for an actual answer.

Maggie heard a low chuckle that slowly morphed into an all-out laugh. *"Hahaha. You mean you don't know? Come on now, you know."*

"I don't know." Maggie responded after a long pause. She had to think hard about it, but couldn't tell where the voice came from. She certainly wouldn't know where in the ship the source could be hiding. "I really have no idea." She asked one more time. This time she got an answer, but not one she expected.

"Very well then. I'm right where you are, Maggie. And if you don't start doing something, you're going to get both of us killed." The voice responded.

Maggie realized right then that the voice had a familiar tone. Like hearing herself in a recording. The voice did not resonate from an outside source. It came from within. She recognized the voice as her own. Except it wasn't hers, not exactly. Something more resolute, more sinister resonated in the tone. She had heard of prisoners in isolation talking to themselves, developing alternate personalities. That wasn't possible for her, was it? Did whoever have her plant something in her head? That had to be it. She ignored it.

The days continued to go by. A small door at the floor would open and a plastic pole with little gripper arms, like the ones someone would use to pick up trash, would push a fresh cup of food in and retrieve the old one. She became accustomed to the timing, to the pattern. She knew when food was about to be delivered out of instinct now.

The voice never gave up. It grew louder and louder. *"You can't continue to ignore me!"*

CHAPTER 1

Ramat–Space Force Guard Ship Catalyst–Razuud Orbit

General Ramat 'Trap' D'Pol sat next to Mark DeCanus peering across the polished metal table to Leader Danuibi. This was the first in-person or alien-to-human conversation between two different species from two different worlds in the history of ever. As far as they knew, anyway. Unless, of course, the Razuuds and the Tartins had met before. But their history was still entirely unknown to Ramat and the humans. The meeting they were conducting right now felt unfathomable. Almost too difficult to comprehend. That is probably why they all sat there in stunned silence. It would have turned into an awkward silence if it weren't for Ramat. He leaned forward and spoke into a tabletop microphone. A small gray box with speakers on each side sat in the middle of the table. Ramat's team didn't have time to jazz it up. Wires protruded from the makeshift box connecting to the exposed speaker. He preferred function over form, anyway.

Ramat introduced himself. "Leader, I am General Ramat D'Pol, this is my friend," Ramat said, unable to come up with a word more translatable than friend and pointed toward Mark. The speaker translated the words into something that Leader Danuibi could hopefully understand. The delay in Ramat speaking and the translator box translating distracted Ramat as he spoke, but he managed to block it out to finish his sentence.

Mark correctly saw that as his cue to introduce himself, snapping himself out of the stunned silence he must have been experiencing. "Yes, I am Mark DeCanus, I am the speaker for the leaders of our home planet, we call Earth. It is a pleasure to meet you."

If facial expressions held any resemblance to humans, Leader Danuibi's face showed that some words probably didn't translate well, but he received the overall message. They were introducing themselves. Ramat shuddered at the thought of these talks continuing on in this way. They wouldn't be able to get anywhere.

Leader Danuibi spoke in a very soft tone. At first, nothing came out of the speakers. A tech had showed Ramat how to make some minor adjustments to volume and also sensitivity. Ramat leaned forward and looked at the device. He found a small gray dial resembling one from a guitar amplifier. A red hand-drawn arrow circled around the dial with a plus sign at the end. There were two dials. He guessed which one was the sensitivity, reached out and turned the dial a quarter of a turn in the positive direction. There was no indication that what he did impacted the device's function. He lifted his hands up off the table in a mini shrug and gestured for Leader Danuibi to try again.

After a pause, it appeared that Leader Danuibi understood what had happened and spoke again. As if he understood why it didn't work the first time, he also spoke a little louder, though it sounded labored and not a natural speaking volume.

Shortly afterward, the translator spoke, "I am Leader Danuibi, Leader of Razuud and all cities and dwellings underneath."

At this point, Mark and General Drobbi, the ship's captain, had already been discussing the events leading up to this point in time. The language barrier still made it difficult to get into as much detail as they would have liked, but what they could gather demonstrated that there were indeed vast similarities between the two species.

Ramat noticed another figure lurking in the shadowy corner. Ramat had his own security in the room with him and Mark as well, and figured it would be the same for Leader Danuibi.

Leader Danuibi must have noticed Ramat looking around. Leader Danuibi followed his gaze and landed on the figure.

"Ah. Please meet Artur Tibambae, one of my oldest friends. We grew up together. Though our paths diverged, they have brought us back together again," Leader Danuibi said.

The figure took a cautious half step forward, nodded slightly, then returned to the shadow.

That's when Ramat realized he didn't wear a uniform. A dark tunic covered his body with a hood draped over his face. Ramat could hardly make out any facial details and definitely could not pick him out of a crowd. Maybe he wasn't ship security, but private security?

Ramat nodded back, then turned his attention back to the leader, saying nothing in response.

Mark had debriefed Ramat on the previous discussions since he couldn't take part in them himself. Coordinating ship repairs, rescue missions, and return plans occupied Ramat's time. When Mark finally explained what led the human fleet here, he felt glad, or maybe fortunate. The Razuud had every right to attack them when the human fleet showed up at their home world. But through a few strokes of luck and good timing, and powerful leaders, they could establish an alternative path for their two species. One that gave Ramat hope. It gave them all hope.

While the meetings between Mark and General Drobbi discussed the past, the face-to-face meeting now between Ramat, Mark, General Drobbi, and Leader Danuibi was to discuss the future. The very near future. Ramat needed to understand what the relationship between these two species was going to be like. There were many answers to that question. Most of which led to more questions, but at least it would get the conversation going. Do they continue living only acknowledging that each other exists but otherwise have no more interaction? Or do they collaborate extensively, exploiting their resources?

Given the dynamics of how the two species came together, there were those that sought war on both sides. Because of the war-torn nature of the Razuuds though, Ramat hoped that those who welcomed help and peace outnumbered those that did not. Or at least a path to peace. Ramat knew that the humans showing up did not automatically stop whatever conflict they had going on with this other species.

"I would like to personally apologize for the events that transpired between our two species," Ramat began, completely throwing out his warning of not apologizing, because it showed that they accepted responsibility. The humans would much rather see it is an accident, which it partially was. But Ramat didn't believe in all of that. He felt sorry that it happened, so he said so. "Although the way we were brought together is regrettable, the chance of our meeting can be positive." Ramat's focus up to this point was tactical. He thought about how he could best keep his mission safe and position the team to be successful going forward, all while doing what was right.

Leader Danuibi paused, probably to make sure he understood the translator, but also to think about his response. Ramat would have done the same thing and sensed a bit of remorse mixed with, what was it? Respect. That could have been his own inner thoughts speaking, but he knew something deep was going on in Leader Danuibi's mind. Ramat felt as if Leader Danuibi would have said something similar. The translator's words confirmed Ramat's thoughts. "The Razuuds feel similar to your species, mister D, D, D…" He struggled with Ramat's last name.

"Please, call me Ramat, that's what my friends call me," Ramat said as a gesture to the leader. He thought about throwing in his callsign of Trap too but decided not to confuse him any further.

"Very well, Ramat." That appeared to be much easier for him to say. Leader Danuibi continued, "I would not be fully truthful if I said we all felt that way. There are some who regret my decision to come to your aid. But, there is much our species' can do to work together. I will not let those few destroy that potential." There was a pause, and Ramat nodded in agreement. This was apparently a universal gesture for them as well. What looked like a smile came across Leader Danuibi's face, as he must have realized the same thing. With the smile, Ramat also smiled, as another realization of similarities emerged. They both laughed. The laughs were very different, but both understood what they were. After another minute, Leader Danuibi continued, "It is my understanding that your people are low on essential supplies and plan to return to your world?"

"That is correct, Leader. Our people have been talking and we're not certain we can get all of the nutrients we need from what you can offer," Ramat told a partial truth. Each species' nutrients would support the other, mostly, but at the cost of morale. Ramat heard many rumors through his command staff, and also confirmed with his own tests that they thought their food tasted terrible. He couldn't put enough hot sauce or spice on it to make it better. They couldn't even get the ingredients to make more when they ran out. They didn't exist on Razuud. Ramat had the cooks and science team check. That would be a note for the next trip, bring lots of seasonings.

"Yes, that is also what I have been told," Leader Danuibi responded. "I would like to make a bold request, I would like to send a team back to your planet with you, if that is agreeable?"

"It certainly is, Leader. I would like to return the gesture as well, with your approval?" Ramat responded immediately. He didn't need to think about it. He and Mark had expected this and were ready for it. They were leaving the following day and had prepared a small team and food to sustain them for a several-month stay.

"That would be most welcome," Leader Danuibi said. Glancing for the first time at General Drobbi, who looked visibly uncomfortable as far as Ramat could tell.

"Great, we'll start getting everything arranged," Ramat said, briefly pausing. "Do you have any information on the ships that attacked us? If they'll return? Should we expect them when we return?"

This time General Drobbi spoke. "I understand your concern, Ramat," General Drobbi said hesitantly, almost coming off as a question. "They took major losses when you arrived. We suspect they don't' have many ships in reserve, but likely will not return in force for some time. If they believe you are still here, it may be even longer so they can build their forces even more. We do not expect them to return for quite some time. We may see scouts, but nothing we can't easily handle."

"Thank you for that information. It does make us feel better about leaving your world." While Ramat was concerned about leaving the new allies with the threat of an enemy looming, he was more concerned about leaving a team with them with a chance they might never return to Earth. Ramat sat quietly, contemplating his options.

MARK

Mark DeCanus sat in the small, impromptu meeting room set up in the airlock of the SFH Catalyst. Both sides decided the airlock served as the best middle ground. Concerns about health and safety, and a warranted distrust between the two species, made the decision on where to meet a delicate one. This central location provided the best mix, allowing for a quick retreat to the safety of their own ships should the situation call for it. There were no decorations on the walls or anything that could distinguish it from a human room or an alien room. The room did not adequately represent the importance of this meeting, but sometimes these things couldn't be helped. The dim lights and soft glow of bioluminescent panels casting an ethereal light set a somber but optimistic tone. While this was the first face-to-face meeting between Mark or Ramat and Leader Danuibi, countless hours of communication had preceded with a smaller Razuud team.

General Ramat 'Trap' D'Pol and General Drobbi, a key figure in the Razuud military, remained seated. Ramat sat next to Mark, while General Drobbi sat across from Ramat. Leader

Danuibi sat across from Mark. Having finished discussing and assessing potential threats, and coordinating defensive strategies against a possible Tartin attack, Ramat and General Drobbi yielded the conversation to Mark, as planned.

Leader Danuibi's eyes met Mark's. His weary expression told Mark he'd been at war for far too long. Mark felt the anticipation building up to this moment. Even though he didn't expect to have a role when this expedition went underway, his whole career had built up to this point.

"Leader Danuibi," Mark began, inclining his head as a show of respect. "thank you for making time for this meeting. I understand how busy you must be."

Danuibi nodded. His expression came off as thoughtful, although Mark couldn't be certain. "Indeed, Mark De, De, Can" He struggled with his last name. Mark took a similar approach as Ramat had.

He cut in, chancing an interruption. "Mark is fine, just Mark."

"Very well, Mark. The affairs of a planet are never-ending. But this meeting is of utmost importance."

"Absolutely," Mark agreed. "We've laid the groundwork for our diplomatic plan, and now it's time to finalize the key points. Our first priority is determining the delegations that will stay here on Razuud and those that will return to Earth. We need to ensure that both our peoples are prepared for the next steps."

Danuibi steepled his furry fingers considering Mark's words, revealing aged, worn claws. "Our delegation to Earth must be well-prepared. The people as you say, must be those who can foster understanding and cooperation. We cannot afford any missteps."

"Agreed," Mark said. "And we need to make sure our delegation is safe from any potential Tartin attacks. Based on what General Drobbi has told us, it appears the Tartins could still be a significant threat, even if a more distant one."

General Drobbi interjected, his deep voice coming out of the translator resonated through the room. "The Tartin threat is indeed substantial, even if it is unknown. Our ships are needed here to defend Razuud. We cannot spare any for an escort to Earth at this time."

Ramat nodded in agreement. "And on Earth, we must be cautious about sending alien ships into human space. I'm sure the recent conflicts have made people wary. We need to ensure that any approach is carefully coordinated to avoid panic." Ramat looked at General Drobbi, trying not to appear accusatory.

Mark could sense the tension building between Ramat and General Drobbi. After all, it was General Drobbi who led the scouting mission that turned into an attack on Earth. Likewise, it was Ramat who led the counteroffensive that caused General Drobbi's retreat, destroying almost all of his ships in the process and killing their crew. Many now knew the attacks were a mistake and misunderstanding, but the animosity still lingered.

Mark turned back to Danuibi. "Given these constraints, we propose a smaller delegation initially that can stay on this battleship, with a more significant contingent to follow once we understand each other better."

Danuibi considered this, then nodded. "A wise approach. We must build trust gradually. What topics do you believe are of greatest importance?"

Mark pulled out his tablet, scrolling through the notes he'd compiled. "First, we need to address the security concerns. Both our planets must feel secure from external threats. For that, we need to understand more about the Tartins."

Leader Danuibi sat silent, seemingly taking in every word.

With no verbal response, Mark continued. "Second, we need to focus on scientific and technological exchanges. There's so much we can learn from each other." Mark attempted to hold back the excitement in his voice. He glanced at Ramat, who had a similar look. Ramat had spoken to him about some of the things he felt the Razuuds were more advanced than them, namely faster-than-light travel. They both were eager to learn more about anything they could.

This time Leader Danuibi stirred in his seat and cleared his throat with a dry, scratchy tone. "Technology exchange would be most exciting," Leader Danuibi said. General Drobbi crossed his arms. Although their body language differed sharply, Mark sensed they agreed. They wanted to share, likely the nukes being their prime trade target, but they also wanted to know they could trust each other better. Mark understood this dynamic very well. He could recall many times in Earth's history when two parties allied together and shared equipment and technology in one war, then turned around and used that new technology against each other in the next conflict.

"We can take that process slowly," Mark responded reassuringly. "And finally, we should discuss cultural exchange programs to foster mutual understanding. We believe a better understanding of your own culture and your relationship with the Tartins would provide much-needed context to the war you are currently waging with them."

Danuibi's eyes lit up at the mention of cultural exchange. "Yes, understanding each other's cultures will be crucial. Fear often stems from the unknown. By sharing our histories, our arts, and our traditions, we can build tunnels of trust."

Mark and Ramat looked at each other quizzically. He remembered that they didn't have large bodies of water, and didn't live much on the surface to necessitate bridges. So it could be that they don't know what bridges are. But they had a similar saying. They built tunnels to connect places, just like humans built bridges.

The conversation flowed naturally from there, with Danuibi and Mark exchanging ideas and refining their plans. Ramat and General Drobbi offered their insights, thoroughly integrating military and security considerations into the diplomatic strategy.

As the meeting drew to a close, Mark felt a sense of accomplishment. They had navigated the complex issues with mutual respect and a shared vision for the future. It went almost too well. He would ponder why he felt that way later, not wanting those thoughts to interfere with the current discussion.

"We have much to prepare," Leader Danuibi said, standing. "But I am confident we are on the right path. Together, we will build a future of cooperation and peace. I have one more request."

Both Ramat and Mark looked at each other silently, then back at Leader Danuibi.

"In addition to continuing negations in a more formal setting, we would like to celebrate our victory over the Tartins with your team. We propose a party, with your original crew, or as much of them as you can manage to return."

They looked back at each other. This was a potentiality they did not account for. They figured they would send a very small delegation to return the Razuud diplomats and pick up the humans before returning to Earth. Sending another fleet back could be challenging.

"Thank you, Leader Danuibi. That is a most gracious offer that we will have to discuss back at Earth." Mark said, shaking the leader's hand. "We are committed to this partnership and will do everything in our power to ensure its success."

"We will see you again shortly," Ramat said. There was a

hint of assurance in his voice. As if Ramat knew the only answer was for everyone to return.

Mark nodded and addressed them formally by name, "Leader Danuibi, General Drobbi, safe travels."

With last farewells exchanged, Mark and Ramat left the meeting room toward the SFG Catalyst, and General Drobbi and Leader Danuibi left toward theirs. They had a lot of work ahead of them, but for the first time in weeks, Mark felt a sense of optimism. The next phase of their journey was about to begin. He, for one, was ready to get back to his old office.

CHAPTER 2

Riley–Space Force Guard Ship Catalyst–Razuud Orbit

Riley sat in his bed, exhausted from another day of patrol and cleanup. Fighter pilots were pulling double duty. He flew escort for a shift, then supplemented the transport pilots to assist them with cleanup efforts for a shift. Opting to get a meal to go from the mess hall and eating it on his way to his bunk gave him a little extra time to sleep. He slept for whatever time he had left on that shift before starting it all over again. This had been ongoing for the last few weeks following the battle. He completed his last shift of transport duty as General Ramat 'Trap' D'Pol, the acting fleet commander, called an all clear for some much-needed downtime. Each of the units was given a reprieve before they departed the next day. Until now, there had been no time to think, no time to feel. Grief and exhaustion were visible on every face in the squadron, but they pushed through it. They had to. There wasn't any other option.

Any pause for rest during the cleanup effort only forestalled what all knew would eventually be needed. More time back home. It wasn't enough to reconcile what they had all been through. They all had lost someone, for the Luckys, that someone was Maggie. There was no trace of her, and with all the wreckage being mostly vaporized particles, it was impossible to find out what specific ship anything came from. They searched until they were compelled to stop, yet many refused to give up. Riley was one of those people. They were closer than many other flight members. He thought he owed it to her or her family to find out exactly what had happened.

There would be more time for that later, though. Now it was time to rejuvenate. The squadron threw a party in their heritage room and living quarters aboard the carrier, and they invited the other squadrons. They all needed to let loose. There was a tiny amount of alcohol, but not enough to get in trouble. At least, that was the idea. Riley thought Trap underestimated the ingenuity of a troop to find trouble, though. He also knew Ramat and assumed he kept a few safeguards on hand just in case.

With the Luckys room ready, people were showing up. Lieutenant Colonel 'Wisp' Broadway, recently promoted from Major after moving up to take Ramat's place as the Luckys commander, enacted the no-shop-talk policy. This would help ensure that nobody talked about the missions they were on which inevitably brought back memories of those lost. There would be time for that later. Or it would lead to a competition to see who got the most kills or had the best flying skills. As he explained it to Riley, shop talk quickly turned to either a bummer of an event or a competition to see who's the best, both of which he didn't want. Unfortunately, the competition part was likely unavoidable. Another unavoidable truth about elite people is they will turn everything into a competition.

Little did Wisp know; Riley had worked with other squadrons to set up a little event around the ship. That event was set to kick off first, and Riley looked forward to the distraction. Since the carrier, SFG Catalyst, sat motionless, and since it wasn't the Kennedy with the spin gravity, everyone was weightless orbiting the Razuud home world.

"Sir?" Riley said as he floated up to Wisp.

"What is it Riley? Shouldn't you be hanging out with the other squadrons, I thought you spent enough time with us?" Wisp responded with a smirk.

"Well, Sir, it's actually about that." Wisp's eyebrows raised in curiosity. "You see, in an effort to, um, bond with the other squadrons, we set up a relay race around the ship."

"Of course you did," Wisp said dismissively, a hint of surprise and concern in his voice.

"Yeah, well, we need you to call the start of the race. Hope you don't mind." Riley didn't give Wisp a chance to respond or shut it down. Riley knew he would if he wanted, but if he moved quickly, he may catch him off guard and get the race started before Wisp could stop it. Not even Wisp would kill the fun for that many people.

"All right everybody, gather around, the race is about to begin!" Riley shouted to the occupants in the room and loud enough for those who had overflowed into the hallway.

So began the inaugural Catalyst relay race. It pitted each flight within the different squadrons against the other. Since it was the Luckys room that the race began and ended, they had to win or suffer the humiliation until the next year. Something Riley wasn't about to let happen.

With the room somewhat quiet now and their focus on Riley, he explained the rules. "The relay race begins and ends at the door. You must start inside the door and the next person cannot leave until both team members are fully inside the room. Follow the routes marked in the halls." The race would take the teams through nearly the entire ship. "Two members from the full team race together at a time. The teams are capped at five members. With three laps, that means someone will have to go twice. Pick your team and your order wisely. We are about to begin." Riley was that someone for the Luckys. His youth gave him that advantage in a couple of ways. First, he was in the best shape of his life. Second, because he was one of the youngest members, command always chose for escort and courier duties, so he also knew the ship best.

The teams broke up into their own sections of the room and in the hall to decide the team pair and orders. The volume of the room continued to rise as the teams competed to hear and in anticipation of the excitement. Finally, something fun they could do, something that was different, but also something that didn't have their life on the line.

Riley and Captain James 'P' Parrant lined up by the main door, along with two other teams.

P was the first to start the trash talk, "Riley, we have to move ahead of them fast, their stench is enough to suffocate someone."

"Hey, I thought we were racing men, when'd the girls show up?" Someone from the other flight asked.

P reached down to his chest and mocked, licking himself. "Oh, you like that chum?" P was getting the best of them, and they wisely shut up and waited for the countdown.

Wisp showed a proud yet embarrassed dad face as he floated to block the entrance of the door.

Wisp called out. "Teams, are you ready?" He glanced at each team, lingering a little longer on P and Riley. "On my mark." Another brief pause. "GO!" Wisp shouted, and the teams went flying through the door. Pushing through and crashing into each other. Riley glimpsed the look on Wisp's face and thought it looked an awful lot like he regretted his decision to allow this race. Too late now, he had to let it play out.

RELATIVITY: RETURNING HOME

The teams disappeared around the corner in a flash, showing their skill in microgravity. A few short minutes later, the first team came screaming around the corner, with P and Riley in close pursuit. Once leg one of the race was completed, the Luckys were in close second place, entering the door and nearly touching the lead flight.

P and Riley momentarily, and maybe purposefully, blocked the door, not allowing the next team to exit the room until they had entered. Pushing through into the room, this let the Luckys next team leave at almost the same time as the first-place team. That helped even up the race even more. The next leg ended with the Luckys, led by Lieutenant Michael 'X' Xavier, in front but by a slim margin. X pushed his way through, blood smeared on his elbows, a perfect pair for the blood on the face and shirt of the person behind him. Riley noticed X's left eye looked a little swollen. As expected, this race turned from just fun to serious fun. An emphasis on the serious.

Riley and Lieutenant Jade 'Star' Starilla took the last leg. Everyone screamed and cheered. Even those not in the race panted from exertion. They all did their best to help their team, even if they weren't racing.

Riley and Star took off and squeezed through the door as best they could, each flight trying to slow the other down, with the net effect being they were exactly where they were before, just a little more tired. As Riley and Star made their way around the ship, the other team pushed Star into the wall, slowing her down. As they separated around a corner, a door quickly opened and someone pulled Riley in. Riley barely led Star, and they were way ahead of the next flight. Riley knew nobody saw what had just happened.

Confusion turned to realization as he understood it was an attempt to sabotage the race. One of the other flights was trying to cheat. Riley and the others who set up the game had tried to account for that and strategically placed some members around the path to help prevent it. This must be a blind spot, or the spotters were in on it too. It wouldn't take long before someone noticed. He also wasn't going to wait long to find out.

As that thought entered his mind, he heard banging on doors and shouting in the halls. It was hard to make out, but he knew they were looking for him. He could hear what sounded like a struggle in the hall, likely an attempt to hold back the other racers from passing as Riley's team searched for him.

At that moment, in a strange twist in his mind, with everything going on around him, Riley had a revelation about something he hadn't thought about in a long time. Something entirely unrelated, but on his mind. What if someone took Maggie, rather than her being vaporized?

In a loud burst, he let out a yell. Part joy and hope, and part desperation. It unintentionally doubled as a shout for his teammates. The door he struggled behind quickly opened, with P leading the way. Riley escaped in the confusion, Star grabbed him as they made their way back into the hall. As he suspected, his flight mates prevented the other teams from advancing. Riley and Star shot around the last corner and finished the race in first place.

Riley had a difficult time enjoying the victory and the rest of the night. His mind raced to work through the thoughts he had. The evening blurred into the background as if set to autopilot, his mind preoccupied. The Luckys celebrated. They laughed. They sang. They mourned.

It was an auspicious time, a time of remembrance, and a sad time. But it was also a time of joy and relief for many. They won and they were still alive and going home. Riley took part passively, his heart not in it. He refused to mourn Maggie's loss if she wasn't truly dead. He couldn't let himself do that, not yet.

After the party came to a close, everyone reluctantly made their way back to their own quarters, all seeming to have enjoyed themselves. Mission accomplished on that front. Hopefully, it wouldn't set in until the morning that they were going to be in the grind until they made it all the way back home. Everything that they had worked so hard to forget about that night would soon come back. Hopefully now there would be some more room for the steam to build up again. For some of them, it would flood back. For others, a slow trickle, gnawing at them steadily until their mind couldn't take it anymore, usually when they least expected it. They were leaving tomorrow, but danger still lurked nearby. The return trip wasn't an entirely short one. And home wasn't a guarantee.

Riley had enough time to follow through with his gut feeling, though.

Riley waited until the next morning at roll call to talk with Wisp. Following the status check for each flight, making sure they all were in one piece following the events of the previous night, Riley went up to Wisp. At first, Riley spoke a normal volume.

As Riley floated up to Wisp, he started talking. "I think I have an idea of what happened to Maggie. She might still be alive." He said matter-of-factly to Wisp.

Before Riley could continue, Wisp held up his hand in a gentle stopping motion. "Hold on there, Riley. We just got done letting her go, don't be too loud about this. Are you sure?"

After a pause, Riley doubted himself. In a way, he felt he had to be right, but he was also only thinking with his emotions. He knew that he wanted to be right. "I'm not sure yet, it was an idea I had last night."

"Listen Riley, I know we all want her to be alive still, but sometimes in battle, that just can't happen. Holding on to hope is ok, but only for a little. We all eventually need to move on. I can't have the entire squadron spun up on this." Wisp paused, contemplating the situation. Hope fluttered across Riley's face, but faded quickly as Wisp spoke.

Riley kicked himself. He hadn't thought it through enough or explained his case. Riley wasn't sure what to do in this situation. "Is that all, Riley?" Wisp continued, indicating that they both needed to get to work.

"Yes, sir," Riley said, letting his disappointment show in his voice. He felt Ramat would have been more supportive. True, Wisp just took over command, but he had one of the best mentors. At least Wisp didn't turn him down completely. Rather than stopping him, he merely suggested he pursue it quietly. At least, that's how Riley took it.

Riley turned and left the briefing room to get ready for his flight. He had been used to a little more support for his ideas in the past. This would be one lesson he might have to get used to. When bosses change, so does their approach to many things. He would not let this stop him from looking into it, but it didn't have the same sense of urgency anymore. He put it in the back of his mind and got ready for his sortie. After all, if he thought of this idea, someone else surely already did too and found nothing to back it up.

With the thought behind him, he climbed into his AIMS and hit the start sequence. Putting on all of his gear and strapping into his seat, he performed the last checks. With all green indicators, he messaged the ground control team that he and his ship were ready to depart. A moment later, the ship moved on the magnetic rails then pushed and released him toward the opening. He took the controls when his ship floated outside the SFG Catalyst and started his patrol.

His initial pass around the fleet just ensured everything was all clear. That no ships threatened their travel. That no debris blocked their route. They were heading back home, and after a long-fought battle of uncertainty, Riley was ready to go home. He needed comfort. Comfort from his family, from Jenn, free of the dangers of this place.

After he completed his route, he looked on. High atop his perch he could see the entire fleet. He called out to Star. "Would you look at that view?" He said in awe.

"That is something else," Star responded.

The view of ships, smaller than their trip out here, but nonetheless impressive, grouped up in a loose cluster. To the unfamiliar, there was no order. To Riley, the formation was in optimal transition formation. There were no overlaps of flight paths. The spread and distance allowed for the best chance of survival of the other ships if one encountered issues. When they reentered normal speeds, they were set up the best to face a threat in a combat-effective posture.

Riley looked at his countdown. The fleet would transition before his ship, then they would catch up and rendezvous mid-flight at faster-than-light speeds.

The countdown approached zero. He saw the light gates detaching from the larger ships, spreading out to begin their sequence. With the darkness of space as a backdrop, the flash as all the ships disappeared stood out in stark contrast. All that remained was the dust of the spent light gates. Riley and Star followed suit and flashed into the darkness.

CHAPTER 3

Mark–Space Force Shuttle–Earth Orbit

Mark DeCanus sat strapped into his landing shuttle. Command ordered most of the crew to remain on their respective ships and receive a debriefing on the previous mission while in orbit before returning to Earth. Mission control blocked or strictly monitored and regulated all mission communications. The Northern Hemisphere leaders wanted strict control of the information that filtered out, for as long as they could, anyway. Mark knew they would subject him to this, but he had other business to attend to first. He also knew that after the crew's orbital debrief, they would likely be confined to an Earth base before being granted any kind of leave.

Mark checked the signal on his personal device. His eyes lit up after seeing the signal bars come in for the first time. Communication monitoring stopped when he left the sphere of influence of the ship and was closer to Earth. Tapping into the shuttle's data link, he began scrolling through the news networks to get a sense of what the people thought of what just happened.

Before he left, if they were successful, he expected there to be parades and celebrations. He refused to contemplate the public reaction and news reports if they failed. But they didn't fail. The success, however, wasn't final or clear. What Ramat and the expedition accomplished could end up being far greater than Mark expected. That wasn't even in the realm of an expected outcome. The problem being, without the right framing, the expedition appeared to be a slaughter with the humans returning with their tails between their legs.

That confusion was evident in the news feeds. Some hosts were saying how disastrous the expedition turned out to be. Others were calling it the end of humanity because we sided with the enemy. Some refused to display any information about it at all. Mark would have snickered if it wasn't for the seriousness of the situation. Earth did not have all the information. Mark's urgent return to Earth was partly aimed to clear the path to revealing the truth. The primary reason was more personal. Rictor needed to pay. Mark knew the truth about Rictor would never get out, so he made it his mission to make sure he couldn't do anything like that again.

Mark couldn't wait for the shuttle to touch down on the ground. He peeked through the small porthole and could distinguish individual houses and streetlights on the ground. Shortly after he felt wheels touch down on the ground. Mark felt the impact more abruptly than on past flights. He had to remind himself that this wasn't an airliner, but a military shuttle, landing from space. He didn't know what the touchdown should feel like. Mark felt the shuttle make a couple of turns as it taxied through the landing area. Before the brakes set, he started unbuckling and heading for the exit.

His foot hit the ground before the back ramp fully opened. He hit what stride he could at his age and made his way to the waiting car.

His shuttle was one of the first to take the crews from the space fleet back to Earth, and he had a bone to pick with Rictor. He knew that if he waited with the crew, officials would direct him to a full debrief, which would take too long. The flight crew hooking the shuttle up and inspecting it yelled at him as he stepped off and ran toward his awaiting car. He couldn't make out their words, but figured they were trying to tell him he needed to debrief, or it wasn't safe yet. Either way, Mark didn't care. He needed to find Rictor before he disappeared, if he hadn't already.

Mark couldn't do much to prepare for his return to punish Rictor. He knew that if he submitted any type of inquiry or filed formal charges, Rictor would catch wind and disappear. To make sure things were prepared for his arrival, Mark compiled all the information that documented the journey, specifically focusing on the parts that Rictor screwed up intentionally. He held this on his personal device and guarded it closely. When he made it back to the office and got eyes on Rictor, he would petition to have Rictor arrested in the most unceremonious way possible. Mark knew that even with all of his safeguards, Rictor could still figure out what was going on.

The car sped through the bustling city, weaving through traffic with a sense of urgency that mirrored Mark's own. The driver, a young woman named Carla, glanced at him in the rearview mirror.

"Sir, what's the rush?" she asked, her voice tinged with curiosity and concern.

"No time to explain, Carla. Just get me to the Capitol building as fast as you can," Mark replied, his tone not allowing any arguments.

When they arrived at the Capitol, Mark didn't wait for the car to come to a complete stop before he jumped out and tried sprinting toward the entrance. He ignored the pain in his legs, holding the cane at the halfway point so it didn't drag while he ran. He climbed the steps to the building entrance, catching the sunset in the reflection of the glass door as he approached. The pristine and stunning colors countering the current mood.

He pushed through the door and made his way right to Rictor's office door. Putting all caution on hold, he felt the unrestraining need to confront Rictor himself. His plan of calling the authorities to go and arrest Rictor could wait.

His now heavy and tired footsteps pounded up to Rictor's office door. Breathing heavily, he didn't delay and flung open the door, only to find it empty. Mark's heart sank. He huffed and puffed, part out of exhaustion, part out of frustration.

As he pondered his next move, he heard shuffling and papers falling around the corner. He rushed to investigate and glimpsed what could only be Rictor going out a back door he had never noticed. He rushed to the door and caught the trail of his jacket around a turn. Mark realized then that Rictor headed toward the exit tunnel. A secret tunnel system below the building that was used in cases of emergency. If he made it there, it would be a simple escape. Mark ran, reminding himself of his time in the army. Being tired was expected. He got into a groove and pushed himself, blocking out all the urges in his mind that said he couldn't go any farther. Panting as the long distance finally caught up to him, he made it to the next door and swung it open.

"Rictor!" Mark's voice echoed down the corridor.

Rictor glanced back, a fleeting look of surprise crossing his face before he broke into a run. Mark chased after him, his military-trained muscles straining with the effort, but his age and the wear of years slowed him down. By the time he reached the exit, Rictor was already slipping into a waiting car. He saw Rictor's smug smile through the window as the car sped off, leaving a trail of dust and frustration in its wake.

Mark pulled out his phone and called security. "This is Marc DeCanus! Lock down all exits from the Capitol immediately. Rictor is attempting to flee."

But it was too late. The local security couldn't act fast enough, and by the time they called in the local police, Rictor would be long gone. Mark stood there, hands on his knees, catching his breath.

"Oh well," he muttered to himself. "that's what I get for being old and lazy."

But he knew that wasn't true. He was getting older, yes, but not old. His body, battered by a tough life in the military, just wasn't what it should be for someone his age. He had to think hard about how old he was, and the effort made his head hurt a little more.

The ultimate purpose was served, however. He had got that liar and cheat out of the government, or so he hoped. Mark now headed to his own office, where he waited for the call that it was his turn to debrief. He did not look forward to what would certainly be a long, painful ordeal. The long walk back allowed him to ponder many things while his body recovered from the recent effort.

Once he returned to his office, he didn't have to wait long for a call. Word got out that he skipped the line and didn't get debriefed. Other staff came to look for him. Mark wasn't hiding, although he felt like curling up in a ball under his desk.

The debriefs lasted much longer and turned out to be more painful than he had imagined. Mark didn't realize he could repeat the same story so many times in so much detail. He lost count of the times and days he spent there. Finally allowed to go back to base quarters, Mark walked back to his small room but still couldn't speak with anyone. Because command personnel were still classifying information, nothing could be shared. Everyone kept a tight seal on this, but Mark wasn't sure what the point was. This information would get out at some point, all of it. As these things went, it was only a matter of time.

He finally thought about something other than the mission. But the mission pulled his mind back in, in a way. He kept going back to when Rictor slipped through his fingers. Mark put some serious thought into it now. He knew that the only place Rictor would be safe from the NHN authority would be in SHUR territory.

While it wasn't difficult to get to SHUR territory, they all knew him and would likely be skeptical of his intentions. Even with an active arrest warrant, the SHUR were too smart for that. They would secretly believe it was a trick and likely not trust him. That was good for Mark because even if Rictor was a complete enemy of the NHN, he still wasn't to be trusted.

The SHUR would likely lead him to believe that they trusted him, maybe even give him some responsibilities, an office possibly. Mark smiled, thinking Rictor would readily fall for it, knowing they would use him. They were all being played. Rictor had access to every damaging piece of information the NHN had. What worried Mark the most, what kept him up and made his mind return to that moment so many times, was what Rictor knew that everyone else didn't know. What secrets did Rictor hold?

Mark compiled a list of potential next moves Rictor could make, people he would try to talk to and convince, and who he knew could get more information. At first Mark thought Rictor was trying to sabotage the mission to get General Sites elevated to a more senior position, eventually the presidency, making Rictor his right-hand man. But Mark started to think that wasn't his ultimate aim after all. Rictor knew about this world they just visited somehow. Much more than anyone else.

What could he possibly want with this information?

The key to figuring that out would be to get a set of NHN eyes on him and track his moves as soon as possible. They couldn't arrest him in SHUR territory, but they could follow him with some NHN loyalists that still lived there. He may not make a move for a while, but he was bound to make one, eventually. Someone like that doesn't just give up. Even if there is no winning involved, he always had to end up being right, even if right was wrong to everyone else and in direct conflict with reality.

Mark sat at his desk in the barracks, the low hum of the military city outside his window a constant reminder of the world he was trying to protect. Eager to get to his own home and bed following this lockdown, he felt grateful for the secure terminal in his room. He activated the terminal and began drafting a message to his most trusted contacts within the NHN.

"Priority One: Subject - Rictor. Immediate Surveillance Required."

As he typed, his mind raced with possibilities. The SHUR wouldn't trust Rictor completely, but they might use him to their advantage. Mark needed to ensure that the NHN was a step ahead. He leaned back, rubbing his temples, and thought about the upcoming days. It was going to be a game of cat and mouse, and he had to be prepared for every twist and turn.

The communicator on his desk buzzed, pulling him out of his thoughts. He answered, recognizing the voice of his assistant, Emily Watkins.

"Mark, your presence is required in the central briefing room. They have new intel on Rictor's movements."

That was quick he thought to himself.

"I'll be there in five minutes," Mark replied, a renewed sense of urgency in his voice.

As he headed out the door, he couldn't help but feel a

flicker of hope. The chase was far from over, but he was ready. This time, he wouldn't let Rictor slip through his fingers.

CHAPTER 4

Jennifer–Northern Hemisphere Nations Central Command–Earth

Jenn walked with a confidence to her dad's office, General John Stanza, that she didn't quite feel. She knew her dad had been aware of her relationship with Riley. Even before she told him about it. He said he was supportive but also worried for her. He tried to explain the emotional swings being with someone in his line of work could bring. Jenn knew that's why he wanted to see her. He knew Riley was coming Earthside today, and he wanted to warn her. At least, that's what she thought.

When she entered, he seemed ready for her. An unusual feeling. She usually caught him off guard. He mostly sat typing away. Or she saved him from a phone call with someone he desperately wanted to be over. This time was different. This time, he waited. No typing. No phone call. No paperwork. She tensed up, prepared for a long lecture from Dad, which didn't happen often. His soft, fatherly tone surprised her. Not the stern one that meant trouble came next. She wasn't a little girl anymore, but this brought her back to a time when she could sit on his lap as he explained the stars to her.

He had a somber expression on his face, a bit of sadness. He seemed genuinely concerned. She thought something bad might have happened, but since she had just spoken to Riley, it couldn't have been about him, could it? She couldn't place his concern. Her? Riley? This mission? He must have had a lot on his mind. But he seemed fully focused on this conversation.

"Jenn, darling, how are you doing?" Her dad began. They both knew it was a rhetorical and impossible question to answer.

"I'm good, excited that the expedition is back," Jenn replied, betraying her current body language. She knew her dad could see the excitement that Riley had returned home and she would get to see him soon. "But also worried." Finally, giving in to her emotions. She shifted to a more comfortable stance, almost instantly feeling safe in this office with her father. A small tear formed in each eye.

Her dad didn't hesitate. He rushed over to her and hugged her. Her face nestled against the hard ribbons and medals of his formal uniform. It didn't bother her. She could feel him patting her on her head, as he had many times before as a young girl after she scraped her knee or got teased in elementary school.

He moved his hands to her shoulders and pulled back just a little so they could speak face-to-face.

He started talking in a soft, nurturing tone. Something her mom had been very good at. "You know, he's been through a lot. I like the kid. He has a promising future in the forces as a pilot. That's a demanding job. The mental struggle that both of you go through will be something that nobody else will understand except those who have done it. Like your mom and I."

"I know Dad," That's all Jenn could think to say to all of

that. She couldn't tell if he was discouraging her or supporting her. Maybe both. The mention of her mom brought up a lot of emotions. Before she died, Jenn remembered her dad being gone a lot. He was a pilot too, but before all of this space stuff. He fought in wars in the air, on Earth. He was gone a lot but they could at least talk. But she knew he understood what she might be going through.

"I know," She repeated, letting him know that she had put some thought into it. She rarely let emotions take full control. This was a situation that needed to be thought through.

"I don't want to discourage you. It seems like you really like him. All I will offer is this; he has been through a lot. A lot of it he won't be able to share with you because it will be classified. Most of the other stuff he won't be able to share with you because he doesn't know how. He lost some good friends, Jenn." He paused and looked her in the eyes. "Just like it's hard for other people to understand what you're going through in your times apart, you'll have a hard time understanding him, and why or what he isn't sharing with you. You weren't there and he'll have a hard time talking to anyone about it, even you. Give him some grace, I guess is all I'm trying to say."

Jenn was not expecting that at all. And that was something she needed to hear. She felt a physical weight lift off of her. The worry and confusion remained, but she felt more at peace with the situation. "Thanks Dad. It's just hard, but I am excited to see him. Do you know when he will be back down?" She responded. She hadn't been looking forward to this talk because of the many ways it went in her head. It turned out to be positive instead of the million negative ways she dreamed up.

He released her shoulders and walked back around his desk. After looking down at his computer, he said, "I had his unit come down a little bit ago. He should be done with his debriefings early. It might be a little before you can see him though. I'll see what I can do to get him to the front of the line."

Jenn lit up. "Thanks Dad." She smiled. She didn't want him to do her any favors, but in this circumstance, she welcomed it.

RILEY

Riley's heart pounded with excitement and anticipation. The cool morning air reminded him of the morning he first met Jenn. He was perspiring more than he should have been considering the weather. He wanted nothing to betray his nervousness. His clouded thoughts also prevented him from being fully present. His mind couldn't focus. The many feelings pulled him in infinite directions. It was uncomfortable, and he didn't know how to handle it.

His parents taught him to be open with his emotions, but he didn't have the vocabulary to express what he felt now. Or the awareness. He only had experience telling his mom he was sad because his pet died, or angry because he lost a game. How could he talk to anyone about the things he was feeling now, especially when he didn't even know what they were? Love and war were new concepts to him, much more personal than reading them on a page. Nothing could have prepared him for what he felt now.

He hadn't seen Jenn since well before he left the surface on his way out on the expedition, possibly never to return. So much had happened since then, both to him and between them. They had shared a lot of deep conversations and laughs and he thought they got to a serious place in their relationship. Even if most of it at this point had been virtual. He thought she felt the same, but sometimes feelings like that can get confused in text or delayed video messages. He recalled many love stories from old Earth's history, stories of soldiers writing to their girlfriends or new acquaintances. They would keep in touch through paper mail, shipped by boats on the water or airplanes across the vast ocean.

In person, he felt completely different. Riley knew that in his last mission, they could have easily counted him among the dead. He lost friends. He lost Maggie; she was like a sister. Riley knew he loved his squadron, but how could he explain that loss to Jenn? Although he presumed her dead, the strange hope of her being alive, combined with his conviction that he alone could prove it, burdened him. All the way back down to Earth, the first thing he wanted to do was see Jenn, to hold her.

The mandatory debriefings denied him that. The different counsels wanted firsthand reports of what occurred. They also wanted to make it clear what he could, and more importantly, could not say.

Riley got a pleasant surprise when command released him from the debriefs much sooner than everyone else. Holding a duffle bag in his left hand, he walked outside the compound. The compound felt deserted. Being the first to be released had its perks, but the silence didn't help his nerves. When the gate opened, the streets were empty, save for one car pulled up on the side of the road in the vast parking lot.

Riley saw Jenn leaning up against her car, looking down at her phone. He paused and forced a cough. He wanted to run to her, but also didn't want to startle her. She glanced up and saw him standing there, a big smile on both of their faces. Riley didn't have to run to her. She quickly slid her phone into her back pocket and ran to him, jumping into his arms with her legs quickly wrapping around his waist. This forced Riley to drop his bag and hold her up. For a moment, they both forgot everything that was going on. Everything that had happened. The pain, the distance, the new alien species and the other new alien species. Everything. It was all confusing. But this moment, right now, was perfect and clear.

After a few moments of embrace, Jenn dropped. A long moment passed as they gazed into each other's eyes, taking in all they had missed. They both realized at the same time that neither had even said a word yet. They both tried to speak, but didn't know what to say. Instead, they both stayed silent and just stared. That was all they needed. A small smile crept on Riley's face before he went in for a kiss. The moment improved. Although Riley wished it could have lasted longer, they released each other again. He backed away, holding onto her hands, taking in the most beautiful thing he'd seen since before he left. Riley eventually released one of her hands and gestured toward the car. "Shall we?"

With a slight nod from Jenn, they both walked to the car and got in.

Once seated in the front of the sleek, silver, four-door sedan, Jenn broke the silence. "Are you hungry?"

"I'm dying for some real Earth food," Riley responded happily as Jenn drove away. "I'm tired of the ship food. It's not terrible but gets old after a while." He caught himself then. Riley wanted to avoid constantly bringing up his last mission and comparing things to it. He thought that might make her feel excluded in a way. So he changed the subject. "How's everything back here? How's your dad doing?"

Jenn paused, a look of concern, or understanding, on her face. Riley couldn't quite place it. Then he realized he asked how her dad was doing. They'd never met yet. Hell, she hardly talked about her dad to him.

"Good. He's glad you're all back. You know, you should meet him." She said, regretting it right as she said it.

They hadn't discussed that at all yet. "Uh…" Riley stammered, surprised by the question, or more like a statement.

"Sorry, I don't know what I was thinking, that's probably too much right now. Don't worry about it. Let's just get some dinner," Jenn cut him off.

He knew she didn't intend to put him on the spot, but feared she would misunderstand his nervous verbal pause.

"No, that would be nice. It just caught me by surprise is all. We hadn't talked about anything like that before. Although I'm not sure why not. It is a little more complicated too because, you know, he's like my bosses, bosses, bosses, boss. Just a little intimidating is all." Riley tried to save it and maybe did a little. He was excited. Why didn't he bring it up first? His mom would love to meet her. She already knew about her and was asking non-stop when they could meet. His dad knew to leave that to his mom.

"Since when has a general intimidated you? Remember Sites, you shoved him in an airlock and ignored a direct order from him," Jenn responded, recalling a time early after the first alien attack. Riley pushed General Sites into the ship, pretending not to hear his orders to get the ship moving, to go back out and rescue more survivors.

"True, but this one's important," Riley said back, with real meaning in his voice. "And I got some payback on Sites."

"Oh really?" Jenn responded, urging him to continue the story.

Riley realized he may have overstepped on what he could say. Jenn must have understood his struggle and saved him.

"Don't worry about it, I know what he did. And I'll figure out what you did and you won't even have to tell me," Jenn said with a smile.

The rest of the evening went about like this. Riley felt a little awkward and clumsy. He felt uneasy with his words and actions. Something was off. He knew she felt it too. He didn't want to think it was something between them, but rather the situation. They would get over it. That's what Riley said to himself, hoping it was reality.

Riley noticed Jenn acted a little strange, though. He couldn't quite place it. Like she was distancing herself from him. Was the reunion not what she was expecting? Was she looking at a different person now, someone she couldn't be with? As they worked their way through small talk, he felt more and more uneasy about their relationship, despite what she said to the contrary. To add to it, he couldn't get his mind off of Maggie. Riley felt he abandoned her. He could have done more to avoid taking the hit that knocked his optical sensors out when he lost track of her. He could have searched better when his ship went back online instead of continuing with the attack. Her disappearance and likely death weighed heavily on his conscience.

He then realized that, if his theory was correct and her ship had been captured, she was a prisoner, assuming she was still alive. She might wish she were dead at this moment, being tortured or worse. He couldn't get the images out of his mind.

"I think it's time I head back, I'm exhausted from all of the interviews and need to catch up on some sleep." The mood suddenly changed. He wasn't lying, but he also wasn't telling the whole truth.

"OK, Riley," Jenn said. A noticeable look of sadness across her face. Riley hoped she didn't think it was about her. But he couldn't bring himself to tell her the real thoughts going through his mind.

They rode in silence the rest of the way back to the compound. She pulled up right where she picked him up earlier. They both got out for one last embrace.

Without thinking, Riley said, "I love you, Jenn."

It was Jenn's turn to be caught off guard. He could tell that she had not expected him to say that. Why would she, considering the car ride they just had? After a brief pause, Riley thought more than enough time for her to respond if she was going to. He continued, "I just want you to know." And then he turned and walked away.

CHAPTER 5

Mark—World Council Delegation Room—Earth

Mark still reeled from just missing Rictor, but he never had time to fully process it. He had been committed to very in-depth debriefings, much more intense than most of the other crew, save for Ramat. Now, leaning back in his chair in his office, he focused on the past. He peered up into the ceiling, trying to find some spot or blemish he hadn't noticed before. It looked as if the ceiling tiles had been through hell and the last few building renovations had missed them. Nevertheless, he had memorized every stain and crack there had been. No new blemishes stood out. He found solace in the consistent chaos. It helped him clear his mind and focus.

That's when he realized. Nothing had changed; he still had his primary goal. Only now, he had less of a roadblock with Rictor out of the way. He leaned forward with a renewed focus.

His next task had to be getting the council to agree to send another delegation out. During negotiations, they had decided it would be best if alien ships didn't appear in the space near

Earth for a little while. And if any did, Earth would assume hostile intent. But the lack of alien ships also meant that the pressure wasn't necessarily on humans to get anything done quickly. Out of sight, out of mind, Mark thought.

Mark did what he did best, planned. He cataloged who would be the most difficult to persuade and who would be on his side. He sent messages and texts to those he needed support from and asked for in-person meetings from those who needed extra convincing. To allow another convoy, he needed approval. But he wanted everyone on board. Not just the majority, everyone.

This was a monumental occasion. Everyone needed to see that. They needed to see that it was in all of their best interests. That's what he told himself anyway, but it didn't stop him from trying. That's what made him so good and likable. He cared, even for those who disagreed with him, except for Rictor. Mark couldn't care less about that slime ball. He still felt like he hadn't heard the last of him, but that didn't slow him down now. When, or if, he had time, he could think about what Rictor might be up to. Right now, there were more important things to do.

Over the next several days he planned, he spoke to other delegates, and he planned some more. He never rested. Not because he didn't want to, although he felt he should. But because he didn't think he could. That the fate of the world wouldn't allow it. If this moment passed and the momentum stalled or reversed, humans would lose their future and Mark would lose his dream. No. Now was the time to push past it all.

In the council chamber, Mark stood before the gathered representatives, his demeanor calm but commanding. He needed to lay out the plan. At this point, he had no clue where everyone stood. He figured it was a coin toss if he got what he wanted. He needed to convince the other council members and sway the political opinion. He thought that to be his last resort to get the fleet approved.

Not only did he need to get the fleet approved, he also needed the original leadership crew to go, himself included. Emphasizing the need for continuity and the benefits of having experienced personnel lead the delegation was the angle he went for.

Councilman Harlan Bespaw was the first to voice his doubts. "Mark, sending the same crew back out is a risk. If something goes wrong, we'll lose our most experienced people. Not to mention being left defenseless at home from the SHUR. You know that last expedition really took a toll on our forces. The timeframe you're talking about we could only send a handful of ships. The rest need to be repaired. And even more of those are still under construction. Are you sure this can't wait?"

Mark expected Harlan to voice concern, he was a strong supporter of Rictor and still carried some of his misgivings. Glad that Harlan didn't make the connection that the SHUR would be the least of their worries if the expedition failed, he let it go. Instead, Mark nodded, anticipating this argument. "I understand your concern, Councilman Harlan. However, the rapport we've built with Leader Danuibi and the trust we've established are invaluable. New faces might jeopardize that. We need to show continuity and strength. To your other points. I only ask for a few ships. This is only a peace delegation, but we should still be prepared. And no, we cannot wait. We must strike while the iron is hot, so to speak. If we delay, the chances of needing that full-strength fleet will continue to go up until we can't afford the bill. No doubt the Tartins are regrouping and planning their next move."

"And why is this our problem?" Councilman Harlan

interjected. Possibly finally getting to his real point, Mark figured.

"It's our problem because the Razuud are now our allies. We don't abandon our friends. While that is a noble reason, we'll also get some great technology and knowledge out of this. Information we will not get on our own any other way."

Councilwoman Jena Durago added her support. "Mark is right. This is a critical juncture. Our relations with the aliens are delicate. We need familiar faces to continue the dialogue. And trust me, we need to continue this dialogue. If we won't, the SHUR would love to jump in."

"I suppose that would help speed up technology exchange. The sooner we can get our hands on their faster-than-light capability, the better," Harlan seceded. Mark probably looked as shocked as he felt at the change of position from a Rictor wannabe.

After hours of debate, the council finally voted. The provision passed with overwhelming support, to Mark's delight. He felt a sense of relief wash over him.

The mission was back on track and mostly everyone supported it. Exactly what Mark wanted. Exactly what Earth needed. What he could get everyone to agree with was that keeping as much of the original crew as possible was best for relations. That meant that Ramat would lead the fleet again. But this time, from the beginning instead of the deadbeat General Sites. There would be a similar contingent of support, fighter, and heavy battleships. A smaller force than he wanted, but with so many damaged ships, it was a larger percentage of the remaining force than he was expecting to get.

The new arrangement for this mission would be a whole delegation of diplomats and negotiators. Mark would maintain the lead. But he would have help. Mark wasn't quite sure yet if that would be a good or a bad thing. He and Ramat had built a great rapport with Leader Danuibi, and everyone thought that would be an advantage. Leader Danuibi likely thought the same thing, but it gave everyone a little more confidence in the situation.

These were uncharted times, so they needed to lead with those who had the most experience, and right now it was those with the only experience. It was a bit of a gamble because if something were to go wrong, all of that experience would be gone. The risk had to be worth taking. With the plans set, now the time came to wait for the ships to be ready and the crew to be refreshed. It could be another long trip.

Mark returned to his office to finalize the preparations. He sat down, staring at the blinking cursor on his screen, and began drafting the mission orders that he would send to Ramat and General Stanza. He paused, taking a moment to reflect on the enormity of the task ahead. This mission wasn't just about diplomacy; it was about ensuring the future safety and prosperity of Earth.

Mark's buzzing phone interrupted his thoughts. He glanced at the name that popped up. His friend's name flashed across the small screen.

"Ramat, how are things going with ship preparations?" Mark asked, getting right to the point. They dispensed with small talk some time ago because they had been in close contact regarding preparations, they knew the stress each other had been put under.

"Mark, the ships are nearly ready. We should be able to launch within the week."

"Excellent, Ramat." Mark replied. "I'd like to brief the crew with you. This mission is too important to leave anything to chance."

Ramat's voice softened. "They'd like that. Most of them got to know and trust you over the last mission." That comment got Mark to think of not just the last mission, but all the time he'd known Ramat. They'd had some close calls together. Some might even say closer than what they just went through. Ramat appeared to be thinking the same thing when he continued talking. "We've been through a lot together."

"We sure have, Ramat," Mark said, continuing to use the first name of his good friend, despite being a general now. "We've got the best team, and we know what's at stake."

"Everyone knows what's at stake. That's why everyone is all in," Ramat responded.

As he ended the call, Mark felt hope stirring inside of him. His eyes lit up, just a little, and his posture firmed in his seat. He got the NHN to buy off on this next mission, but having the SHUR on board would make it much better. He hadn't addressed that part yet with the other council members. Mark skillfully changed the topic every time it came up during meetings. He hadn't wanted that discussion to bog down the NHN support. Now he couldn't put those talks off anymore.

The SHUR hadn't been very involved in the first trip. Because the SHUR didn't lose any ships or people then. They said they didn't think it had been their fight to take part in. Now that news of everything that had occurred trickled in, they wanted in on the action, and potential technological gains.

When Mark embarked on the first mission, the two sides had established a short-term treaty to hopefully ensure cooperation while the main NHN contingent fought an alien species. It had been a risky maneuver but ultimately paid off.

Mark didn't want the inclusion of the SHUR to undermine the efforts made up to this point. For this next step, Mark believed that including the SHUR reduced the chances of them attempting a transfer of power while the NHN fleet was deployed. He also strongly believed the two sides would be better together, contrary to many of the NHN members' feelings. They didn't need ships, although it would help, the SHUR ships could not be outfitted with light gates fast enough and they did not possess that technology on their own. This stood as the first proper step toward unifying the two hemispheres, something he had been looking forward to for quite some time.

After all was said and done, the SHUR sent a contingent of delegates. They would represent the SHUR even though they had no standing with the Razuud. As far as the Razuud were concerned, there was no NHN or SHUR, it was one world, just like Razuud. Mark wanted to keep it that way as long as he could. He knew one person at the SHUR could help him do that. He met her long ago and had intermittent contact with her. It also helped that she was the chosen leader of the SHUR. Shani Chuma. If he knew one thing, she also wanted peace between the two but she distrusted the NHN. Mark hoped he could be a conduit for change because she trusted him. Positive change.

CHAPTER 6

Riley–North American Mid-West–Earth

Riley had been enjoying his time off. Sure, he wanted to see Jenn, but he knew he would have time to do that later. He may not get another chance to see his parents and grandpa. His parents were rarely home at the same time but they were again in this case. Just as fortunately as they were before he shipped out the first time.

Riley's dad had sent him to the small corner store in the quant town to pick up a few items for lunch. Riley would be returning to the compound later that afternoon but wanted one last meal together. After stopping at the store, he drove the all-too-familiar roads back to his house. The last time he drove this route he remembered feeling on top of the world. He just graduated from college, commissioned in the Northern Hemisphere Space Force to become a fighter pilot. He threw caution into the wind then, taking autopilot off and driving the car himself. He was invincible.

Now, with the knowledge of all he had gone through and how at-risk Earth really was, he couldn't be so positive. He also no longer felt invincible. He had nearly died and lost friends in the process. Now, when he drove these roads he was reminded of a simpler time, a time he could never get back, only remember. The closeness of the car around him, the oncoming traffic, the smells, they all reminded him of something else now. No longer childhood memories, those were replaced with an uneasy fear. Not something he was scared of, but something he needed to face, and would face without hesitation. Even though he wished he didn't have to.

Pulling up to the driveway the pleasant sight of his grandpa on the porch sitting next to his dad stood out. This brought him back to the present, although it still felt different. He couldn't explain it. Not to himself or to anyone else. Riley forced a smile on his face and stepped out of the car. They both looked at him with this knowing look that Riley couldn't escape.

Then it dawned on him, he wouldn't need to explain it, they all knew what he felt and thought. They all felt it before. That simple notion helped him relax and feel all around better about his situation. He wasn't alone.

Walking up to the house he heard his phone chime. Knowing that his unit was on high alert, he had his message volume turned up to make sure he didn't miss anything. When he checked the message, Jenn's name popped up. He clicked on it and read, *'Are you free tonight? I want to talk.'* Riley thought for a moment. He should be free. He had to be back to the compound so he could meet her. He just wouldn't be able to leave.

His most recent notice that put them on high alert had everyone returning to the base by 1630 to be prepped to leave within the next several days. High alert usually meant that nobody could leave the base and needed to be prepared to depart within thirty minutes of any notice. He couldn't tell her that because it was sensitive information. But he could tell her he can meet but not leave. He figured that after a couple of days they would lift it and they could go back to a more normal routine. Command had been running these drills non-stop it felt like. After this next drill, he'd get to spend more time with Jenn during his off time.

Riley typed his reply. *I'll be back to the compound in a few hours. Should be free tonight but can't leave. I can meet you at the gate?'* He planned to be at the compound just before the report time so he could spend as much time with his family as he could. He and Jenn thought there would be more time to see each other before he left again so they didn't push to meet after that first date when he returned.

She responded. *'I'll see you at 5:30?'*

'See you then.' Is all he could say back. He wanted to meet with her now. Something about the message felt off. Like this wasn't going to be a great conversation. He tried not to let dread overshadow the next couple hours with his family before he had to make the trip back to base.

Riley walked up the porch and greeted his dad and grandpa. "Hey pops, they had those mini baked apple pies you like," Riley said as he fished one from a bag and tossed it to his grandpa. A smile came over both of their faces. "Don't let it spoil lunch," Riley added.

Just then, another message came in. For some reason he felt the ring and the beep more prominently than before. He reached into his pocket to fish out the phone and looked at who it was from. It was a fleet number. From his short experience, that wasn't a good thing. He hesitantly opened the message. *'All fleet personnel must RTB immediately. Fleet departure is imminent.'* "Oh crap," Riley muttered out loud. What could have happened? The thoughts must have been clear as day on Riley's face.

"What's wrong, son?" Riley's dad asked.

"Oh nothing. We're getting recalled now. Can I get a ride to the station?" Riley responded.

"Sure son, let me grab my jacket."

When he went into the house, Riley's grandpa spoke. "Now that you've been through it. Now that you've lost someone. You know what we carry. Your mom, dad, me." Grandpa Riley paused for a thoughtful moment. Clearly considering his next words. "We wouldn't wish this upon you, Riley. But this is your calling and we couldn't stop you as much as we wanted to. The harder we tried the more entranced you became. It only gets tougher from here, dealing with everything. What you do with that knowledge is what matters. What really matters. Make your time count."

"Thanks grandpa," Riley said back, feeling at a loss for words. "I'm going to go grab my bag," Riley said, then went into the house. He heard his dad and mom exchange some words but couldn't quite make them out. He went to the hallway where his bags sat ready with his mom and dad talking. "He can't know right now." Is all Riley could make out. Then the conversation stopped. His dad looked up and spotted Riley. His dad kissed his mom then headed to the door, passing by Riley with no jacket. Riley thought that was strange and figured the conversation was why his dad needed to go into the house.

"I'll meet you at the car," His dad said moving past him through the hall.

His mother stood over his bags.

"Off to save the world again, are we?" His mother asked.

"You know me, mom. I'll be careful," Riley responded, giving her a hug and a kiss on the cheek.

"Nobody in the family has ever been accused of being careful. Reckless, yes, but not careful. Just come home to us safe."

"I will mom."

"And bring that girl of yours with you next time, will ya? I'm dying to meet her," His mom replied.

Riley didn't know if they were still a thing but couldn't bring himself to tell her that right now. Nor did he have the time.

"I promise," Is all Riley could think to say. Riley turned and walked toward the front door. He pushed the door open, bag in hand.

His dad had already started the car. Riley made his way down the porch and along the sidewalk. He walked to the passenger side of the car, stepped inside, and put his bag in the back seat. His dad selected the route and it began backing out of the driveway.

"Watch out for the neighbor's cat," Riley said.

His dad smiled and continued to back out, pulling onto the road and heading toward the interstate toward the base.

Riley pulled out his phone and clicked on Jenn's contact. He pushed the call button. Putting the phone to his ear and listened to the ringing. She didn't answer. He tried again. Still no answer. This time he left a message. "Hey Jenn, I know we're supposed to meet tonight but I just got recalled, we're leaving now. I'll try calling again later." He ended the message and typed out a similar message in a text. He hit send and waited a moment for a response.

His phone chirped while he waited. Another notification, this time from Major Broadway, his squadron commander. It was a squadron-wide text. *'We're being recalled. Report directly to the shuttle landing pad. We're headed back to The Spin. We leave as soon as the entire squadron has arrived.'*

He took a second to process that. Why did they need to leave so soon? Something must have happened. Riley guessed he would figure it out soon enough. He opened Jenn's contact again and sent another text. '*Another change of plans. I'm heading to The Spin right away. Sorry we didn't get to meet up. Can we talk when I get back?*' He was hoping the answer would be yes and not something like don't bother. He waited for a response, still having received nothing from the first message. When nothing came after a moment, not even a notification that she read it, he put his phone away and turned the radio up.

The rest of the drive went by in relative silence. Riley wanted to ask his dad what he and his mom were talking about in the hall when he wasn't around but decided against it. They said that he couldn't know right now. Which to Riley meant that he could know at some point in the future. He figured that when that point came around, he would know then. Until then, no need to worry about it.

Riley's dad pulled up to the main gate curb. Coming to a stop, Riley reached to the back and grabbed his bag. Pulling it to the front seat he grabbed the door handle and opened the door. He stepped out and closed the door behind him, leaning over to look back through the lowered window.

"Take care dad. I'll let you know when I'm home," Riley said.

"You too, son," He responded, then hesitated. "We're proud of you Riley. Your mom and I. We just want you to know that."

"I know dad. Talk soon," Riley said, then walked up to the guard. He showed his identification and the guard waved him through. Riley didn't have a long walk to his barracks to grab the rest of his flight gear. The hustled pace of those around him got Riley's adrenaline pumping. He quickened his pace, getting to a jog before he made it to his barracks. He changed and headed to the shuttle pad. At a run, he found the shuttle waiting, ready to go. Riley had been the last to arrive.

"Feel free to take all the time you need, Riley," Captain 'P' Parrent said with a crooked smile on his face.

"Always the jokester, P." Riley found a seat on the side of the shuttle next to Jade 'Star' Starilla. He secured his bag under his seat and then strapped himself in. The shuttle was uncharacteristically quiet for some reason. He looked around and spotted nervous faces.

"Why the sour mood?" Riley said, hoping to get some intel on what he missed or what they were doing.

"Don't know yet. I think everyone's mad about their plans being canceled. There's a rumor we're headed back to Rutaun soon," Star said. She was the only one that didn't look upset or concerned, or both.

"Back, already?"

Star just shrugged and went back to her tablet.

Riley took another look around, then shut his eyes. He didn't know when the next time he would get quality sleep would be.

CHAPTER 7

Jennifer–Northern Hemisphere Nations Central Command–Earth

Unlike the last meeting with her dad where he requested her, Jenn intended this meeting to be a drop-in, much like all the others. In the past, though, she knew his schedule and made sure it was a time she could walk right in. The opportunity, or realization rather, that she needed to go on this next mission came to her mind so abruptly and at the last minute that she didn't have time to waste. She needed to get approvals and convince the right people of the importance of her presence. Jenn wasn't at her dad's office to convince him though; she didn't need his approval. She wanted his support, personally, as her daddy, not as a general in the NHN Space Force. Although he could probably get her kicked off if she didn't play her cards right.

She approached his office; the large dark red wooden door was closed in front of her. The security light shone red above his door, indicating he was in a classified meeting. Jenn glanced over at the receptionist who had been on the phone and just noticed her.

"Oh, hi Jenn. He's in a meeting right now, should be finishing up in just a minute," The receptionist said covering the end of the phone up so the listener on the other side didn't hear her talking to Jenn. She promptly went back to the phone conversation.

Jenn knew that just a minute could be just a minute or fifteen. She sat on the soft cushioned chair outside his door. As she sat, she pondered everything that had gone on and would go on with Riley. When she first spoke to her dad about Riley, she was unsure how that conversation would go. He made her feel better about the situation, but now she didn't know how to go about giving him his space. She felt like her first attempt of giving him space when she picked him up at the compound, and that night at dinner, had come off more as pushing him away. This worried her and she didn't know how to tell Riley. That night ended with Riley being too exhausted, or frustrated, to do anything after dinner and Jenn feeling defeated. Why didn't she respond to him? He said he loved her. And she could say nothing. All of it confused her. Jenn wasn't sure how to bring up this next bit of news to Riley. Especially with how everything just went.

Her attention turned to this next conversation with her dad. It made her nervous for an entirely different reason. It wasn't about the matters of love and war, but about her career. At least, that's what she told herself.

As she contemplated this conversation, the red secure light above her dad's office door turned off. A moment later, the door opened. A couple of uniformed men, and a woman left the room, her dad followed close behind but stopped at his door. He caught notice of her just then.

"Jenn, I wasn't expecting you. Is everything alright?"

She didn't say anything. Surely that meant that everything was not alright, at least she hoped he would catch on.

"Come on in angel. Missy, can you hold off my next meeting for a few minutes please?" General John Stanza said to the receptionist. She nodded in the affirmative. Jenn stood and made her way into her dad's office. He followed behind her and shut the door.

"What is it?" He asked as the door latched.

"I want, no, I need to go on this next expedition. This story needs to get better attention, it needs someone who knows what's going on and can report on it. The people on Earth are scared, but they don't need to be." Jenn jumped right into it, ripping the band-aid off.

Her dad's body language and tone shifted slightly. It seemed he went from dad to commanding officer. She stood back in his office—the same place she'd gotten fatherly advice moments before—but instead of hugs and comfort; he delivered a stern lecture.

"Jenn, I cannot support this. I will not let you risk your life to go prove something. This mission is dangerous and no place for you," Her dad was in the middle of saying.

"You won't support me, or you won't let me, Dad? I'm not a little girl anymore. This is important to me!" Jenn responded. Knowing full well that he controlled the list of people that went on the next delegation mission.

"I can't support putting you in harm's way. What I mean is I won't be pulling any strings to get you on that mission. You'll have to do that on your own. I'm worried that you have a good enough argument. I just wish it were someone else."

"Dad, I know you do. But you know I'm good at what I do, and this is the last piece missing from this mission. I've worked my whole life to be in this position, documenting world-changing events, and now I have a chance of really making a difference." She paused. She didn't want to get wound up too much. Jenn knew he would always be there for her. "I don't want your help, I just want to know you'll be there for me when I need you."

"Of course I'll always be there for you kiddo," He said without hesitation. She could tell that he wasn't sure where this was going, or if it had already run its course. "I just don't want you doing this for some boy, that's all."

Jenn was a little shocked that he took that approach. "Some boy? Riley isn't just some boy. But I'm not doing this for him, Dad. I'm doing this for me, for the good of the people back at home who are left in the dark about all this stuff that is going on. Somebody needs to tell the story, the real story."

"I didn't mean it like that, Jenn. I know you'll do a great job. I don't want you going on this trip just so that you experience the trauma that they, that Riley is going through, so that you can connect with him better. It doesn't work like that. You won't get what you want that way."

Jenn stood in shocked silence, again. It showed on her face this time. Not in anger, but in realizing that her dad had just uncovered the root of her desire to go, before she even knew herself. The shock wore off, diffusing into tears that rolled down her cheeks.

Before one could fall off her jawbone onto the floor, her dad was right there to wipe it away.

"Does he know?" Her dad asked, gently.

"Know what? About me wanting to go?"

"No, about how you feel about him?" He responded. The wisdom of a father showing through. She detected a hint of her mother's training in there as well. He always did a great job of taking her viewpoint after she passed away. Jenn loved that he tried.

"No. And I don't know how to tell him."

"Jenn, sweety. You need to talk to him before you go. And not to add any pressure, they're leaving soon. All I can say is, be yourself. That's what he likes about you. Forget everything else I told you, be yourself."

As if he knew he got into her head, he tried to get out of it and let her be herself again. Let her figure this out on her own.

"Thanks daddy." They hugged. "Sorry about the tears on your uniform," Jenn said, half sarcastically, "I need to go see Mark."

"Of course you do," Her dad responded. Knowing full well that if anyone could get her added to the mission, it would be their old friend Mark DeCanus.

Jenn left his office and made her way to the street. As she walked out, she put in a request for a rideshare to get her the short distance to Mark's office. She normally walked the distance, but she was in a rush this time. The car pulled up to the tall building edged with marble pillars. She made her way inside and right to Mark's office.

Convincing Mark to include her in the delegation had not been difficult. He had agreed with everything she said. Mark supported the idea, thinking the skills of a talented journalist and investigator would be perfect for transmitting the information to the people on Earth in an easily understandable way.

"You know, I'm a little upset I didn't think of this idea myself," Mark said in response to her argument. The argument it turned out she didn't need to make. Mark was convinced from the beginning. "The only problem is, we're leaving to head up to the ships in two days."

"Shit, I need to get home and pack. And tell Riley."

"And tell Riley? You haven't told him yet?" Mark replied in shocked disbelief. Jenn had told Mark about Riley and her, but she didn't know if he knew anything else about him.

"No, it's complicated," Jenn responded a bit too defensively.

"I see. Well, sort that out. I'll send you the information for the flight up. You'll tag along with me. We could leave any day now."

"Thanks, Mark."

"Don't thank me, you did this. You deserve this."

Jenn smiled and turned away. She had a lot to do and very little time to do it. She raced to her apartment. Fumbling with the keys trying to get into her apartment, all the remaining tasks scrolled in her mind. Getting the key in the hole, she twisted to unlock it and then pushed the door open. She put her bag on the counter and pulled out her phone. No new messages. She opened the latest message from Riley and said, *'Are you free tonight? I want to talk.'*. Short and to the point. After hitting send, she realized it sounded bad and tried to go back to the message and delete it. She wanted to take it back but Riley already read it. She wanted to meet him to talk. She needed to talk to him about her going, but she also needed to talk about them. What they were. With their departure imminent, they needed to meet before time ran out. They had spoken several times since their last meeting but hadn't seen each other. Riley went out to see his parents and grandpa, and they both had been too busy and not in the same area to even meet.

Jenn squeezed her eyes shut tight, clinching her jaw. She relaxed her face and opened her eyes. As much as she wanted to throw her phone out of her apartment window high in the sky, she placed it face down on the counter. She had too much to do to beat herself up over a text. She went to her room and flung open the closet and drawers. Finding her suitcase, she began stuffing it with things she thought she would need. The trip would be long, but there would also be a formal event. The dress was her biggest concern.

As she shuffled through her hangers of clothes and dresses,

Jenn heard a chirp from her phone on the counter. She went out to check it. One new message. From Riley. She dreaded opening it. After a moment's hesitation, she pressed the message icon. *'I'll be back to the compound in a few hours. Should be free tonight but can't leave. I can meet you at the gate?'* Why couldn't he leave? Was he not saying something and waiting until they met in person? She hoped it was because of all they needed to do to prepare for the mission. Jenn felt both relieved she would get to see him again but also scared of the outcome.

She responded. *'I'll see you at 5:30?'*

'See you then.' Came his response.

Now Jenn had to figure out how she was going to break it to Riley. She cared for him, and so far felt like she'd done a terrible job of showing him. But in her mind, telling Riley what she was doing could go two wildly different ways, and she was nervous about both. She didn't want Riley to think she was just trying to get and stay close to him, and also didn't want him to think that she was doing it just for her career. But which one was better? And why was she doing this?

She was going to have to think of something fast. She and Riley had only seen each other that first night before Riley went to spend time with his parent and grandpa. The turnaround for this mission had been extremely quick. They had planned to see each other again when he got back, and she hoped they would still be able to, but the redeployment sounded like it would get sped up. So they needed to change plans. She wanted to spend more time together. To figure out what they were.

She threw everything she thought she needed into the suitcase, grabbed her tablet and left her room. Locking the door behind her, she made her way to her car. She started the hour's drive to the city's edge where they had set up the compound. Jenn wanted her mind to be clear, free of all distractions. She had to think and also get into the right mindset. She needed to be prepared for any outcome. Either way she would go on this mission and she needed to be prepared for the worst-case scenario with Riley. She silenced her phone and turned the radio up. The vehicle hummed along the road as it drove her to the compound. With the windows down, her hair waved about. She felt connected. Connected to the city, to herself.

Quietly humming to herself, she pulled up to park in the parking lot. This time it had been fairly full of cars. Mostly from the personnel that were soon to be deployed. Though cars filled the lot, she couldn't see a single person. Not even Riley. Jenn parked the car. Leaving her bag in the car, she walked to the gate. He wasn't waiting there. The eerie silence made her feel like she was standing in a ghost town. In the distance far beyond the gates in the base, shuttles took off. She checked her phone. She had made good time and got here when she said she would. Usually very punctual, Riley was nowhere to be seen.

That's when she noticed all the missed messages and calls. She was so focused on how she would talk to him about her coming on the mission and so nervous just to see him, that she hadn't noticed her phone going off on her drive. She kicked herself for silencing it. Most of the calls came from Riley. Another one from her dad and from Mark.

That caught her attention. Her vision closed in and she felt clammy and flush. She felt hot suddenly. She desperately hoped nothing bad had happened. Taking a deep breath, she checked the ones from Riley first. The first one she got told her she didn't need to come anymore. Riley was being sent to the Kennedy early to start combat patrols leading up to the departure of the convoy. Her heart sank. She was also worried. Did that mean that there was a threat? More than before, anyway. Before she continued down that train of thought, she closed her eyes and took three long, deep breaths.

Letting the final breath out with a whoosh she opened her eyes again. Checked her other messages, they all said the same thing. She needed to get ready to go, and soon. The council was getting uncomfortable and wanted to get the fleet out as soon as possible. They wanted to be established there before the enemy arrived if another attack on Rutaun occurred.

It now looked like she was going to have to tell Riley the one way she didn't want to. Her heart sank. She was going to have to tell him in person, while underway to the alien world, on the ship he did not know she was on. If there was one way that screamed she was doing it only for her career and that she didn't have any feelings for him, it was this way. By showing up as part of the fleet, and not telling him on Earth, face-to-face like anyone would deserve. This would not be good.

"Damnit!" Is all she could scream in the parking lot. Her voice echoed off the parked cars. Her mind went on autopilot. She needed to get her shit together. She had to hightail it to the shipyard to meet up with Mark. This would be one hell of a ride to space.

CHAPTER 8

Rictor–Southern Hemisphere United Republic–Earth

Rictor Inagru had been hiding out for too long. He ditched the multiple tails that seemed to collect around him. The tails were a good sign. That meant they weren't out to kill him, just observe him. At least not kill him yet. They could have just been building a pattern of life. A pattern that Rictor had been careful not to create. That only made this next part more tricky, but he'd spent a good portion of his life hiding things from other people. He prepared for what came next. He looked through his paper files; Rictor trusted nothing electronic right now.

His notes brought him back to a day long ago. Back when he didn't have everyone breathing down his neck about what needed to happen next, who was bad, who was good. Back when he was invisible. Nobody knew him. In a way, he liked that much better. But he knew that to get what he wanted; he needed to be higher profile. The jump to politics was the best logical next step for him.

He took these notes, was it thirty years ago? It had to be.

RELATIVITY: RETURNING HOME

Sometimes it felt like yesterday, in others, it felt like an eternity ago. He took solace and comfort in knowing that everything that had happened over the last couple of years was his doing from thirty years ago. Hard, meticulous planning. A sense of pride overcame him. The longest of long shots worked.

He had been a young, up-and-coming engineer. In charge of identifying and cataloging trajectories for the faster-than-light tests. He remembered his old commander, Colonel Johnson. He chuckled at the name, so generic, but it made it easy to remember. That man didn't know the first thing about orbital mechanics. Which made his deception and manipulation all the easier. Rictor got the most sophisticated computers to crunch through data from deep space scans from the last two hundred years.

While Rictor's primary job had been to find safe trajectories for the faster-than-light trials, which he found plenty, he looked for ones that could cause problems. In particular, Rictor had been looking for a planet, one with a high likelihood of being habitable. That was difficult because humans had never seen one before. With all the advanced technology at his fingertips, the likes of which humans had never centered on a singular problem before, Rictor could discover a few. A few worlds that had not only a high likelihood of being habitable but being habitable by intelligent life. Advances in artificial intelligence assisted modeling and analysis of existing data made these discoveries possible. But Rictor hid the data from everyone.

Anyone would expect to be excited about that prospect and tell everyone they knew. Not Rictor. No, Rictor covered up the data. He tweaked the algorithms to make sure they would not be discovered for a long, long time. With that information covered up, he became free to recommend trajectories for the tests. Some trajectories were worlds with the potential for intelligent life. He played the long game. The very long game. He knew how long it would take to impact those sites. And if they even did, there would be no guarantee that intelligent life could do anything about it. He never fancied humans. They all disgusted him. He had no actual relationships, none that didn't end in embarrassment for him, anyway.

When the technology of the faster-than-light trials was far enough along that he thought it might be successful, he added some of the worlds to the trajectory list. One world would turn out to be Razuud.

He waited and waited. Years went by. He thought the test failed at first. The probes had some ability to steer. Scientists programmed them to steer into a sun or away from any planets or moons to avoid accidentally destroying something important or habitable. Rictor manipulated the guidance systems on these particular probes to do the opposite. He had them steer into the planet.

He didn't want to elicit any suspicion that a planet or something may be in the path as the probe approached, so he only sent one probe to each location. It would have been easy for someone to spot the trail if he were to aim at the same planet. Because the distant planet had been orbiting its own star in a distinct part of the galaxy, Rictor had to lead the planet. This would look very obvious from Earth's perspective. So he didn't target that area again. Surprise and relief overcame him when an alien attack occurred. He knew, long before anyone else, what was going on. He had been stockpiling what he knew would be the currency of this conflict: data. Any and everything that could be useful to trade with an alien species.

Right now, though, his plan to start an all-out war with the aliens had not worked out. The end effect being intentional contact with an alien species. He knew that if he got the chance to speak with them, he could get what he wanted. He enticed them to attack Earth thirty years ago. Well, less considering the time it took for the test ship to make its way there. That seemed to work. The humans sent a retaliatory strike, but despite Rictor's best efforts to sabotage the mission, instead of attacking the alien world and starting a major war, they became friends. Even Rictor didn't expect that. But now he knew of another species, or at least that's what it looked like right now. That was a common enemy to the Razuuds and the humans. That meant they could be potential allies to Rictor. But there also remained the possibility of spoiling the relationship between the Razuuds and humans.

His job remained unfinished; he had more tricks up his sleeve. His watch chirped. The time had come.

He shuffled the papers back into their folder and closed it with a string. He briskly left his room on the second floor of a pay-by-the-hour motel and headed across the street to a bar that hardly looked open.

Rictor entered the bar and sat in a corner of a small back room. He was there because he was sure nobody would expect him to be there, and nobody that was there would recognize him or care about his outlaw status even if they did know who he was. They all probably had their own official or unofficial record, anyway. This was a place for outlaws, for those who didn't want to be found. He had set up a meeting and his mark was just about to arrive. Rictor knew this because he set up cameras and microphones throughout the building. He couldn't be too careful.

He scanned the dingy, smoke-filled room. Through the haze, he noticed nothing out of the ordinary. Not out of the ordinary for a rundown bar like this, anyway. Two men with tattoos and ripped-off sleeves engaged in a stare down, probably over some drinks or a girl. A middle-aged couple in a booth were arguing over something Rictor couldn't quite make out. From the looks, the man was losing, whether or not he was in the wrong. Rictor smiled inwardly. He mused that this was the reason he'd never had a relationship. That kind of mindless bickering that completely disregarded the facts was insufferable. The woman in the argument paused long enough to glance over at Rictor. Their eyes caught. She gave a sort of, mind your own business kind of look, and Rictor obliged.

Rictor's eyes turned to the video screen he held in his lap and stayed locked on that as the woman approached, keeping a close eye on her route, making sure she didn't look nervous or brought company. He could sense when people were uneasy or when something was off, but with her, everything seemed normal. A good start.

When she sat down, they didn't even bother with introductions or small talk. Rictor spoke right away. He had a sense of urgency, almost as if he was in his death throes and was making one last attempt to stay relevant, important. He needed to prove that he could still make waves with the north, so that the SHUR would see him as more valuable, more trustworthy. His immediate goal, since he could no longer influence the north by being part of the north, was to influence the NHN by being part of the SHUR.

He played a dangerous game.

"I need you to take this," Rictor said, handing her a clear tube that had actual paper rolled up inside of it. "Don't look at it until you have boarded the delegation ship. Everything has been arranged. You leave tomorrow morning with the second shuttle. If you pull this off, I'll double your compensation to your family. If you come back and receive it yourself, I'll triple it." He knew she would not make it, and he knew he only had to pay the first half up front and could likely ignore the second half, regardless if she succeeded or not. The amount was not too significant to him. Triple would be, though. She nodded, took the tube, and slipped it into her pocket. She stood to walk away. "A lot is counting on you, don't screw this up, Helena," Rictor said as she turned to leave, using her new fake identity he set up for her.

She glanced back, without stopping and said, "I don't fail." Her voice sounded cold and confident.

As she exited, Rictor felt a shiver of excitement and dread. This was his last card to play between the humans and Razuuds, a last gamble in a game that had been decades in the making. The fate of two worlds hung in the balance, and Rictor was determined to shape it to his will. He planned how he would meet with this new threat. They would be most interested in the information he obtained. Right now his fate hinged on a woman that the only thing he knew about her was that she hated the Razuuds and the government. He didn't care why.

CHAPTER 9

Maggie–Unknown

Maggie lost count of the days. She had nothing to write on or mark the walls. She tried tearing the bed sheets, but she couldn't. They felt like cloth but were much tougher. She didn't have the strength. Not now. She had eaten the last cup of mush for the day not that long ago. Following her routine, this meant the lights would dim and she would fall asleep.

Maggie liked to fall asleep with the lights still on. She found some comfort in that, knowing what her surroundings were before she dozed off. She didn't sleep through the night, but whenever she woke up, she didn't move. To avoid detection, she didn't let on that she was awake to whatever or whoever might observe her. She either didn't move or couldn't move. She never tried to find out. Maybe some childhood fear was the reason. If she stayed still, the monsters would leave her alone. A childhood fear. She paused at that. Something about that felt familiar, painful. It brought knots to her stomach.

The voice grew louder still. She made her way to the bed, curled up in a fetal position facing the wall, and tried to sleep.

But sleep didn't come. The voice. Childhood fear. Face. It couldn't be. She shoved those memories so far down, there's no way they are still alive. She needed to find out. She needed to test to see if this was some nasty trick, or her past coming back to haunt her at the worst possible time.

If she was going crazy and this voice was her own, there was only one way to know, at least she hoped. Without any other indication, she responded. Except this time, instead of speaking out loud, she spoke internally. "Who are you?"

No response. Partially relieved, partially disappointed, she thought of ways to counter this mind trick that these aliens must be trying to play on her. As soon as she came up with her first idea, she heard a response. Something she dreaded.

"I'm you, of course. Your old friend. You used to call me Face." The voice responded with confidence, like they truly were old friends. Now she remembered. She remembered Face. Not the one everyone else knew. But the one she had locked away a long time ago. It was the picture of the person she wish she could have been during those dark times, the stronger one, the better one. The one that got her through tough times.

Maggie couldn't say anything. She became numb to her surroundings. So numb that she didn't notice someone approaching the door.

"Maggie, someone's coming." Again, the voice reached her ears. She couldn't remember the last time she heard it. She almost didn't make out what it said, surprised by the sudden intrusion. *"Yes, I'm back and someone is coming. Get ready."*

Maggie rolled and sat up in her bed just in time to hear an unfamiliar noise. With the lights still on, she peered at an area by the food slot to investigate the source. She saw a crack appear where she hadn't noticed one before. Light flooded in at the floor and along one edge. A larger section of the wall next to her food port slid away. She stood up quickly next to her bed, ready for anything.

A figure walked in. Slightly smaller than her, covered in short stubby fur and a robe-like uniform. She recognized the creature instantly as a Razuud, or at least she thought that. She couldn't be too sure about anything right now. The size of the creature also made her feel better. With it currently in the room alone, she felt she had the upper hand if it came to a physical altercation. While she wasn't too tall herself, she made up for it in skill and experience. It resembled the aliens she had seen pictures of. She remembered mostly pictures of the dead ones from the Earth attack, but she had seen some just before going into battle with them alive. She thought they were her allies. They must have turned. Maybe it ended up being some kind of trap. She received very little in the way of intel on them or the aliens they fought against.

Maggie had been thinking about the Razuuds and this other species they were helping the Razuuds fight. She knew she didn't have the entire story. What if these were Razuuds, and they were allies? It would not be unheard of or entirely unexpected for allies to do experiments on friends. After all, the humans had done experiments on those aliens killed on Earth. They weren't allies then, but humans did still research to identify them and, more importantly, discover how to kill them. Keep your enemies close and your friends closer. Wasn't that the saying?

She had also been thinking a lot about whether there were other prisoners. There had been no sign yet. But then again, she hadn't left her room since her arrival. The situation was totally screwed up.

Maggie didn't know what to do, but they had her backed into a corner. She could fight, but to what end? A soldier or guard of some sort stood in between her and the door. She didn't see anyone else but knew someone had to be outside.

The creature slowly walked toward her, acting friendly.

As if some switch got flipped, Maggie heard the voice again. "*I got this.*" A look of realization at the dangerous predicament the creature had just stumbled upon crossed his face. His mouth went slack and his eyes opened wide. Nothing had changed in the room except for the look and feeling that she gave off. But it wasn't Maggie that made the change. Maggie had no control at that moment. Face took over. The creature, surprised to see this human that once cowered in the corner, now flew at him. The creature had no time to react.

Face flew at it with blinding speed, leaping forward with her knee to the chest of the unsuspecting demon. This pushed the creature back, grasping at its chest in pain for air. She followed it up with a right elbow to the creature's stubby snout, careful to avoid the teeth. It appeared to have the same effect as hitting a human in the nose. Its eyes watered and blood rushed down its face.

Face, noticing the muscular legs, sidestepped a kick that would have put her into the back wall. She lunged forward and behind the creature to grab it from behind. Hoping the air and arteries worked the same, she moved in position to choke the creature out.

That's when she felt the zap, zap, zap of what must have been a taser. The same type that had knocked her unconscious when she first arrived. She expected something, and this time it didn't totally knock her out. But it brought her to her knees. She felt at least two creatures grab her by the arms on either side and drag her to her bed. The damage had been done to their friend. The creature coughed up what looked like blood as more of it poured out from several places on its face as the other two dragged him out of the room.

With large sticks, the two other guards came back into the room, ready for an attack. Face, recovering from the taser strike moments ago, stood at the ready. The guards must have thought twice about their decision to attack, and what could happen to them, and quickly left the room. They wouldn't get revenge right then. The doors hissed and shut. Any sign of a door disappeared. But now she knew a door existed and where it opened. She learned something new.

"What the hell was that?" Maggie said out loud. No response. She repeated the question. This time in her head. *What the hell was that Face?*

"Like I said, I got it. The way they were violent to you, pulling us from our ship. We needed to return the favor. Show them who they were dealing with. I saved you." Face responded confidently.

You could have gotten me killed. You can't take over like that. Maggie said back, keeping the conversation in her head.

Maggie didn't get a response.

The room went pitch black. The sudden switch in environment thrust Maggie back into her cockpit. She flashed back as terror gripped her mind and pulled her in. She froze in place. Somewhere in the middle of the room with no reference point. She couldn't bring herself to take even a single step in any direction. Maggie couldn't move to find a wall, her bed, anything. She needed to sit, but couldn't bring herself to.

The lights came back on, blinding her. She heard a voice in her head again. *"It's my turn again. You don't need to see what happens next."* Face emerged out of the light.

The door hissed again and opened. Only this time, it wasn't one small alien, but four. And there was nothing nice about what they were doing. They rushed in and knocked her to the ground. As three of them pinned her down, the fourth restrained her with what she could only compare to hand cuffs. Shouting at her all the while. It sounded as if someone muffled the shouts. The image of these aliens holding her down, softly yelling at her, coupled with everything she had been through so far, actually made her laugh. The sound they were making, trying to be forceful, was hilarious to her. This did not help her current physical situation at all. But it helped her strategic and mental situation. She got in their heads, right where she wanted to be.

Dragging her out of the cell, they forced her into the hall. Her body hit the hard black composite floor, a stark contrast to the pristine white in her cell. Before she could react, the guards had her by each arm again, forcing her to her feet.

They walked. Face stumbled the first few steps, not sure what they wanted her to do. Were they taking her on a tour, or something much worse? She did her best to remember all the turns they took and the doors they passed. She noticed little indicators that they still had her on a ship currently underway in space. A large ship at that. It must have been bigger than the Space Force Guard Ship Catalyst. The last ship she served on.

Slight movements or changes in gravity gave it away. She felt close to zero gravity only briefly twice. Like she would feel just before and after a transition to and out of light speed. It is not uncommon if they were making a long journey. She ruled out a centrifugal ship like the Space Force Platform Kennedy, which would have been already in orbit somewhere. Those, no matter how large they were, always gave a slightly disorientating spin in her head. Her ears, eyes, and body couldn't quite come to a consensus of what she experienced on spin gravity ships. Annoying, but manageable. She didn't feel that here.

Face recited each turn, and doors passed on repeat. Adding each additional detail as she continued, determined to memorize the layout on the first try. She may not get another chance. They eventually came to a somewhat large holding area. It looked like a small hangar, not dissimilar to the one onboard the Catalyst. There were a couple dozen smaller ships moved off to the side, all smaller than her fighter.

Rows and rows of chairs filled with aliens occupied the center of the room. Maybe a couple hundred. She avoided calling them Razuuds because she refused to believe her people had been betrayed so quickly. She needed to hold on to some type of hope that humanity still existed. That either someone would look for her, or she would have someone to go back to if, no, when, she escaped.

What was this? A parade? An execution? The thoughts didn't stop streaming through her mind. The aliens were bringing her around, everyone stared at her. She didn't hyperventilate or lose her cool. She remained calm, defiant. Face hadn't realized how dry her mouth had gotten from the exertion and no water until she went to speak, but nothing came out. Face wanted to tell them how ugly they were and how she'd make them pay. She didn't expect them to understand her; they hadn't seemed to so far. But it sure would feel good to get it off her chest.

The two guards, having to pick up more of her weight now, brought her to the front, where everyone gawked at her. She heard little murmurs here and there. Were they hushed whispers or speaking? She didn't know because, based on their screaming, they could have just been talking normally. That made her laugh out loud again. Or try her best, at least. She had better luck with the laughing than the talking.

She felt a blunt jab to her right ribcage that knocked the wind out of her. But she kept laughing. She didn't want them to see any weakness. She continued to laugh, until one of the larger aliens, still only about her height but with legs like tree trunks, stood in front of her. He brought one of those tree trunks back and kneed her in the stomach. The alien's knee forced all the air from her lungs, causing her to dry heave. Spit streamed out of her mouth onto the floor as the guards let her drop to all fours. The two guards lifted her back up. She spat what little she could toward the guard that just kneed her.

He raised his leg again when she heard one of them speak just off to her left side. She hadn't noticed him before. The kick never came. The voice halted the alien's next blow. He hesitantly put his foot back down and moved behind her. She heard the same voice continue to speak, this time into a microphone. Because of her proximity to him, she heard both his voice and his voice over a speaker system. She turned to see, but the guards forced her head back forward. Whoever spoke must have reached the end of what he wanted to say. As soon as he stopped speaking, the guards forced Face to her knees. She knew this was the end. She did everything she could to get her throat wet enough to insult them as best she could. One last act of defiance.

But nothing happened. After a few moments, she tried looking around again. They allowed her to this time. The aliens then laughed, or what she assumed was laughing. The motion and noises had all the right feeling of a laugh, it just lacked the familiar sounds and volume. All of that captured in a strange alien form. It must have been laughter, although she couldn't imagine what someone would laugh at during a time like this. These aliens were super weird. And that thought made her laugh too, uncontrollably. She thought the executioner stood behind her to deliver a fatal blow, but as of now, they spared her. She might still be dead, just not right now, not yet.

Without lifting her back to her feet, the guards dragged her back through the middle aisle of chairs and out the same door they arrived through.

"That wasn't so bad. Now they know who they're dealing with." Face said to Maggie.

Stop doing that shit. I want to mess them up as much as anyone but

81

it's going to get us killed in here.

"We're already dead Maggie. Just a matter of time." Face responded.

No we're not. I need to get back. Maggie said back, willing herself to be in control again. Maggie needed to see the next part. She needed to remember everything, from her point of view. She needed a plan.

They exited the hangar and made their way through the halls. At first, it felt like the same route. She recited the turns and doors in her head, trying to go backward. Almost like reciting the alphabet backward. She had to go forward from the beginning repeatedly but got to an earlier letter each time.

Then they stopped unexpectedly. They were on the same route; she felt certain of that. At least as certain as she could be. Her room should only be a couple of turns up ahead. They turned her to face a door. One guard leaned forward and pressed a keycard to a panel on the side of the door. It opened. They forced her in the door, being careful not to let her go as they squeezed in behind her. The large partially lit room, or hangar, held a familiar shape.

She immediately recognized her ship, or what remained of it. It lay in pieces. Scattered everywhere. The aliens laughed, cueing off of her reaction. A reaction she hadn't realized she had projected. She tried hard to keep her thoughts and feelings internal, but she couldn't resist at this sight. This laugh felt different. A more guttural, ruthless laugh. This wasn't funny to them, or maybe it was a little. No, they were telling her that her situation was hopeless. Then she pinpointed it. The laugh was an evil laugh. Like a villain out of a movie.

Maggie collected her thoughts and composed herself. This seemed to set off the guards. Their laughs stopped, and they turned to snarls. They could not hide their disappointment. Whatever plan, they had backfired. Maggie noticed a lot of activity going on around her ship. She held out hope that if she escaped, she could get to her ship and get out of this place. She hoped the ship would heal itself enough to at least protect her and get the engines working. That chance currently stood at zero, with her ship scattered across the floor. Humans did the same thing. Whatever advantage they could gain from better understanding their enemy. Maggie tried to stay and see as much as she could before they took her away. She thought this might be the last time she would see this place. She thought they were trying to tease her, get her sprits down, make her feel hopeless.

Maggie made a conscious decision right then. Maybe she couldn't do it alone. *Face, we need to work together. We have to get out of here and warn the others. Warn our family.*

The aliens' attempt to discourage her didn't work. It did the opposite. In the hangar's corner, she saw a few of the aliens shooting something at pieces of her fighter hanging in the air. As they took her away, she couldn't help but think that it didn't look like a weapon she had seen before. The energy looked different. Even accounting for the synthetic vision her fighter gave her, it still looked different. It looked as though it melted away from her like melting ice under a hot torch. The metal composite dripped down. She could see a glimmer, which she hadn't seen from this view before. She thought the glimmer had to be some type of energy shield, probably mimicking her ship's shields. They appeared to be doing nothing against this new weapon. They were building something to defeat the human ships. She had a new purpose. She needed to warn her friends.

"Let's kick some ass." Face said back.

CHAPTER 10

Jennifer–Space Force Guard Ship Redemption–In-Transit

Jennifer Stanza didn't let her nerves show, or at least she didn't think she did. That was something she prided herself on, staying cool under pressure. Sure, she got nervous all the time, more so lately. But this, this was different. The ship had been underway for almost a week and she had been hiding the whole time. Why would she do that? She was allowed to be there. Was she hiding, or was she avoiding? She supposed it was both.

She knew when she confronted Riley for the first time it would be bad. Why wouldn't it be? What would make it worse would be if it was not on her terms, but by accident. She wasn't just hiding from Riley, but from anyone that had regular interactions with him. She didn't want to put anyone in a situation where they felt obligated to tell Riley that she was there. So that meant Star, too. That also meant Mark, but the ship had sailed on that one. She knew he wouldn't say anything because he had told her as much. It had to be on her terms. It had to be soon.

She couldn't figure out how to tell him she was here, on the ship, with him. Every minute she waited made it worse. Every minute she waited, she felt worse. She could get ahold of him easily, but then he would know that she was on board. Jenn hadn't been responding to him, because she hadn't been getting any of his messages. She left her phone back on Earth like everyone else because they didn't work up here.

The fleet issued her a communication device and a personal computer that could link up with the ship's comm system. This way she could communicate with anyone within the fleet in real time, but also access the ship's database. She could send and receive messages to and from Earth using the scheduled comm drones. She just received an email from him and wanted to respond. But would she act like something happened to her phone or what? She couldn't take it anymore. The time had come. She needed to talk to him in person today. The schedules finally lined up.

That time quickly approached. She had to confront him, and whatever happened, however he took it, that's what was going to happen. Butterflies were an understatement.

She snuck through the halls. Functionally, the layout of the ship was the same at every level, but she hadn't been to this level yet, where all the pilots stayed. Lucky for her, they didn't venture off of this level very often other than to eat. The gym was on this level, so Jenn hadn't gone there yet. Not being able to exercise did not help her anxiety about this situation.

As she stood in an outcropping for a door, her comm device buzzed in her pocket. She looked down to check if it was the message she had been waiting for.

"*Coast is clear.*" She received a message from Mark DeCanus. He understood her situation and agreed to help set up a meeting. Even though he spent most of his time near Ramat in the command section of the center of the ship, and

Ramat no longer had his quarters in this section, Mark's old room from the previous mission hadn't moved. It sat right next to the Luckys ready room. Right where Riley would be.

That was the message she had waited for. He didn't spot anyone in the halls, and he would be the only one in his office. She had to move fast. Jenn stepped out and around the corner. Keeping her head down just in case someone stepped into the hall, she made a direct path to Mark's office. Mark held the door open, waiting just inside so as not to raise suspicions.

She stepped through the threshold and Mark closed the door behind her. Jenn felt a sense of relief, but at the same time her nerves went into overdrive.

As if Mark could sense what ran through her head, he reached out and placed both hands on the sides of her arms, gently squeezing as he looked into her eyes. "Everything is going to be just fine. He will understand."

"Thank you Mark. You don't know how much this means to me," Jenn replied.

Mark dropped his hands with a slight chuckle. "This is nothing kid. I have to broker a deal with aliens later on, the least I could do is help you out. Now, I better get running, I have a meeting with Ramat." They both smiled at each other.

Mark pushed the button to open the door and stepped into the hall. The door closed behind him with a quiet mechanical slide and he was gone. Her emotional safety net walked out the door. She just hoped she wouldn't need it later.

Mark had requested a meeting with Riley earlier that day, asking him to go to his office after his shift was over. They occasionally met up, mostly to talk about Riley's grandfather, so the situation wasn't out of the realm of possibility.

Riley must be on his way. She knew that. They had set the time, and it quickly approached. She was sitting in Mark's chair. The door to his small crew cabin and office were closed.

What should her facial expression be? Should she be smiling? Did she smell alright? How was her hair? Damnit. Now she was in her own head. And acting very not cool, going against everything she wanted to be feeling at that moment.

She heard two sharp knocks. She panicked. Should she say enter? Really, what the hell was going on with her? She closed her eyes and took a deep breath. As she breathed out, she said to herself, *you got this*. When she opened her eyes, Riley was standing in front of her. She was so lost in what she would do that she hadn't heard the door open. Riley's facial expressions were flashing as rapidly as her racing heartbeat.

She no longer had to think about what to do, what to say, how to act. She melted. Tears started forming in her eyes. Jenn stood, not sure she could keep her balance. She used the desk to brace herself in the low acceleration gravity, following the edges to make her way around the corners so that there was nothing in between the two of them. She stood face-to-face with Riley, someone she felt like she loved but betrayed.

RILEY

Riley stood in shock. He knew that his facial expressions were confusing her. His emotions were confusing him. While he had figured out that she was on the ship, he wasn't expecting to see her here and now. His heart pounded in his chest at seeing Jenn instead of Mark. For certain she could see it. After how things transpired the last time they saw each other, and her not returning any of his messages over the last week, he thought things were ending between them. Before they ended, though, he knew he needed to see her one last time.

He just didn't expect it to be right now, on the way to a potential major battle against an alien species. And he hoped it wouldn't be the last time.

Anger flashed over Riley's face when he first saw her. That mirrored his initial reaction when he found out she was on the ship a couple of days into the journey. After he hadn't heard from her the first couple of days, he started checking the manifest to see if there had been anyone else on board his or another ship that knew her. He contacted them to see if they heard from her. He hadn't seen Mark yet or he would have asked him. When he started his search, he came across her name pretty quick. How could she do this to him? Not tell him or give any kind of warning she had joined the mission. To make matters worse, they had assigned her to the same ship as him. Why did she wait so long?

This line of questioning brought on confusion. Some things made sense, while others didn't. He was glad he had a few more days to figure out how he felt, because if this was the first time he knew about it, his first reaction would have taken over and this wouldn't be a great encounter. It still may not be. But at least he was somewhat prepared, and possibly more understanding. He went through all these emotions a few days ago. His body and mind were reliving those feelings now but much faster. He thought he was ready to see her, but the reality of the situation was something different. Riley settled now on what he eventually settled on before. He felt resigned to whatever fate lay ahead of him. His facial expression and body language showed relief and a little confusion. But not anger and not hate. There was a good explanation, and he was going to give her that opportunity. He had to assume the best intentions and see her for who he knew her to be. Someone he cared for. Someone he loved. She deserved that much, even if everything was about to end.

That's when he broke the ice. With his eyes slightly squinted and a quiver in his voice, he spoke. "Hey, you're not Mark, I don't remember him being this pretty," He said with a smile, the door closing behind him.

Riley could see a wave of relief come over her. She rapidly closed the distance between the two of them as she wrapped her arms around him. He did the same. Everything seemed to be better for Riley. Even though he wasn't certain yet, he just felt relieved. After a few moments, the unease of the situation surfaced, and he decided that the time to talk had finally come. He needed to get this part over with. To see where this was going, all of it.

"This seems to be a common thing for us. Long hugs with no words," Riley said with a short laugh. Maybe he went too far with the last joke, but Jenn's response told him she didn't care. She was just happy to see him. They were happy to see each other. Relief washed over both of them. The weight of this encounter finally came to a head. Even though neither knew how it would end up yet, they didn't have to wait anymore.

Jenn spoke. They talked for quite some time. Jenn explained the series of unfortunate events, what she felt, thought, did, everything. Riley understood, he understood it all. And if he was being honest with himself, this was the best-case scenario out of all the situations he dreamed up. He just never thought of this one.

"Mark will be back soon; we should get going," Riley said.

Jenn sat there for a moment in thought, her pointer finger resting on her chin, looking down at the ground. She looked up and reached her hand out to Riley.

"Here, follow me," Jenn said. "I've been trying to keep a low profile on this ship for a while now, so I found some pretty cool places on the ship."

Riley got spun around by her pull, but quickly regained his balance and stepped to follow her. She led him down corridors that Riley wasn't even aware existed. Within a couple of minutes, Jenn stopped in front of a door. It read 'Maintenance' but in small unsuspecting letters. Not like the other signs he'd seen that were large and bold and grabbed your attention. Jenn felt around the door and a little hole gave way to her finger. She pushed it in and slid open the door.

Shelves of broken equipment and electronics lined both sides of the small room. But at the end of the room, Riley spotted why Jenn took him here. A small view port extended to the outside. This was one of the few places offering an actual view of space, not a camera-relayed screen view. Riley's jaw went slack. He hadn't seen space without some screen in the way. He had trained on how to look through access ports for troubleshooting a shuttle, but never needed to use them.

Riley smiled widely. "This view is incredible," Riley said, looking at Jenn. Riley had everything he needed right now. He wrapped his arms around her, wishing he didn't need to let go anytime soon.

CHAPTER 11

Mark–Space Force Guard Ship Redemption–In-Transit

Mark DeCanus used the small amount of gravity from the ship's acceleration to aid him in sitting down. The chair in his office on board the SFG Redemption wasn't quite like the one in his office back on Earth. This one was much nicer, newer, and more comfortable. He somehow still missed his old chair. The chair, bolted to rails on the floor, had built-in straps that he wrestled with, throwing them over his shoulder and waist. He pulled the chair closer to the desk, waiting to hear the soft click indicating it had firmly locked in place.

He squeezed his thumb and forefinger on the bridge of his nose, trying to rid himself of a migraine. He looked forward to dealing with the Razuud, and maybe even the Tartins. It sure beat acting as the school principal for the petty squabbles of the NHN and SHUR. It was strange to Mark how different the two human halves were in their ways. So far, there had been no fights on board the ship, but only time would tell if that stayed true. He always felt diplomats were the most difficult people to get along with. They always had some kind of hidden agenda. Some angle that nobody else could see coming.

Putting his hand down and opening his eyes, he pulled open his screen to check his messages. Mostly unremarkable, as usual. Everyone thought their messages were a priority, so to Mark, none of them were.

Except one. One message caught his eye. It was from his aide, Emily Watkins. *'Check high side.'* That's all it read.

That meant Mark needed to go to his account on the classified network. The message must be too sensitive and classified to be sent along with the rest of the mail. Because of his position, he had the luxury of being able to convert his room into a mobile secure room. Mark placed his phone and tablet into a lockbox in his drawer. He reached under the desk for a button. Fishing around for it for a second since he never had to use it before, he finally found it. Pressing the button made an audible click in the door and a red light above the door illuminated he hadn't noticed before. It read *'Secure'*. Mark pushed another button on the desk and this switched the computer he used to a different computer, one only on the secure network. Forgetting his long drawn-out password on the first attempt, he thought hard and reentered it. Luckily, it worked this time.

Waiting for the slow, outdated system, further bogged down by endless government bloatware and security measures, he opened a bag of coffee. He clicked on the desktop icon for his messaging system and watched the icon spin in circles as it tried to process his request. He sipped his cooling coffee. Finally, it opened. Surprised to see even more needless emails, he searched for the message Emily wanted him to see. It popped right out to him. *'Intelligence Report'*.

He forgot he had been waiting for this. Mark put a tasking out sometime ago to follow Rictor in SHUR territory. He forgot about it because he had difficulty tracking and maintaining eyes on him. Just before they left, Mark got word that Rictor had been spotted and a team would surveil him.

"If you were going to reveal a plan, just before we left Earth would have been the time to do it," Mark said out loud to himself. His words dying against the walls.

Mark opened the message. He skimmed the classification markings and skipped right to the assessment and sources. Ground intelligence, from internal agents. High confidence in accuracy. No need to double confirm.

'Message intercepted that set up a meeting with an unknown individual. Agents set up at the expected meeting place and observed and recorded the exchange. Background noise and the short notice made it impossible to make out the full conversation.'

Mark continued reading. Then he saw what was so important.

"I'll be damned, Rictor snuck someone on board this ship."

CHAPTER 12

Riley—Advanced Individual Maneuvering Shuttle—Razuud Orbit

Following the meeting with Jenn, Riley felt the weight of the situation lift from his mind. Their reunion earlier in the trip put him at ease in one regard but heightened his senses in another. The knowledge of her being on board gave him a renewed focus—a different type of pressure, to be sure, but one he'd rather manage than what he'd felt before.

Riley's rotation in the flight schedule had him on the first patrol as the fleet executed the final portable light-ring transition to the Razuud local space. Now, traveling at normal speed, or speed more normal than what he had been traveling mere seconds ago, he checked and rechecked his ship's status. Everything looked good. His system checks all showed green. His radar didn't have any indication of an enemy threat. He paid close attention to any unknown objects on the scans. The Space Force did their best to work with the Razuuds to catalog all the ships and their signatures to make it easier to identify friends and enemies. An unknown ship didn't necessarily mean an enemy, but the chances were much higher.

"All status looks green on my end. No enemy in sight yet," Captain James 'P' Parrant said. This prompted Riley to check in as well.

"All green here too. Running deep scanning protocol," Riley responded. He heard Star's response in the background.

Lieutenant Colonel Charlie 'Wisp' Broadway had been silent on the trip so far. He was lead, as the Luckys commander and overall highest-ranking member in the squadron. He always put himself in the toughest, and least desired flights whenever possible. Something Riley noticed General D'Pol did as well. Thinking of Trap made Riley think of Maggie, and the support he would have given him to look into finding her.

As if Charlie had been reading Riley's mind, Riley saw a private channel open up between the two of them.

"Riley, how do you read?" Charlie asked.

Caught off guard by the direct message and the use of his first name and not his call sign, Riley responded, "Loud and clear, boss."

"Listen Riley. I thought about what you said. Last time we were out here and heading home. About Maggie. I talked to Trap." There was a long pause. Riley didn't know what to say, so he said nothing. "How can I help you?" Charlie continued.

Riley didn't expect that at all. He had mostly put the thought of finding her in the back of his mind, instead focusing on having lost her. "Uh, sir, I haven't put a lot of thought into it since, you know."

"I know it's been hard on you, on all of us. I'm sorry if I've caused you to lose hope. But I'm listening now. So if you have any doubts about anything, or wild ideas, tell me, and I'll support you. Whatever I can do."

Riley was silent again for a moment. "Thanks. I've not given up hope. It's just hard to see the positives all the time." Then he paused again. "Does it get better? The feeling. When you lose people like that," Riley asked.

"I wish I could tell you it does. But it doesn't. It just moves to a different part of your mind. You have to find a way to hold on to the positive memories and make sure they outweigh the event and the hole that's left behind. You have a good head on your shoulders, Riley, and a good heart. Try your best to keep that."

The line cut off, they had work to do.

Looking back at the scope and landmarks, or space marks, key navigational aids, like the planet and moons, Riley oriented himself to where he currently flew. It was all very familiar to him. He had been on patrol in this very same area for countless hours during the attack and subsequent cleanup during the first expedition. The Razuud system had been a complete unknown at the time and they were certain they were entering hostile territory. While that ended up being partially true, they also ended up making an important ally.

Last time, they entered normal space well away from Razuud to assess the situation and develop a plan. That turned out to save all of them. This gave them just enough time to establish communications with the Razuuds and set up a temporary alliance. Without extra time, the Razuuds would have destroyed the Earth fleets.

This time, they knew where they were going and a scouting party had sent back an all clear. By getting much closer before going into normal space, they saved a lot of time traveling at slower speeds. They could also map and predict where all the planets were going to be. The Earth fleet didn't have that luxury before.

As expected, there wasn't an enemy fleet waiting for them, but there was a welcoming party. "Would you look at that? They certainly pulled out all the stops with our return. I haven't seen that many ships to welcome a fleet before," Riley said to Star, who currently flew by Riley as his wingman.

"They must really love us," Star replied.

With Earth's fleet's imminent arrival, Riley and a few other fighters were tasked to make sure the arrival zone was indeed safe. Once they confirmed the area was all clear, they continued to provide protection from any threats that might appear. They at least needed to clear a path long enough for the primary defenses to get online and for additional fighters to launch should an enemy poke its head up.

Riley looked down at his screens looking for indications of anything out of the ordinary or a hazard to the fleet. While he did that, the flight computer initiated an automated flight profile to scan all sectors of space with the greatest efficiency. The deep scan protocol. So far, he only got friendly returns. That was the hope and expectation.

His flight computer continued to scan, sector by sector. It started with the sectors most near where the fleet would enter normal space and it expanded outwards from there. Focusing on small sections at a time. The complete capabilities of the Razuud systems were unknown, so the humans relied on their own systems and used the Razuuds as backup or confirmation if they found anything.

"Have we figured out how the Razuuds travel faster-than-light yet? It seems way different than our systems. I haven't seen them use light gates like we do," Riley asked Star and P.

"Tobias has been trying to figure it out. He said it uses Tachyons, or his closest approximation of them," P responded.

"Aren't Tachyons made up?" Star asked in return.

"They were a theoretical particle that could travel faster than the speed of light. Theoretical until the Razuuds apparently found it and tamed it, that is," P responded.

"I would love to ditch my light gates and shed that weight,"

Riley said back.

"You and me both," P said.

"That makes three of us," Star added.

When Riley's computer finished scanning a sector just behind where the fleet was to enter the orbit of Razuud, he noticed a small irregularity. It wasn't a ship per se, or a structure, but it could be. It looked like a dead spot on the radar. Stealth was possible, theoretically, against their scanning systems, but extremely unlikely. Multi-directional scanning or scanning from both the human systems from one location and Razuuds or human systems from a different location, made stealth nearly impossible. At least, it is impossible for human technology. Riley never wanted to count out what he didn't know.

His reports showed no Razuud defenses existed in that particular dead spot on his scans. The Razuuds must be stretched thin if they couldn't set up defenses in that location. Or they were expecting an attack from somewhere else. Riley needed to verify what he saw with the others.

"Are you seeing that dead spot in the scans behind us?" Riley asked on the open channel. It was possible it was an error. But it was also possible it was something the ships and sensors closer to the Razuud planet missed. Because Riley was part of the advanced escort team, his ship's additional sensor packages extended and enhanced its capabilities. It also contained a more advanced artificial intelligence that could process much more raw data. This helped build him a better picture of the battlespace.

"I see it," P said back. Riley could see that P remotely accessed his ship and worked the settings, enhancing the scan and focusing both of their ship's sensors on that dead spot refining the accuracy. Using his knowledge of the flight software, P worked to clean everything up and figure out what they were looking at. They were all very capable of manipulating their ship and sensors to see things that might want to stay invisible, but P was on a whole different level. After a brief pause, P's voice came back over the speakers. "It's not an error. Initial messaging with the Razuud fleet says they don't have anything out there." A bit of his southern drawl coming out.

"What's the call Wisp?" Riley asked. Even though Riley knew what they needed to do. Wisp was the flight lead on that mission as the squadron commander. And as the flight lead for the scouting party, it was his sole responsibility to ensure the safety of the entire fleet as they transitioned.

"Let's go check it out, shall we?" Wisp responded.

"We shall," Riley said as he steered his fighter in that direction. They had to kill all momentum and reverse course or make a slow arcing swing. Depending on the situation, one might be faster than the other. In this case, it was faster to flip the engines and burn hard until their velocity was zero, then continue to burn hard until they picked their speed back up. Speed is power continued to be as true a statement in space combat as it had been in air combat. They needed to clear the area soon before the main fleet arrived. There wouldn't be enough time to warn the fleet and have them extend their flight or transition sooner, so they had a better vantage point to assess the situation. Riley's job was to clear the area, whatever the costs.

As they approached, alarm bells blared in their cockpits.

"We have lock on, multiple enemy missiles are released and targeting us. They're coming from that dead spot," P said to the flight.

Wisp took over. "Rip, take Star and jump to the other side of them. P and I will continue on this route. Let's catch them in a trap," Wisp said, using Riley's callsign.

"Copy that," Riley responded. Then he switched over to a private channel with Star. "Star, you ready? Link our ships up, let's get over there."

"Ready, linking now." Star responded.

Riley was excited to use the new light gates. They were supposed to deploy quicker, and he had more of them onboard. That just increased their tactical advantage and allowed them to do quick shifts and attacks like the one they were about to perform.

"On my mark." Riley input a countdown to jump on his computer. "Mark." With no need to say anything, the ships simultaneously jumped and reappeared on the other side of the blip on their sensor screens. "Shit, that was fast." As quickly as possible, they turned their ships in an arc. They were now on the other side of the enemy targets but traveling in the wrong direction. Aware they had likely surprised the enemy; they aimed to keep their ships confused. They also wanted to keep as much speed and momentum as they could. Burning to zero would be a big mistake in this situation. As they were accelerating into the arc, their ships locked onto all enemy targets.

"Fire!" Riley said as soon as he saw both of their fighters had a lock on what he could now see as four smaller ships.

The four smaller ships split off in different directions. Wisp and P had closed the distance with a quick transition of their own and were now engaging the ships that were fleeing in that direction.

As Riley's missiles arced away, guided toward their targets by optics and other sensors in their noses, Riley began evasive maneuvers. Some enemy missiles changed course and continued to follow their ships after the transition, likely confused at what just happened. New missiles were launched toward them when they reappeared at the rear, adding to the volley.

"Get ready for evasive maneuvers. If the updates don't work, go to manual," Riley said to Star.

Engineers applied new software updates to the ships, hoping to improve evasive maneuvers and release decoy measures at a more appropriate time. Instead of it being too late. This would be the first combat test of the updates. That made Riley a little uneasy. These missiles with the laser warheads were all too familiar to him.

Just on cue, his ship took over and began rotating to dissipate the laser on his shields and armor. The violent twists and turns and hard banking brought him to the verge of blacking out. It brought him to a time and place he never wanted to go back to. A time he lost his last lead, Maggie. *Not this time* he said in his head. He fought to regain his focus and targeted the missiles with his Gatling gun.

He snapped off two quick shots, taking out two missiles. Star took out the third. The fight had been intense but ended quickly. They destroyed the four ships. With no time to consider what just happened, he, they, needed to get back on patrol.

"That didn't seem like an ambush, almost like a scouting party that didn't want to be seen," Riley said.

"Agreed," P said, "Let's keep looking for more."

Just then, a couple of signatures lit up their screens. But they were not threats, they were transition indicators. The computer picked up their signature as Razuud signatures, and they were outgoing. Because they were Razuud, they could have also been Tartin, since they had the same faster-than-light system.

"Looks like the enemy is going to make it back to report after all," Star chimed in.

Just as she said that, many more signatures showed up on

their screens. This time, inbound. This time, friendly. The Earth delegation fleet had arrived.

CHAPTER 13

Helena–Center Staat Building–Razuud

As everyone entered the main room of the Center Staat building, where it seemed not too long ago the leaders had witnessed an object rain down and destroyed part of their city, she slowly filed into the corner. Her name tag said Helena Darwin. Whoever that was. Rictor was a strange one, and she only assumed that he had a perverted reason for choosing them. It didn't matter. All that mattered was that name got her onto this delegation. She no longer had any ties to her previous name, anyway. Maybe she would keep it.

The tour of the city started on the outskirts, on the edge of where the destruction was worst. Where the reconstruction had shown the most progress. It led them toward the center, following the path of collapse. Only a select few on the delegation team received the tour. Seemingly at random, but from what Helena could tell, only people who didn't have an official role to prepare for the banquet later that night didn't get to go. The rest of the official party would make their way planetside and join them later. The actual banquet was to be held in the underground city, just on the outskirts of Rutaun. Helena stood in a conference room on the top floor of the building, looking out over the city. This is presumedly where Leader Danuibi stood when the impact occurred. Also, where Leader Darnwich sat. She hadn't seen him yet, or didn't think she had. They all looked similar to her. But Leader Darnwich was precisely who she was looking for. She read the reports that the humans received of the incident. The classified reports. That was one of the ways Rictor found out about her, in fact. He admired her skill in retrieving those details. If it wasn't for the fact that Rictor had put a special tag on them for the very specific reason of finding someone interested in that report, she never would have been caught.

She thought to herself that, if the faster-than-light test had malfunctioned with power levels just one thousandth of a percent in either direction, it would have hit the city directly or missed the planet completely. Knowing what she knew now, the pain it brought her, she would have preferred it to hit the city directly. She didn't like it here, none of it. The atmosphere was too dry for her. The people, or whatever you wanted to call the Razuud, too much resembled rodents and were coming off way too polite for a species the humans nearly destroyed. It brought back too many memories. She had never seen one before in real life, but ever since they caused her so much pain during the attack on Earth, she wanted nothing more than to see them dead.

She didn't need the money from Rictor; she needed the opportunity, the ride, to get here. The money was just a bonus, although she didn't believe she would make it out of here alive. She also didn't have a family for Rictor to pay on her behalf. The money would be funneled to a charity or something of that nature, Helena couldn't remember anymore. She also believed he would not follow through with his promise.

RELATIVITY: RETURNING HOME

As much as she hated the Razuud and the human leadership that befriended them, she had enough practical sense to understand she needed to play nice for the time being. Rictor told her that one of the Razuud, Leader Darnwich, was an ally to her cause. She would use both of them as along as it served her purpose. The Razuuds caused her unimaginable pain. She now had an opportunity to do something about it. Make the leaders pay. The leaders from both sides.

She sneaked into the delegation shuttle back on Earth, where she traded places with someone who conveniently could no longer make it. Now that Rictor had done his part, it was up to Helena. She had an official role as the delegation coordinator. Which meant she didn't have to do anything and could go where she wanted to, when she wanted to. This gave her free access without unwanted questions coming up about who she was and what she was up to.

She didn't mind this game so much, as long as it had an end point. She couldn't put on this act for much longer though. The thought of cozying up to a bunch of strangers to gain political favor and climb the ladder made her nauseous. She couldn't grasp how anyone could do that and think it was enjoyable.

She stood at the window looking over the landscape, dust swirls circling the barren plains. Even more dust was created by the ongoing construction. She wasn't at the window to gaze over the desolation that was being rebuilt, although she enjoyed the damage that had been done. Helena turned and looked out over the crowd. She was at the window surveying the political landscape. Figuring out who was who and who knew what and who she needed to know. She had her mission and would use every skill and trick that she had picked up over a very extensive career, doing very similar things. Although, this was the first time doing it in an alien world.

It didn't take her long to piece most everything together. Where she stood now had been a designated meeting spot by Rictor. The first of only a couple of opportunities to meet with her contact. If she didn't meet someone now, or at the next location, she would have to improvise. That didn't bother her so much. She needed the help, but the need to trust an alien species, one she was currently trying to kill, made her uneasy. One document Rictor gave her was the location to stand and what to do when she got there. There were two possibilities. Rictor wasn't certain that they would meet at the Center Staat building, but it was the first and likely best opportunity without being too obvious.

For the first step, she needed to remove her nametag. She had only met a couple of Razuud at this point, and thought she could keep them straight. Any new Razuud that approached her but also knew her name had to be the contact. Reaching up to her chest, she acted as though she needed to fix her jacket button. In doing so, she reached inside her jacket and removed the magnetic clip holding the front in place. With her off-hand pressed against her nametag, faking holding her collar, she allowed the nametag to slowly slide inside her sleeve. Once there, she lowered her hand and placed it into her jacket pocket, the nametag falling unnoticed inside.

Now to notify the contact which human he should approach. She needed to identify herself by twirling her hair. She couldn't believe Rictor had made the instruction when she first read it. While it would be a simple thing to describe to an alien to spot, it would also be a great way to bring attention to yourself from the other human men. An attractive woman amongst a bunch of men that have been cooped up in a ship for a few weeks, doing something just like that would turn some heads in her direction.

Nevertheless, she reached up, expertly placed an

outstretched finger across her forehead, found a free strand of hair and wrapped it around her finger. She had performed this action many times, usually to get a free drink, or to distract a mark from what she took from their pocket. Sometimes she would pull the loose strand behind her ear, others she would allow it to fall back into place. This time she tucked it behind her ear. The soft tickle of it gliding across her forehead at every movement was beginning to annoy her.

As soon as she did it, sure enough, an unsteady Razuud made his way to her. He looked nervous, almost like a boy going to speak to a girl for the first time. Nerves get people killed in this business, though. Helena already didn't like him.

"Ah, Helena, a pleasure to meet you," The Razuud said, working his translator volume down so as not to be overheard.

He didn't wear any formal gowns like the other leaders she had seen. This led Helena to presume that Leader Darnwich had sent a messenger on his behalf. She introduced herself and exchanged pleasantries, which seemed to be a similar custom as on Earth. She clarified she was interested in speaking with and getting to know Leader Darnwich.

"I'm really interested in meeting the other Leaders," Helena said. She hoped this Razuud would know what she meant.

"In due time, down at the banquet. He had some unexpected matters to take care of," He responded, fidgeting with his hands and the translator box while he glanced around. Apparently her reputation had preceded her, or Leader Darnwich was as brutal as her. Either way, it looked like he didn't want to upset either of them. She only tolerated them because they enabled her to do what she came here for.

The premise of the plan had been simple, along with the outcome. She needed to stall the talks. Bonus points if she caused the Razuuds to attack the humans. The only problem with the execution of the plan was that she hadn't been to this planet before and she needed supplies and information. All of that needed to be given to her by someone she didn't know or trust. On Earth, this would have been a hard pass. But the situation dictated a little more risk tolerance than would be acceptable on a mission on Earth. She also had nothing left to lose.

The Razuud, who she had been talking with, slowly stuck out his arm, trying to conceal something in his hand. As far as Helena knew, a handshake wasn't a normal gesture for Razuuds. Their clawlike fingers and small palms made that gesture unnatural to them. She caught on quickly and reached out to take his hand. She caught a glimpse of something in his hand before hers made contact. Feeling an item between their hands, she palmed what he had. Helena put it in her pocket for later viewing. She resisted the urge to look around to see if anyone noticed this obvious exchange.

Helena had some time, but not a lot. She made her way around to many others, focusing on those who allied themselves with Leader Darnwich as best she could. There were surprisingly few who were open about it. She didn't ask per se, but judged their allegiance based on their reaction to bringing him up. She also needed it to look like she was going with the party line and not going to cause any trouble.

She did that by talking with and agreeing with the leaders currently in power. She wandered around the room. She came across one Razuud that intrigued her. He looked different. Not just appearance, his robes were more worn and darker. But also his demeanor, cautious, calculating. She approached him. Before she made it more than a couple of steps in his direction, he turned and left. She couldn't follow his path and lost sight of him almost as quickly as she noticed him.

After a short period, the head of the group turned his

translator up and spoke, "Attention, we will begin transitioning back down to the banquet hall to get prepared for the party."

Helena made her way with the group to the elevators. Once at the bottom of the building, a larger transporter waited on the street. It drove them down a tunnel and into the underground dwellings that started on the outskirts of Rutaun. For all intents and purposes, the transporter appeared to be a city bus. The size and shape on the outside shared enough features that a reasonable human would make the connection. The tires seemed like rubber tires. The similarities struck her as odd. The separation in physical space between the two species, even the very way of life being vastly different, and yet the mode of mass transit still looked familiar.

When they moved, she couldn't notice the whirl of a fossil fuel engine, more of the whine of an electric engine. She didn't think, or care, to look to see if it charged at a station or while on the road. Some human roads started including the capability to charge the vehicle through contacts underneath the car while driving.

She positioned herself at the far back of the bus. Placing her bag in the seat next to her so nobody could sit there. There were what she could only describe as adapters in the seats for humans to sit. The seats that contoured to the Razuud physiology did not look compatible to Helena. She appreciated they hadn't overlooked the detail. As they rode, she focused less on her surroundings, occasionally raising her head to orient herself, and more on the paper someone had given her.

It contained a simple message. *'Fourth Door Down, Left Side of Banquet Hall. When the Leaders speak.'* Simple enough, she thought to herself. A meeting location, with Leader Darnwich presumedly.

She ripped the paper up into little pieces. Splitting them

into different pockets, intending to scatter them in various locations after she exited.

Helena needed the meeting to feel natural; she couldn't appear as if she were on a mission. The bus pulled up to a dimly lit stop in the underground tunnel. Much of what she saw after entering the tunnel was the side of the rock walls. She occasionally glimpsed vast caverns where the tunnel passed close to openings. Those brief views surprised her. She did not imagine the underground cities to be that large. Or maybe it just appeared that way because of how they traveled through the tunnels.

Exiting the bus, she entered a set of main doors. She expected to walk some distance or take another shuttle to reach the banquet hall, but happily discovered it was right there. The bus dropped them off right at the entrance. She looked down the hall and spotted four doors to her right. 'Could it be that easy?' She thought to herself. The fourth door is down on the left side of the banquet hall. She couldn't go straight there, so she followed the rest of the group through the first door. The vast open room stunned her senses.

Expertly carved and polished stone formed the walls. The brown undertones gave the feeling of an ancient wood. The arches themselves felt old yet supremely powerful. An elevated section toward the back, toward the fourth door, held a line of tables overlooking the rest of the room. Round tables filled the space, leaving enough room to pass between. It indeed appeared to be a banquet hall. With a feast and all. She only hoped the food was human and not Razuud. She heard stories of how bad that tasted. That would be enough to drive her to attack, if she hadn't already.

She wanted to scout the meeting location before the intended meeting time. She didn't want to go straight there though, so instead, she surveyed the room and planned meetings with others as she made her way through the great space.

She sucked up some more conversation. Just a little longer and she could be done with all of this. Helena migrated around the room. Nodding, smiling, and saying very little while she listened intently. All the while making a plan in the back of her mind. She knew the supplies she would get from the sources. Some of them were repositioned, some would be handed to her. There's no way she was going to carry out any distractions in this room without someone noticing, even if they were a bunch of high-level suck-ups. She needed to draw attention to certain directions at certain times to allow her to move where she needed to go. First to the hall to get the supplies. Then to the leaders' positions to execute the plan. She needed to slip past guards and over observant onlookers.

After what she felt was far too much meandering and people-pleasing, she spotted someone she didn't expect. Helena found Leader Darnwich. Or she could say he found her. They were both next to each other, talking with different delegates. A simple turn by both, and they now faced each other. As natural as she could have ever wanted. Perfectly executed by Leader Darnwich, Helena thought, thankful he appeared more skilled at this than the last Razuud.

"I heard you were looking for me?" Leader Darnwich said, even more quietly than their normal voices carried.

"That's funny, I heard the same thing about you," Helena replied. "Is everything set up?" She questioned. They were in the open, but nobody would have a clue what they were talking about. Helena played off of his tone and worded her conversation to make it appear they were discussing the party. In a way, they were, just not how anyone would have suspected.

"Just about. Are you ready?" Leader Darnwich responded.

Then followed his question, "I need to know I can trust you."

"You can trust me. Just make sure everything is set up."

Leader Darnwich paused, appearing to assess Helena, the agent that Rictor had sent him. He started reaching for something, then stopped. After a moment, he continued his movement and reached out with something in his hand.

"The party favors, I believe is the term I've heard used, are set up around the perimeter. Try not to be there when you use the box," Leader Darnwich said, apparently deciding he could trust her.

Helena immediately reassessed Leader Darnwich as not good at this at all. Again, he unnecessarily risked this type of interaction when there were far better, safer ways to pass information and items. She looked around briefly, flustered. Helena calmed her nerves and quickly reached out and took the small box. She put it in her shoulder bag. Helena plastered on a fake smile, hoping Leader Darnwich would get the expression but expecting he probably didn't. He was going to single-handedly ruin this. She would not go down for it, if that was the case. She needed to take some extra precautions to cover her tracks if it wasn't already too late.

"Is this everything?" Helena asked. She expected something else, specifically a gun, to execute the main part of the plan.

"You will get the rest when the note said," Leader Darnwich replied. Helena, initially stunned by seeing Leader Darnwich now, recalled the note. Fourth door on the left, when the leaders speak. She nodded then brushed past the leader. She started moving toward the edges of the room, remembering she saw signs for a bathroom. She needed to clear her head and concentrate on what came next.

CHAPTER 14

Jennifer–Center Staat Building–Razuud

Jenn had worked her way into the delegation on her own terms. She was not a diplomat, although her job required her to be diplomatic from time to time. She was not a people pleaser. Her job required her to be a truth teller, even if it hurt the ones closest to her. Fortunately, she hadn't had to do that too many times. The most damaging story she had on a loved one happened in high school when she laughingly 'exposed' her father that he would play dress up with her when she was a little girl. Makeup, dresses, the whole bit. Of course, Jenn had done the makeup before she had fully developed fine motor skills. The dresses she picked out were robes and homemade crowns. That article quickly made its way to his new command, who then posted pictures of it everywhere on base. He didn't live it down for a while. It never seemed to bother him.

The latest article she wrote or had been in the process of gathering facts and writing had been about the old Mino commander, General Sites. That ended up getting interrupted by this whole alien invasion, turned galaxy alliance. As she thought back about the events that led her to where she now stood, overlooking the sprawling underground banquet room, she couldn't help but think how strange and dynamic it all had been. At the beginning, she met a cute and captivating young space force pilot who at first declined to give her a ride up to the orbiting ship. She suspected he knew she was there to expose the corruption of General Sites. That trip quickly turned into working to expose a whole new corruption of General Sites and Rictor, which could have doomed Earth. Not to mention the host of people she, Riley, and Star had saved doing search and rescue after the attack.

Snapping back to the present, she turned to continue small talk with another delegate. She attempted to get to know as many members of the delegation in as much detail as she could. That made her appear kind, which allowed her to get close. She understood they all also had their own agenda. Knowing full and well her role on this trip, most were cautious to share information. Jenn had a way of getting people to spill a little too much without even thinking about it. This skill came in handy more times than she could count already on this trip.

"The view at the top of the Center Staat building was amazing, wasn't it?" An older man said to her, standing next to a Razuud wearing a light-tan tunic draped all the way to the floor.

"I don't think we have a view quite like that anywhere on Earth. We have some landscapes that are similar to what you have above ground, but no city built like this. And certainly nothing like what you have underground. It is quite impressive," Jenn said with a smile she hoped would translate. She recalled similar conversations earlier in the day, visiting the tall skyscraper above the city. From there, she overlooked the sprawling concentric city, averting her gaze from the section a human probe recently destroyed. She could partially relate to the destruction and loss of life given the previous events, but wasn't sure how that would come off, so she said nothing.

"I would certainly like to see your landscapes, as you put it," The Razuud responded through the interpreter box. The interpreters had improved significantly, including programs that were on everyone's personal devices. These stand-alone translators, like the one being carried by this Razuud, were little brown and gold boxes that swung around their neck on a loop of string.

"I would love to see a point where we could visit each other's beautiful worlds," Jenn said. Indeed, she found the view stunning, especially from above. Something about a bird's-eye view revealing the complete picture made Jenn feel calm, even thinking about it like she did now. She had been in the middle of responding when she noticed someone she wasn't able to speak with much yet. She had seen this woman up in the skyscraper earlier during the tour and she didn't approach her then.

It wasn't the woman that caught her eye, rather, what she had just done with another Razuud. She noticed something similar up in the skyscraper, but it didn't register until now when she saw it happen again. She had gotten somewhat used to the basic customs of the Razuuds. Shaking hands had decidedly not been one of them. At the top of the tower, she assumed it was a Razuud mimicking a human gesture. This time, she clearly saw an exchange. Her senses went on high alert. The hair stood up on the back of her neck. The conversation she was just in the middle of went silent to her ears, even though the others continued speaking.

Two handshakes and at least one exchange. Nobody else had shaken her hand or given anything to her. Nor to anyone else that she could tell. She hadn't been jealous; the action stood out as unordinary. Her reporter senses were tingly, on the verge of screaming at her.

This piqued her interest even more. Now's as good a time as any to approach her, Jenn thought. She nodded at the two she stood with. "Excuse me, I just remembered I need to speak with someone." She did her best, and as inconspicuously as possible, to make her way toward the woman. Jenn didn't go directly. She paused at another Razuud she met earlier to greet him. Then she meandered to the drink table to see the selection of refreshments. After picking up a glass that appeared to have water in it, she continued on this indirect path. All along the way toward this woman.

Eventually, she arrived. Jenn just hoped it wasn't too soon after the handoff she witnessed. Jenn could tell the woman was startled. But she couldn't tell if it was her arrival or from the situation she just witnessed. Jenn got the sense it was the latter. This woman could suspect Jenn caught her during the exchange, so she tried to play it off as normal as she could.

When Jenn started speaking with her, she couldn't quite place what about the situation felt off, besides the obvious exchange. Something about her seemed out of place. She didn't fit in with everyone else. Her demeanor felt different, the way she carried herself. She looked confident, but not in the way a diplomat would. More in the way someone who was formally trained in deception needed to be. This woman also didn't appear to have an actual role. It had been easy to find information about nearly everyone else. But not her. What she had found said Helena had been assigned as a secretary, essentially. But she didn't report to anyone. She got people and things to places they needed to go. But she didn't have anyone to do that for. The details of her file flooded back to the forefront of her mind.

Jenn kept her knowledge of that to herself for now. Few people had access to that information without a lot of work. Jenn figured out how to gain access, which took a lot of work. She used other resources to get even more. She wanted to get to know her a little more, though, to see if there had been a reason to explain her actions and background. Maybe the woman was just a little off, and that was that.

Earth only sent the best of the best in each respective field. Jenn reminded herself of that. Earth couldn't afford people that were a little off right now. She put the thought aside for the moment.

"Hi, I'm Jenn," Jenn said with a welcoming smile. "I don't think we've formally met, but I've seen you around the ship on the way out here," She lied. They weren't on the same ship, but Jenn wanted to see if she noticed. She tried to catch the woman off guard. Jenn looked down, but didn't notice a nametag where it should be. The nametags were in English, or the wearer's native language. They also included the pronunciation of the Razuuds, to help them say everyone's name.

"Jenn?" Helena responded after a slight pause. The slight pause was unusual to see for Jenn because diplomats always had a canned response to being greeted. They could blurt it out in their sleep almost if someone startled them awake. "I'm Helena. It says you're a reporter? How'd you manage to get out here?"

Interestingly enough, Helena was the first to ask her that question. Maybe everyone else was being polite, or maybe Helena didn't have manners she cared to use.

"Fair question," Jenn responded quickly. "This story needs to be told. I was at the right place and time to be the one ready to tell it. I was on my way to the Mino when it got destroyed. It's a story that has two sides. When all is said and done I'm sure it has more sides than that, probably just like most of the people in this room. Wouldn't you agree?" This time she brought the question back to Helena, maybe a little too forward with her accusation.

"We all have secrets, after all we're human," Helena responded.

"I bet you've wanted to go on this trip since they announced they were taking people?" Jenn asked in response, continuing to probe her background.

"Since before that. Since the attack itself," Helena said, then continued. "But I was a last-minute swap on this trip. I took the place of someone who was unfortunately unable to go, family problems or something like that."

Jenn didn't know she had been a last-minute swap. Alarm bells sounded in her gut. Jenn thought back to the message she received from Mark. Someone here doesn't belong. Jenn didn't want to tip Helena off that she just figured something out about her. Something that Helena certainly didn't want or couldn't allow anyone to know about. One of Jenn's real friends was supposed to be going on this trip, in fact in the same shuttle from Earth even, but she never showed up. It wasn't like her. Jenn tried to reach out but never got hold of her. Jenn had been worried about her but wasn't able to figure anything out. The trip quickly dominated her priorities and concentration. Now her worry resurfaced.

Jenn had read up on every human going on this mission. Some people were straightforward, and she stopped digging after she put together a brief biography. Others, she did more digging. She recalled what she found on Helena. And what she recalled was that she dug and dug and found nothing. Almost like she didn't exist.

Helena stared into Jenn's eyes. A squint and a scowl showed through the once-smiling face. Helena didn't give

Jenn a heartwarming feeling. The look said back off. Helena's look warned and threatened Jenn.

Just then, the preparation chime sounded. The shuttles from the orbiting fleet were about to land.

"Good timing," Helena said as her expression turned back to friendly. "Time for me to go to the ladies room before this gets started." They nodded at each other. Jenn forced a smile back, then they parted ways.

Riley's ship should come down to the surface with this wave, Jenn thought. She along with all the other delegates, we're going to greet those in the fleet that were attending. They had set aside some preparation time before the festivities began. This would give Jenn and Riley some time alone. She hadn't seen him for about a week and they had had little time to talk or send messages. Besides a few other things, she wanted to talk to him about this Helena. Everything that just happened got her tipped off about Helena, like she was up to something more than just maneuvering for a better job.

Following a crowd of humans and Razuuds, she made her way through some smaller tunnels and up an elevator. The elevator stopped just at the surface of the landing pad. Dust flew across the top and partially obstructed their view of the incoming craft.

Holding her hand to her eyes to block the lowering sun as much as the blowing dust, Jenn watched as Riley's AIMS did a quick pass over the shuttle landing pad. Her hair whipped around in the turbulence. She used her hands to re-secure her hair behind her ears, before bringing them back up to block the setting sun. Riley came in for a landing on the pad right next to the shuttles, where the final delegates exited down the ramp. Jenn had been the only one waiting for Riley, so she stood off alone next to where his AIMS stopped, waiting to greet him. She had mixed feelings about her encounter with

Helena, but didn't want to give off that anything felt wrong just yet. Not until they were together, alone. She put on a smile as best she could as she brushed her hair out of her face again, noticing she still had streaks of red and blue flowing through. She had recolored it, keeping the same theme she had before.

As Riley stepped out of his ship, they approached each other. She wanted to be a good example of human behavior to any Razuud watching. All those thoughts left when the emotions of everything going on rushed up to greet her, just as Riley did. So she grabbed him and held him close. They separated for a moment, but only to go back to kiss him. To hell with anyone watching. This was her time, their time.

It felt like what an old homecoming from one of the great world wars from Earth's history would have been. But they had only been apart a week. Trap had talked with them about their relationship, and about how they could help to show the Razuuds at least one example of what humans are like. Since they were the only couple on board, or at least the only couple not hiding it, they would have to be on display. Jenn figured Riley thought she put that talk into action. What Riley didn't know was that her last interaction with Helena had startled her and Jenn was happy to see him. She felt safer around him. She could hold her own, but things were always better with him.

CHAPTER 15

Riley–Banquet Hall–Razuud Caverns

Riley followed Jenn to one of the many small side rooms lining the halls on their way to the banquet hall. They were transformed into some type of changing room. Riley couldn't tell what they were before this. Hand in hand, which Riley knew was technically against regulation, they made their way inside the room. In the spirit of showing human interactions to the Razuud, he decided to ignore regulations. Public displays of affection, or PDA, weren't a strictly enforced rule which he thought had been stupid to begin with, so it left his mind as quickly as it came.

Riley needed to get changed and ready for the evening. As they made their way to the room, Riley felt a sense of urgency as they walked. Instead of walking next to him, she led him, pulling his arm. Her pace quickened.

When they got in the room, Riley was ready for Jenn to continue what she started out at the ship. But instead she broke down crying. Riley misread the situation.

He did nothing at first, just held her. Her reaction confused

Riley, but he didn't probe, not yet. He would if he needed to. At this rate, he couldn't put his finger on what the issue might be. He didn't think he did anything. Had something happened to her while she toured the city? He waited for her. He still couldn't place the underlying emotion that drove the tears. As he continued to hold her, he could feel a slight tremble. She was neither happy nor upset. Something had scared her. Something had scared Jenn. He wanted nothing more than to figure it out and take care of it. Resisting the urge to solve the problem right away, he held her closer.

After several minutes, he finally asked, "Jenn, what is it? Something's got you scared, what's going on?"

She held still for a moment, almost as if Riley had freed her from an endless cycle of torment. With her mind back in the present, she told Riley everything.

"I think something is about to happen, something bad."

Confusion spread across Riley's face as he tried not to show it. Riley knew many things were going on, many of them not good, but what could be so bad that got Jenn scared? Certain she had a good reason; he prompted her to continue. "What makes you think that?" Riley asked, as he continued to comfort her as best he could.

"I don't know for sure, it's a lot of things." She paused. "Helena. Something is off with this girl I met today."

"Who's Helena?" Riley asked, letting her know he was engaged, but also genuinely confused. He did not know who this was and why it got her so shook up.

"That's just it. I don't know, nobody knows. I met her today and something was off. She took Cindy's spot."

"Cindy? Your friend from back home. Did you ever get ahold of her?"

"No, I haven't heard from her. Nobody has. Theres another thing. I saw two Razuud handing her something, two different times. At least I think I did. Something is wrong, I can feel it," Jenn said, getting more and more agitated as she went.

Riley knew at this point to trust her gut instinct, and his. He made a call to Major Adam Thompson, the head of security. Riley got to know Major Thompson much more after he helped him apprehend General Sites the last time they had been by this planet. The expedition appointed Major Thompson as its head of security. In that role, he lead security for the human delegation that went to the planet's surface on Razuud. With Trap being planetside, Major Thompson wasn't taking any chances.

If anything could be done, Major Thompson could figure it out and stop it. At least that's what he told Jenn, hoping to give her a little peace of mind.

"I sent a message to Major Thompson, he'll take care of it." This seemed to help for now. They finished getting ready to go. They were determined to not let this ruin their evening. A banquet awaited them, after all.

This time, Riley led Jenn out to the hallway and into the banquet room, pulling on the large round door. The oversized polished black rectangular plate acted as a handle that accented the light-gray stone door. The door appeared as if someone had cut it from a mountainside. Not a local mountain, there weren't any mountains like this anywhere near here that Riley knew of. This giant slab of stone had to have been transported from another world or a moon. Riley hadn't seen a stone of that color yet. Everything he'd seen had been red or reddish brown. Luckily, the door had a much lighter touch than it looked as he swung it open for her, grazing his hand low on her hip as she passed by. He remembered his dad always teaching him to open doors for ladies; he practiced on his mom every chance he got. An old human tradition that was all but lost in today's world.

The banquet hall in the underground portion of Rutaun had large bulbs hung high in the ceilings, giving off a low gold hue. This lighting condition seemed much more natural and comfortable for the Razuuds given that they evolved in cave systems. It wasn't exactly necessary anymore, but their bodies and minds still urged for that connection with their past. Riley learned about parts of their cave network; orbital scans showed a small portion of their vast network. The entrances sat naturally concealed by the backdrop.

There was a circle of tables set up, draped with tablecloths and outfitted with plates and what he thought were utensils. There were sizable gaps between each table so people could make their way through without bumping into anyone eating. Riley heard an audible hum coming from speakers in the wall that fluctuated frequencies, giving the feel of some strange alien music. Riley couldn't tell if that was what the Razuuds called music or if that had some historical significance to their species.

In all honesty, Riley had been dreading this event, but this news from Jenn gave him a new purpose and focus for the night. He wasn't dreading it because of the banquet or to be with Jenn. That was a much-needed break and a date night that he had been looking forward to. What he wasn't looking forward to was the shit he was going to take from the squadron for being the only one going. He talked to General D'Pol, Trap, about it when he first told him. Trap tried to explain that they needed a somewhat normal human couple to show as an example. And that him being there would far outweigh the grief he would get from his team. Riley thought that had been a line just to convince him to go. Although, if Ramat couldn't convince him, he would have just ordered him. Ramat was exercising the number one rule of a good leader.

Don't make your people do something that you yourself haven't or wouldn't do.

Even though he had a new purpose for the evening, it bothered him that Jenn was upset about it, and he wanted to help her fix that. It appeared to be open seating, although almost nobody had sat down yet. Ropes cordoned off a section of tables on a raised platform at one end of the room. Riley assumed those would be for all the leadership and distinguished guests. All the special people, Riley thought.

As they looked around, Riley felt a small squeeze of his arm from Jenn. When he looked down at her, she nodded subtly toward a girl sitting at a table somewhere in the middle of the room. Not right next to the leadership tables, but not very far away. Based on how Jenn reacted, Riley knew this to be the girl she just told him about, Helena.

Riley didn't want to give away the fact that they were keeping an eye on her, so they didn't sit at the same table, as much as he wanted to. For whatever reason, he got the urge to place himself between General D'Pol and this girl. Riley nodded to Jenn toward a cluster of tables that were situated just where he could monitor the room, specifically Helena, but also between Helena and the leadership tables.

The leadership tables sat elevated at one edge of the room. The center of the room sat below the edges by several feet. Steps ran through the whole circumference of the oval-shaped room. As Riley looked around the room more, he noticed someone had hung the lights from rock formations throughout the ceiling. These formations may have formed naturally here, or they could have been Razuud made to resemble structures found in other parts of the cave system.

"Check those out," Riley said, pointing to the ceiling, a smile on his face.

"This style of architecture is not like anything on Earth, it's amazing," Jenn responded.

Riley led Jenn over to a chair and pulled the chair out for Jenn. Jenn sat in the chair and he pushed the chair in or tried too. This part had always been awkward. With someone sitting in the chair, it made it difficult to slide forward without almost tipping the person out of the chair. He finally scooted her all the way in.

Once they sat down, Riley pulled out his personal comm device and texted Major Thompson again, letting him know the location of Helena. The tables were filling up, and Helena no longer sat alone.

Each seat had a program sitting on the plates in front of them, outlining the sequence of events for the evening. Riley glanced through the program, chuckling to himself because it looked oddly familiar to many Earth military balls. He had only been to a couple in his short time, but those, along with Dining Ins, Dining Outs and many odd military traditions, all carried a similar feeling.

Riley heard chimes come out of the speakers around the room, his experience telling him the official program would begin shortly. This would be the time to use the restroom or get a drink if anyone needed to. Riley glanced at Jenn, who stayed in her seat. She knew the drill. Riley knew she must have been to far more events like this than he had. They were all set. Riley also didn't want to leave if he knew Helena remained in the room.

Once the final chimes sounded, the music, or what Riley assumed had been music, went silent. Someone at the head tables stood and began addressing the crowd. Riley didn't pay attention to what the person said, because as soon as he spoke, Helena stood and walked toward the side of the room.

Strange, Riley thought. Of all the times that Riley had been to a traditional event, nobody got up to do anything at this stage. It even said not to on the program. So when Helena stood to make her way to the exit, Riley decided that there were too many suspicious coincidences going on. Once she fully exited the room, Riley stood to follow.

Jenn gave him a quizzical look but understood why he got up. She had to have noticed Helena, too. She may be even more familiar with the traditions than he was since she grew up around her father. Riley even got a look from Ramat. He mouthed 'sorry' and just hoped his hunch was right or he would hear even more shit than he already would.

None of that mattered. Something didn't feel right, and he needed to figure it out. When he reached the edge of the banquet room, he made his way to a different door than Helena had used, just in case she stood right outside. He didn't want to run into her and whatever was going on. The next door stood about fifty feet farther down. This distance was far enough to avoid detection, but close enough to observe any activity.

As quietly as he could, Riley pushed on the metal rectangle and forced the large rock door open. Just as effortless as before, he controlled its movement enough to squeeze out the door and shut it again without making much of a noise. He looked down the hall back toward the door as Helena went out. Nothing. He didn't see her or anyone down in that direction. Riley then pivoted his head in the other direction just in time to see Leader Darnwich handing Helena a small object and a bundle of loose cloth. He couldn't make it out at first. Helena unfurled the cloth and draped it over her shoulders and pulling a hood over her head, partially obscuring her face. It donned on him what the other object had been. His eyes opened wide in surprise. A gun. A human gun, if he wasn't mistaken.

They weren't even being careful about it. Either they didn't think they could get caught, or this Razuud and Helena were both terrible at being sneaky. Either outcome was useful information to Riley.

But Riley wasn't very good at this either, being a pilot after all. The space force spent little time in spy craft training for its pilots. In fact, Riley never had any training on the subject. The duo must have sensed that someone had watched the transaction, or they glimpsed Riley out of the corner of their eyes, because they both looked right at him at the same time.

Riley froze. What was he supposed to do? He didn't have to wait long to see what they were going to do. Helena raised the barrel of the pistol and fired a shot. Riley recognized the situation he had just landed in and before the bullet whizzed by, he dove behind a stone planter that was filled with red-brown dirt placed next to each door. He remembered thinking to himself, why is there no plant in this planter as he crashed to the floor, the bullet glancing off the pot and continuing its ricocheting path down the hall. The bang from the pistol was not all that loud. They must have used a suppressor. Not silent, but people inside would likely have heard nothing.

Riley risked a peek as soon as he regained his composure. He slowly lifted his head and didn't see anyone. In the hallway ahead, he could see a light on the ground where they were. It appeared to be emanating from the banquet hall, and it dimmed rapidly. He peeked even farther in time to see the large stone door closing.

It was time to act again. He stood and rushed for the door, hoping she wasn't still standing there. As he got closer, relief washed over him when he saw that nobody had waited there for him. This also meant that she likely made her way into the banquet hall to do whatever bad thing she came for. He braced himself for whatever possibility lay on the other side and swung the door open.

CHAPTER 16

Ramat–Banquet Hall–Razuud Caverns

Ramat sat overlooking the extravagant ballroom. From this vantage point at the head table, amongst the distinguished visitors and leaders of Rutaun, he felt a strange sense of misplaced power. Or, his seating was on the normal level, and everyone else had to step down to get to the center where they sat. He wasn't sure of the meaning behind that and Razuud culture, but he didn't like it. He much preferred to be among his troops, at the same level.

He gazed out, both inquisitively, trying to take in all he could from this alien culture, but also from a military perspective. He tried to perceive threats, identify exits, and determine strategies he could take in case of any unexpected events occurring. This happened naturally. It wasn't always like this, but the longer he spent in the military, the more he did this and the better he got at it. He had a great security team, and he trusted them with his life, but on this alien planet, he didn't know quite what to expect, so the extra vigilance helped put him at ease.

The speaker, a younger Razuud that Ramat didn't think held the title of leader, gave opening remarks. Ramat had a more detailed script of the events than everyone else at the other tables, so he already knew what the speakers' remarks were. The typical welcome and introductions. Laughably universal. Leader Danuibi, Ramat, and Mark would get into the details of why they were there soon enough. Leader Danuibi would lead the speeches, but not until after the food had been served. Nothing made a speech more unbearable than to have that stand in the way of a good meal. People, and it appeared Razuuds, were much happier when they were eating.

Ramat glanced over at Tobias, who declined a seat at the head table, in favor of mingling with the crowd. While he wasn't a social person by nature, his wealth and fame forced him to adopt it as second nature. He looked right at home. He laughed and conversed with everyone near him, unfazed by the agenda of the evening.

Shortly into the speech, Ramat saw a young female stand and make her way toward the exit. Ramat understood the tradition and showed respect, but the rule requiring everyone to remain seated during this portion or face ridicule never made much sense to him. He noticed but cared little. This type of thing only happened occasionally.

The odd part came next. He saw one of his own, Riley, also stand. Riley stood to walk in the same direction as the girl, leaving a somewhat-shocked-looking Jenn sitting at the table.

He looked over at Riley again, who caught his eye. He had a strange look on his face, one of concern. Or was it apologetic? Riley mouthed something to him. It didn't matter; Ramat would need an explanation at some point.

Ramat continued to scan the room, a little more on edge now. Something about what had just happened felt off. On the opposite edge of the room he noticed another figure making its way across to where Riley had gone. He looked closer. The figured glanced up and caught Ramat's eye then turned his head back and continued his trek. Ramat recognized the figure, although he couldn't recall his name at the time, he knew it was Leader Danuibi's friend. The one he met during the first face-to-face meeting. Something definitely wasn't right.

He was midway through another look around when Leader Danuibi stood and spoke into the microphone. Servers came out of doors that Ramat hadn't noticed before, blending in with the walls with astonishing precision. They all carried trays and pushed carts filled with steaming hot food. The aromas filled the air. Some smelled familiar, while others did not. Listening to the leaders had been the point of the entire trip. To show unity and resolve in the face of a common enemy, the Tartins. Leader Danuibi went first because he was the leader of his species and they were at his home.

Leader Danuibi began by thanking the humans, which Ramat expected. He criticized some of his own species—those who had initially wanted to destroy the humans—a move Ramat hadn't expected.

As Leader Danuibi spoke on the topic of joint trust and moving forward together, Ramat saw someone reenter the banquet hall. The smaller, more slender shape suggested a female form. The cloak covering the head and shoulders made it difficult to tell. Could this be the same person who just left? She could have reentered a different door than she left. Maybe that wasn't that strange. But she also wasn't going back toward her seat. So maybe it was someone else.

The figure appeared to be heading in his direction. The direction of the head table. She mixed in with the other servers. It was at that point that Ramat noticed that all the servers dressed the same as this new person. It would be hard to tell if he didn't catch her from the beginning. She would be the only human, so the shape was much thinner and a bit taller. The cloak may have covered her head and shoulders, but not her dress. Ramat could finally see the dress and knew then that it was indeed the same girl.

Maybe most people wouldn't notice a human girl mixed in with the alien servers just because she wore the same outfit, but Ramat noticed. At that point, Ramat saw Riley abruptly enter the ballroom from the same side door that this woman had entered. Something had to be going on now. There had to be a good reason he broke in.

His gaze shifted back to the human female, quickly approaching their table. His heart skipped a beat before hastening. His senses heightened; his focus sharpened. The smells of the room went away. With a threat identified, his instincts blocked everything out that wasn't important.

She had broken off from the normal flow of servers at this point and made her own path. She got closer, working her way behind the head table. The whole head table faced overlooking the rest of the room, so unless Ramat looked behind him, he would see no one there. But Ramat looked behind him, following the girl. Alarm bells sounded louder, their high-pitch screech in his head. He glanced down at her hands just in time to see her pulling something out of her bag.

A gun registered in his mind just as he saw Riley in a full-on sprint toward the lady. Ramat looked back to Leader Danuibi and yelled a warning as he attempted to stand. Ramat, being the closest to the leader, started putting himself in front of Leader Danuibi while pushing him to the ground. He looked back just in time to see Riley flying in the air across the backdrop and violently colliding with the woman.

As Riley and the lady were crashing to the ground, he heard

a pop and recognized it instantly as a gunshot. Unless the aliens had similar antiquated technology, it had to be of human origin. Before anyone else fired, Riley seized the gun hand but hadn't yet broken her grip. Riley twisted around behind her, the gun hand still in his grasp while he wrapped his legs around her waist. He took his free left hand and began maneuvering the crease of his elbow around her neck.

Only seconds had passed. The struggle felt so surreal. Like he witnessed it unfold in front of him in a movie theater. Trap quickly looked around to assess the situation. He could leave Leader Danuibi's side and go help Riley, but what if there were other attackers? When he looked over to Leader Danuibi, he glimpsed another leader, clutching his stomach. He couldn't remember his name. The bullet must have found a target after all.

Ramat saw part of his security team approaching him while a couple more were heading toward Riley. They could assist him. As all of this was going on, Ramat pieced together the preceding minutes and why Riley was doing the things he had. He briefly thought that he had a great crew, and he was very glad at this point to include Riley on the banquet team.

He relaxed too soon. Ramat could see the woman struggling still as Riley maintained his choke hold around her neck, just as the two separate security teams made it to both Riley and him. As his security team grabbed and secured him, he saw the other team by Riley removing the gun from her hand and helping Riley up. The woman still struggled with the guards. They were working to put her hands in some type of cuffs.

Ramat caught Riley's eyes, but as soon as he did, Riley's attention frantically looked around the room. To Ramat, it appeared as though he was looking for Jenn, making sure she was safe. Trap would have done the same thing. But he soon realized that wasn't the case. Riley was looking for someone in particular, not someone that was in danger, someone that was a threat. He wasn't frantic, like someone would look for someone they cared about. He methodically studied each person before proceeding. Like he was looking for something specific that would separate one person from another.

Then Riley's eyes lit up. Whatever he had been looking for, he found it. Riley pointed at one of the Razuud, just a couple of people down from Ramat. Riley said something. No, screamed something. All the commotion drowned out his words.

Riley rushed closer, the words becoming more clear. "It was him! It was him!"

Ramat wasn't sure what that meant but turned to where Riley pointed, anyway. His gaze landed on a shocked-looking Leader Darnwich. Beyond Leader Darnwich, he noticed the shadowy figure rushing up behind him along the wall, but still too far away to do anything. He didn't even know if he could trust him.

Ramat looked back at Riley, hoping to pick out some more of what he tried to say. Ramat looked past Riley. To his amazement, the woman had freed one hand and held something small in it. Her outstretched arm beyond reach of the guards who clawed at the device.

Time stopped. No, that wasn't quite right. It slowed, but so did his motions. His brain seemed to work at normal speed, but everything around him slowed down. He noticed things he had never had the time for previously. Or his mind noticed them and stored the thoughts away for later. The strange flowers in the large bronze vases that lined the back wall. The red stone pillars that cornered the room, and that they didn't reach quite to the ceiling. Animals and extravagant designs covered their surface. An unusual grin showed on the woman's face, almost as if something pleased her. She held something in her hand, almost imperceptibly. But Ramat understood what she held right away. He witnessed the small button on its surface depress, just a small fraction. It had been enough. Time returned to normal. That's when all hell broke loose.

Ramat couldn't tell for sure but at least two, maybe three separate explosions around the perimeter of the room rocked the banquet hall. Chunks of rock flew around, not stopping until all of their energy had dissipated, whether that was the opposite wall or a human or Razuud. Dust filled the room. Small fires remained from where the blasts emanated.

Hopefully, the many people that already fled from the initial gunshot reduced the number of casualties. It also could have made it worse, as there were many more people closer to the perimeter trying to exit when the explosions came.

Ramat's security really moved now. Violently grabbing him and forcing him to the exit. Standard procedure at this point was to get him to his ship as quickly as possible. That's when the calls started coming in. He ignored them at first, assuming it was about the situation he just witnessed and experienced. He glanced down and saw a code that he hoped he would never see at any point, especially while off the ship. The message caused chills to run down his spine and froze him in place. Even his security team couldn't make him move.

This must have been a coordinated attack. The Tartins were back in orbit, and on their way in force.

CHAPTER 17

Riley–Banquet Hall–Razuud Caverns

Riley's head hurt and his ears rang. Or were those alarms sounding? He couldn't tell or concentrate with all the ongoing commotion. Utter chaos flooded the room. The series of explosions threw Riley to the ground as he ran toward Leader Darnwich. Riley didn't know what triggered the event but looked out over the devastation as he shook his head to clear his vision.

He looked around, this time trying to spot Jenn. Where did she go? Riley saw bodies scattered around the perimeter of the banquet hall. Some were still, others held parts of themselves, screaming and bleeding or too in shock to do anything else. Humans and Razuuds mixed. He looked as best he could, but he couldn't see Jenn. Too much debris littered the ground. Too much dust and smoke filled the room.

He needed to find her.

From what he could tell and what he remembered; the explosions came from the perimeter. Jenn had been in the middle of the room when the explosions went off. *Stop* he told himself, *what would she do?*. She wouldn't leave the room. If she didn't get hurt in the initial blast, she'd be looking to help others. That's just who she is.

Riley shifted his focus. Instead of following his initial fear and looking for her amongst the injured, he turned his attention to those who were bent over those injured rendering aid.

His gaze stopped on a crowd of people. Ripping part of her dress off and wrapping it around a Razuud's leg, blood soaking it almost instantly, he spotted her. Tobias was next to both of them, doing his part to dress other wounds. Riley rushed over to her, passing by Ramat and his security detail. They were lifting him up off the ground to his feet. Ramat looked ok from what he could tell, so he didn't stop or talk to him. He felt better knowing that both of them appeared unharmed, but he also knew that danger still lurked.

"Jenn!" Riley shouted, trying to get her attention as he ran over.

"Riley! Here, help me with this," Jenn said as Riley slid on his knees to her side. He helped her finish dressing the wound. Wrapping more cloth around the thick leg the flow of blood slowed. They both worked to help the Razuud to his feet, Tobias moved on to another. Riley got the attention of someone running by and stopped them to help.

The Razuud resisted. "Let go. I can walk on my own," The alien said on his own, without a translator box. "Thank you for your help," He said, then limped away.

Figuring there was nothing else they could do for that Razuud, Riley turned to Jenn. "Are you hurt, are you OK?" Riley asked, grabbing her by the shoulders and looking her over for injuries. Satisfied that he didn't see any, he brought her in for a tight hug.

"I'm alright Riley. Just some scratches," Jenn responded.

Riley brought her back out at arm's length, just to make sure she told him the truth. He couldn't think of losing her. Riley thought of home. He was unwilling to lose a single person.

They both looked at the chaos that surrounded them. Debris fluttered down with bits of paper and tablecloth still burning and smoking. The chaos scattered tables and chairs in every direction, leaving almost nothing in its original, meticulously placed position from minutes before. The acrid smell of burned hair and flesh mixed with charred rock assaulted his nostrils.

Riley looked back to where he saw Ramat then let his eyes wander to where he had struggled with Helena. He couldn't see her. When he last left her to go after Leader Darnwich, she was being held by the guards who took over for him. He thought they would secure her, but he didn't see anyone there.

"We need to get you somewhere safe," Riley said.

"I'm not going anywhere without you. I didn't see where Helena went after the blast. I need to stay with you." She would not leave his side, Riley knew. It wasn't even worth arguing with her about it now, even if there were time. He needed to make her safe. The best way to do that now was to get up to the ships as quickly as possible.

"OK, come with me," Riley said.

As he grabbed her hand, he could make out a distinct and familiar voice. At first, the voice sounded distant, but then, unexpectedly, it shook and spun him around, appearing directly in his face.

"Sir?" Is all Riley could get out.

"Are you OK Riley?" Ramat yelled to make sure Riley could hear him.

Riley winced and shook his head, still trying to clear his hearing.

"Riley?" Ramat repeated.

"Yeah. Yes, sir. Just my ears ringing," Riley responded. He didn't mention his own shaken state after the near-death experience or the fear of losing Jenn. Somehow, it was different when he wasn't on his ship. In his ship, he knew and accepted the risks.

"Figured the last part," Ramat responded with a little smirk in the corner of his mouth. "I need you to come with me. The enemy fleet is inbound. We have to get back to the ship," Ramat told Riley.

"What, the enemy fleet is here now?" Riley asked, realizing he might have known this if he'd checked his phone earlier. He began to look down at his personal device but Ramat interrupted him.

"No time to explain, but there's something going on. We need to get everyone in the Razuud command center where they'll be safe. Then you and I need to get back up to the fleet," Ramat said, pushing toward the door, his security team clearing the way all around.

"We don't know everyone will be safe here for sure. What about Jenn?" Riley responded with concern in his voice.

"Jenn can stay down here with the others. She'll be safe down here. I need you to come with me now, Lieutenant," Trap said, sounding like he was losing his patience. Riley didn't care. He was letting emotions take over and he needed to protect Jenn.

"Sir, we don't know that it's safer down here," Riley repeated. He followed it up with a more personal tone. "I can't leave Jenn down here. The fleet is the safest place."

Trap looked to be deep in thought for a moment, considering his options.

Riley knew what the options were. He wasn't going anywhere without her, so she needed to go with Ramat.

"Alright. Jenn, come with me and Tobias. We'll take my shuttle up. Riley, get in your AIMS and provide cover for us." Trap ordered this time. Then he turned to run toward the hallway that led to the landing pad.

With no more arguments to be had, Riley grabbed Jenn's hand, and the two chased after Ramat.

They sprinted down the hall, up the stairs and out into the open, dry Razuud air. It hit their faces like a furnace. The scene that unfolded in the sky brought the information they read on their phones to stark reality. The view was simultaneously stunning and horrifying. They observed missiles streaking upward into space, and others headed for them. They made a mad dash for the landing pad. It was impossible to tell how much time they had and what the missiles were targeting. Riley knew one thing for certain, he did not want to be on the ground when those impacted.

As they ran, Riley initiated the start sequence on his fighter through his linked personal device. He received conformation that the command had been accepted and the computer took over. He slid the phone back into his pocket and picked up the pace.

In a matter of minutes they were all at the shuttle, breathing heavily from exertion and fear. Riley held short at the ramp's entrance. Jenn, being ushered in by Ramat, paused. With one foot on the ramp, Jenn turned and rushed back to Riley. She hugged him. They kissed, almost as if it was the last time they ever would. Riley hoped that was not true. Riley knew that time was of the essence, so he cut their embrace short. As Riley turned to run away, he could hear Jenn yell his name.

"Riley!"

Riley stopped and turned around to face her. Her hair swirled in the downdraft of the spooling engines. Her voice came across muffled, but he could still make out the words.

"I love you, too."

It was Riley's time to be silent. It had just dawned on him she hadn't responded the first time he said those words to her back on Earth. Now he got his answer. With that, he smiled, kissed his fingers, and blew them in her direction. He turned and made his way to his fighter.

As he approached the fighter, the belly opened for him to climb in. He strapped into his seat, finished the startup sequence, and took off, pushing the spacecraft to its absolute limits. Riley wasn't about to let anything happen to that shuttle.

CHAPTER 18

Maggie–Unknown

After the excitement of her hangar tour, the routine of the day returned. Maggie welcomed the routine. It gave her time to think. Face became restless. She wanted to act. The lights would turn off just after dinner. She assumed this represented a day. Her body became accustomed to it, whether it was her day or the ship's day. The lights would dim in the morning, then turn bright. She usually woke up just before this happened. Shortly after, someone would place a meal through the tray door on the floor. She would eat. Sometimes she would eat fast, sometimes she would eat slow. Not that she didn't like the food. For prison food, at least that's how she thought of it. It wasn't too bad. The speed at which she ate more had to do with her mood that day. Sometimes, in the night, she would get an idea. Those days she would wake up excited to try it or plan for it, which led her to eat fast. Other times she felt stuck, abandoned, forgotten, which led her to eat slow. Those days, she only ate because she knew she needed to.

RELATIVITY: RETURNING HOME

Occasionally, she could hear someone approach the door. She would tense up and stand at the ready. Usually nothing happened. On rare occasions, the door would open. She would always try to get to an angle where she could see something of value. The door always closed too quickly to do anything about it or get a good view. She could glimpse an alien peering in from time to time. She tried to time these occurrences, to see if they happened at a certain time or were random. If they were on a schedule, she could be ready next time.

On even more rare occasions, a pair of what she assumed were guards would come into the room and approach her. Face liked those days. Those days, Face took over. It meant she got to get some energy and aggression out. Along with a little much-needed exercise and practice. She wouldn't let them touch her without paying a price. They didn't seem to learn. More would cram into the room to drag her out to even the odds. They could get more aliens attacking her at one time in the hall. When exhaustion set in and she couldn't muster the energy to fight back, they would stop fighting, too. The group would then drag her back in and leave. Laying there, heart pounding, unable to move for what seemed like hours afterward.

It often took the meal door opening with her dinner to knock her out of her daze. They fed her the same meal each time. Although it didn't taste terrible, it was getting old. Eating the same thing every day, twice a day, no matter how good, was getting annoying. They didn't give her the option of any seasoning or anything. Maybe they didn't know, or more likely, they didn't care. She picked up the cup, held it to her lips and let the thick mush slide into her mouth. They never gave her any utensils either, so the last bits would remain in there, uneaten. She needed all the extra energy she could muster, so she brought the cup over to her sink. Adding water to the cup and swirling it around to collect and mix with the mush was something she started doing recently. The first time she tried it, she couldn't finish it. The mixture emitted a distinctly spoiled taste and smell. She didn't get sick, so she continued to do it for the energy. She knew she needed to.

Shortly after her second meal, the lights would go out. Then she would count the day. She couldn't quite remember how many days it had been. She wasn't sure that entirely mattered. If she ever got out of here, when she got out of here, she reminded herself, she would ask. The walls were too hard and smooth to make any marks to help her keep track.

The next morning, she woke up before the lights turned on. Unusual after a day like she had previously. She typically slept past the light turning on, waking up to her breakfast already sitting on the floor by the wall. Although her body felt tired and sore, her mind couldn't wait to get to work. She sat on her bed staring toward the opposite wall. The pitch black made it impossible to see the walls, but she knew exactly where everything was. Where all the seams to the panels were, the sink, the toilet, the food slit, and now the door. One night, she tested the small grooves or seams of the panels to see if they were weak spots. She couldn't pry them apart. Even the bare white color of the room, or maybe they were slightly off-white, gave off any sign they surrounded her in the pitch black. Everything in the room was the same color. Shadows were the only thing that cast a different hue.

This morning just felt different. The lights came on; she didn't move yet though. When the food came, she quickly picked up the cup and drank it as fast as she could. Going to the sink, she swirled the water around and drank what remained as fast as she could, trying not to taste or smell it. She wanted to move onto thinking. Maggie had a new grasp on her purpose. She wanted to live. She wanted to escape. Realizing that she had a lot of problems to solve on the way, she needed to get to work.

The first problem revolved around getting out of this cell. She had only left the cell a few times, and only one of those occasions led her away from her cell through the ship. That time they took her around to show her to the rest of the crew, like a farm animal at a petting zoo or worse. They thought they were insulting her, degrading her. Unfortunately for them, it only made her more focused and angry. It also gave her a layout of the ship. But she couldn't rely on that happening. She couldn't force them to give her another tour of the ship.

We have to figure out how to get out of here, Maggie said in her head. In case the aliens were listening, which she assumed they were, and they couldn't understand her, which she wasn't sure about yet.

"We know one way to get out," Face responded.

Yeah, but there's always too many of them. How do we get out into the hall and break free from all of those guards? Maggie asked.

She could force their hand to bring her out to the hall. All the other times she left the room were her doing. Anytime she beat the crap out of guards, they brought her outside the cell to control her better. They couldn't fit enough guards in the cell to handle her, so they dragged her out into the hall so they could get more attackers on her at one time. They then threw her back in after they returned the favor.

"We'll find a weak spot, we just need to keep trying. Not to mention, fighting them is kind of fun, it's my entertainment for the day," Face responded. They both smiled.

The fights helped her get some energy out, exercise and stay sharp with her mind and combat skills. She also wanted to show them she wasn't a pushover. But these were veiled reasons. The real purpose was to find any weakness in their response. Something she could exploit. Being outside her cell also let her gather information. How many people were there, what was their response time, what weapons did they have? All of this she kept in her mind to use in her plan. Every little thing helped.

I haven't seen any weapons on the guards besides the sticks. Maggie observed.

"*Their response time is getting slower too. The last time it took them a minute before more rushed in to help. If we can get the two guards into the hall before that minute, maybe we can get out before the reinforcements show up,*" Face said.

What, we let the two think they are standing a chance and hope they think to drag us out? Maggie asked.

"*What if we just focus on one, only keep the other at a distance? Then when it seems his buddy is going to die, if his friend tries to drag us out, we let him,*" Face said.

That might work, Maggie had to think about that one some more. A lot of different things could happen or go wrong with that approach. She admitted it wasn't anything she'd tried before. *What if we time it for when they enter? Pull them in and leave before the door closes? Lock them out and run?* Maggie asked.

"*Worth a shot. I prefer the fighting plan though.*"

If she wanted to escape, she didn't think that getting beat up and exhausted was the best start. But the only time she ever left besides the tour around the ship was when she fought. She was trying to think of any way to get out of her cell, either to learn more about the ship, or to find possible escape points. It could be possible to defeat a group of them and hide somewhere on the ship. But she may have already ruined that opportunity. Hiding somewhere wasn't escaping, and it would be only a matter of time before someone smarter realized that pulling her out of the cell wasn't a good idea. If only she hadn't been so hard on them at the start, they would have underestimated her.

Taking it easy and giving in just wasn't her style, though. All out or nothing, that's how she lived. She had to think of something else. While her brain pondered that, she thought about what could happen next. What would she do if she got out of the cell and could make it to some other part of the ship?

So we get out of the cell with the odds in our favor and we escape. What next? Where do we go? What do we do?

What she learned about security from her fights was that they weren't right outside during the initial skirmish in her room. They sometimes didn't wait for the door to close. It took at least a minute for a response team to show up and assist. They were monitoring with cameras somewhere that she couldn't see. When they took her into the hall, it was usually just the two original guards and at least two to three more. Nobody else was down the hallway that she could see. Both hallways turned a few doors down from her room. There was another hallway across from her that ended just off-center from her door. When they removed her from her room, they usually took her to this intersection, probably for a little more room to deal with her. She couldn't see anyone and nothing stood out down that hall either.

"We only know one place to go," Face said.

The hangar. Maggie said back, their thoughts acting as one. The only place she knew where to go, because they brought her there the first time she got out, was the hangar. They brought her in front of what must have been the pilots and their ships and part of the crew. That's where she wanted to get back to.

Good thing I was paying attention.

"I know, I'm going to run into the wall until I knock us out if I have to run through that route one more time," Face said back.

Luckily, Maggie had been alert enough to remember that route and thought she could get back there if she had a chance. She remembered much about that path, as much as she could, and rehearsed how she would move. Maggie went through that path hundreds, if not thousands, of times. She had committed it to memory. That was the only part she felt comfortable with. Once she got out, she would make her way to the hangar and get on a ship.

What ship are we going to get on? We know mine is torn to shit.

"*I can fly anything, just get me on board,*" Face said back.

I can fly anything. But we don't even know if those fighters have a spot for people. Out intel always said they were remotely operated.

"*Sorry Maggie, you're not gonna get a fighter. You'll need something more like a shuttle. You know they have to have at least one.*"

She felt confident that if the ship was ready to go, she could fly it. The Razuuds' anatomy was similar enough that controls must be similar. It might be an issue if she needed some type of password or key or something. She didn't know if they had artificial intelligence. She didn't think that was likely. Her interactions and learning before her capture didn't suggest that. A key or code to fly one of their ships was certainly possible, though.

"*Do you use a key or code to start your fighter or to fly one of your shuttles?*" Face asked, both knowing the answer.

No. Knowing the system and being able to follow the procedures to start the thing up is the password. I can't understand what they're saying so there's no chance I could read a procedure.

"*Not true. Your fighter might be that way, but your shuttles do most of it for you. And the parts it doesn't, there are nice pretty pictures on the screen to show you what to do.*" Face said back, sparking Maggie's memory.

Maggie hadn't been the pilot on a shuttle for a long time, almost all the way back to initial pilot training. She didn't know how she knew, but she must have seen or read something about a new procedure. Or she saw it sitting in the jump seat but didn't think twice about it. Face noticed. When Maggie thought about it, she knew.

Ok. Let's say it's that easy. We get to a ship and it turns itself on for us. If we leave this battleship or whatever it is, then what? We're flying around in a stolen ship and we stop to ask for directions? We have no idea where we are and if the ship can even go faster-than-light. We could be stuck.

"We could be the first hijackers of an alien spacecraft, how cool is that? It reminds me of when you stole what's his face's motorcycle after he tried to hit you. Just as long as we don't get the same outcome," Face said.

Yeah, he deserved that. I didn't think ditching it off the bridge would feel so good. Maggie said, looking down at the scar on her forearm from the road rash she got as she slid on the pavement, letting the bike careen off the road and into the canyon below. The thought of that time in her life made her go quiet.

That's about when Face came around for the first time. Face shielded Maggie from things in her life. Face always got her through it.

"So, we're flying in our stolen alien spaceship, probably the first person to do that in the history of the universe, but where do we go? I know we have felt several transitions to or from faster-than-light speeds. Let's say there is some kind of ship log on a shuttle. We might be able to find some coordinates or something. But for that we need to know where to look in time," Face said.

I know what you're doing and thank you. Maggie said, knowing Face was bringing her back to the present, away from all the bad. Bad that she would give anything to get back to, but not in her memories. Maggie continued. *But the days in here are a blur. It's been more than one hundred days. Maybe a hundred and twenty, maybe thirty.*

"That's close enough."

She started working her way back through the plan again. If she waited for guards to enter her room and take them by surprise, she might close them in her cell and run down a hallway toward the hangar before anyone else responded. She could hide in another room, but she would have no idea if she was entering an empty broom closest or the mess hall. That plan wouldn't do. She may only get one chance at exploiting that weakness, so she needed more confidence in it. At least something else to help her explore the ship a little more. She would save that plan to use when she figured out another way to explore the ship.

As she thought through other ideas to escape her cell, she felt a transition. She had felt several before, so that part was not out of the ordinary. The alarms she heard were out of the ordinary. The constant wail of a siren echoed throughout the ship and in her room. She had to cover her ears at first. As she sat with her ears covered, knowing it would do no good to get off her bed to look, she had a sudden and startling flashback.

She recalled another fragment of her memory. Sitting in her cockpit as it got cut open from the outside. She remembered hearing a dull drumming. She thought it was part of them cutting into her ship but now, thinking back; it sounded vaguely familiar to what she was hearing now, just muffled. When they breached the hull of her fighter, she now remembers they had the same sound. She heard that sound as they knocked her out. When she last heard this sound, they were in combat around Razuud.

Are we back where they picked us up? Maggie asked, knowing there were many possibilities.

"It could be. Assuming there's only one other alien species to fight. Because we transition, this ship is likely on the offensive. We're either

back where we were taken around the Razuud home world, or at Earth. If we're back at Earth, at least they saved us the trip," Face said.

I don't know what would be worse. If they are attacking us on Earth, humans are in big trouble. Maggie said with a bit of hope sprouting in her mind. At least her chances of getting out and rejoining the fight were looking better.

CHAPTER 19

Darnwich–Battleship Gracium–Unknown System

Leader Darnwich huddled in the corner of a cold dark room. He tried to make himself as small as possible and to stay as quiet as possible. Unable to keep his mind on the current predicament, he thought to himself about many things. He'd never had to get himself out of trouble before, so he wasn't sure what to do at this moment. He couldn't call his dad; not even miserable pain could help get him out of this mess.

He supposed he wasn't a leader anymore. Somehow, he felt some relief at that notion. Darnwich got a thrill out of the climb to the top, but not the responsibilities that came with it. He had done the only thing in their laws that could have caused his title to be removed. It wasn't just that he attempted to overthrow Leader Danuibi. It wasn't even that he failed at doing it. Previous offenders had done all of those things and usually faced only a slap on the wrist as punishment. The problem was he got caught red-handed. He got caught out in the open and he had nothing to persuade anyone otherwise. To make matters worse, a human caught him.

When he heard the footsteps outside the banquet room, not knowing what else to do, he rushed back inside to his seat at the head table. He planned to make an exit if this human woman didn't make a move soon. Next thing he knew, he heard a gunshot ring out in the banquet room and the same human from the hall was yelling at him. He froze in that moment. That embarrassed him thinking back on it. He wrapped his cloak around his head and he ran. He ran as far and as fast as he could. He didn't remember ever running like that before in his life and hoped he never had to again. The chaos of the explosion worked in his favor, because no one chased him. But yet he still ran.

Everything happened so fast. One thing he knew was he was accused of attempting to assassinate leader Danuibi, which had been factual. If he stayed, he wouldn't be able to avoid execution. He didn't quite know how he got here but it felt like the next time he opened his eyes, he was running to the nearest shuttle. His familiarity with the ports paid off at this moment. Because his city, or what used to be his city, was across the planet, he frequented these docks any time he had to make a trip to the Capitol. In the chaos, he spotted a shuttle that looked like crews were just finishing checks on, and passengers hadn't yet started loading. He rushed ahead then closed and locked the outer doors.

His dad came in handy just then. Against his desire, Darnwich's dad had made him take flying lessons. He ended up liking them and excelled. They paid off now.

He guided his hands over the controls, manipulating them as if this were his ship and he had done this countless times. The craft came to life and began the slow roll that would turn into a rapid ascent into space. He turned on the radio to check and see if anyone had noticed him taking the ship yet.

Out of a stroke of luck, or one of the other leaders had a

plan he didn't know, he heard over the radio that a Tartin fleet had just shown up. Any time the Tartins came into the system an announcement came across all channels, so he couldn't have missed it.

Darnwich didn't like the coincidence, but figured he would try to capitalize on it. He was not much of a believer in things happening for a reason like the older leaders, but this time, he took it as a sign. Darnwich couldn't fly back to his city. He wouldn't be safe, not even there. His people were loyal, but they had limits. He thought he landed on a solution to all of his current problems. He knew where he might be safe, celebrated even. The Tartins.

He idolized them in a way and always read about them in the history books. He took all that happened as his sign, his time to take the next logical step. Everything at that point made sense. Why was he spending his time and energy, his life, trying to change the Razuud to something they could never achieve, when the Tartins were already doing it? Why hadn't he thought of this earlier? He was a Tartin. The old ways were the right way. Relief washed over him. His path had just been revealed and everything he went through in life up to this point made complete sense.

With the incoming Tartin fleet, it didn't surprise him when nobody even tried to contact his shuttle, let alone chase him down and destroy him in a fireball. As he got farther and farther from Rutaun and the Razuud home world, he let himself relax. Thinking he just might make it, Darnwich let his guard down. He intently scanned the instruments for any sign of threat, but no alerts came.

No, he let the guard down in his mind. The ones guiding his thoughts. The ones that should have stopped him from going in this direction. He panicked back on the planet. Instead of relief as he left Rutaun, he started to feel as though he made a mistake. Now that he approached the Tartins, and they were within firing distance to shoot his shuttle, he couldn't change his mind. A churning feeling in his stomach manifested into a dizzying nausea. He failed to see it from their perspective until it was too late. If he were truly a Tartin, he would not allow a deserter to enter his ranks. From where he sat now, he was certain he had made the wrong decision.

He briefly considered turning around and probably would have had he had more time to think about it. But while he contemplated it, he received a communication request from a quickly approaching Tartin ship. A fighter. The request sounded more and more urgent with each passing second. Then a lock-on alarm chirped that accompanied the request. Having no choice, he decided he had to answer. He had to keep moving forward or else they'd kill him.

With a quivering voice, he answered the call. "This is Leader Darnwich, don, don't shoot. I, I have information that you need." That is all he could muster out. That's all he could think to say. Just moments before he had been confident and certain with his life, now he feared for it. He hadn't thought this far ahead. His mind started spinning, trying to get ahead of the situation. He keyed the mic to talk again, trying to plead his case, but he got cut off.

"Shuttle, follow my wing to the Gracium. You will dock there. Do not deviate or you will die," The Tartin pilot said to Darnwich, giving him very clear direction.

This gave Darnwich some hope. If he went to the command ship, which he remembered from his intelligence briefings, that the Gracium was a command ship, then the commander would be there. In Tartin culture, the commander outranked a leader. If they even still had leaders. Some reports suggested everyone had to be in a military unit.

That is great news, Darnwich thought. He could surely

reason with him.

He made the approach, just as instructed. As the shuttle worked its way into the bay, Darnwich hit the auto land function and prepared himself. The recent action left his clothes torn and dirty. He looked through a couple of cabinets, but all he could find was a garment that didn't fit him. Darnwich draped it over his shoulders, which made it cover most of the worst areas of his current tunic. He found a mirror and attempted to brush off any dirt that remained on his face.

The shuttle made an audible notification through the cabin that touchdown would be momentary, and he needed to secure himself to a seat. With his time up, he had done all he could. With the moment of truth upon him, he would soon learn if he made the right decision or made his last mistake.

He hoped for a grand greeting. A gesture from the Tartins rewarding him for his bravery. After all, that had been his entire life. Instead, he got the most unwelcome and jarring experience in his life. Even considering what had just happened with the bombs on the planet.

The door to the shuttle opened and two guards threw him to the ground. Or maybe it had been three. It didn't matter. They smashed his face into the ground, a knee on his neck. His arms were being bent and pushed up into his spine toward his neck behind his back. They pinned his legs, and he felt someone placing shackles around his knees and ankles. A metal rod linked the set together so that he couldn't kick with his powerful legs.

Darnwich pleaded with the guards. Begging, crying, screaming. Anything he could think of to convince them he wasn't a threat, not only that, but that he was an asset. He began yelling that he knew information about the humans. Information that any of their reports, or spies he knew they had, could not get.

That didn't seem to matter. They hauled him up by his shoulders, which felt like they were about to be ripped from their sockets, and pulled him along a hallway, his legs dragging behind him. He felt humiliated, unlike any other time in his life. But just like every other time of his life though, he continued to talk. He felt that was his only chance to save himself.

They dragged him down one hallway, then another, then through a door. It didn't seem to end. A strange sight caught his eye as they made their way through what he hoped would be the last doorway. Two Tartins, with their hands on their knees, blood dripping down their faces. They looked like they were just in a fight, but not with each other. He tried to look closer, but the guards whisked around one more corner. As he lost sight of the two Tartins, he glimpsed what he could have sworn looked like a human. That couldn't be. There were no reports of missing humans or Razuuds.

He didn't have time to think about it. They continued to drag him until they finally arrived at the command deck. The place where the fleet leader often stayed, this time being no different. When Darnwich looked up and saw the leader, his presence alone silenced him.

"Please, please, this man should not be in shackles, remove them at once," The Tartin leader said. Darnwich did not know of this general but knew he must be the one in charge. Darnwich spent no time getting familiar with the Tartin uniforms, so he couldn't even guess at what rank he held.

They immediately took the shackles off, to Darnwich's relief. He crashed to the ground, not expecting the sudden change of fortune. He tried his best to rise gracefully, but he swayed, still unsteady on his feet from being dragged through the ship. His ankles and legs were already sore from the tight shackles bearing down on him, holding him in an unnatural position.

"Forgive them, they were just following protocol. I'm General Tragdor, the ship's Captain. Now tell me, Leader Darnwich, what brings you to my ship?" General Tragdor asked.

"Ss ss Sir. I seek refuge and position amongst your people. As a show of loyalty, I have information that you will not find amongst any source. Information that will allow you to destroy the human enemy and squash the Razuud," Darnwich said, certain that would do the trick and get him anything he wanted.

"Is that so? I'm intent to hear it."

"Sir, the huma—" Darnwich began, about to tell them everything he knew he thought would be of use. But General Tragdor cut him off.

"But right now, I have some other important business to attend to. I'm sure you understand. We'll hold off our attack to gather some more information, from the battlespace and from you. But in the meantime, we have an execution planned."

Shivers went down Darnwich's spine, feeling that he may have been referring to him as the one to be executed. The leader must have sensed his fear secretions and continued speaking.

"No, not you leader, you are much too valuable, and one of us now. No. I'm speaking of the human. We are to make an example out of her. We will broadcast it live to that fleet, and they will be powerless to stop it."

So he had seen a human prisoner. Those words did not relieve Darnwich as much as he expected, or as much as they should have. Something felt wrong. He got the distinct feeling that the general was playing him, or his words were not truly being considered. These were all new feelings for him.

Confusion overwhelmed his thoughts. He needed to stall as much as he could.

CHAPTER 20

Ramat–Space Force Shuttle–Razuud Orbit

While Ramat knew Riley had the best sensor suite on his ship to see the battlespace around him, he lacked a wingman to help him sort through data and watch his back. There also wasn't any genuine type of space combat command, feeding him the bigger picture. Colonel Archer, the duty officer for the fleet, focused on the larger ships and the picture surrounding the main fleets. True, they spent some resources making sure that Ramat arrived at his ship unscathed, but when Ramat first saw what they were dealing with, they all had their work cut out for them. They didn't appear to be in direct danger, but only because the rest of the fleet was surrounded and the planet they were leaving was the backstop. The main human fleet was just about in between the planet and the Tartin fleet so his shuttle didn't need to traverse enemy battlespace. But once Ramat got back to his ship, to his command, the only thing they could do was fight.

With all of that in mind, Ramat decided he would act as Riley's lookout until he made it back. Both combat command,

and wingman. Even though he couldn't do anything besides point out problems and give advice. This would give Riley a better idea of what to expect and figure out how to react to anything that approached. Ramat could hear some information flowing in from the main fleet, but he knew from experience that it wasn't exactly what Riley needed. He hoped it wasn't necessary, but knew Riley could use all the help he could get.

Ramat also knew that his team onboard the ship had everything under control. That didn't stop him from checking in and making sure all aspects were being considered. Acting as Riley's combat command also helped him get up to speed on the battlespace. From what he saw, this force that now surrounded them, consisted of numbers the Rutaun didn't think were possible.

This brought him back to days when he had been more in the weeds. It wasn't that long ago that he would have been right with Riley in a fighter, engaging with the enemy. A much simpler time, he reminisced. To ensure a seamless transition back to command, he needed to understand the full situation before arrival.

Mechanics outfitted all the landed ships with return boosters and refueled them while the others were in the banquet hall. Fortunately for Ramat and the other human guests, this process didn't take very long. The mechanics went to work when everything appeared to be going normal. The first sign of trouble forced them to speed things up. These additions, along with their oscillating pulse engines, allowed them to return to orbit and back to the human fleet without any other additional help. While the Razuud world appeared smaller to Earth, its density gave it a similar gravity well.

Because Riley's ship was lighter and more maneuverable, equipped with the same boost engines, it made it to orbit much quicker. His stronger ship also meant he didn't need to slow down for the max Q phase, or the maximum aerodynamic pressure, that the shuttle needed. Riley began maneuvering along their path, his sensors on full blast, trying to detect anything that may lurk in the dark.

"You see anything out there yet, Rip?" Ramat asked over their comm link. He established a single line that only they were on.

"All clear, sir. I'm scanning for everything I can."

"Good call. We're almost up and on your tail," Ramat said, his nerves at their vulnerability showing through. He decided to not say anything else. Partially so his nerves didn't transfer to Riley, but also to let Riley focus.

Ramat focused on the flight paths of his fleet and the Tartins. He checked the relation between those and his flight path. He did that repeatedly for what seemed like forever but had just been a couple of minutes. They were almost in orbit. That is how the beginning of the flight went. A balancing act between staying up to date with the enemy and fleet movements, all while being Riley's wingman. It brought him back to the days when he was sitting in that very cockpit, or better yet, his air-based fighter. That thought, that feeling, brought a sense of nostalgia, pride, something that he had lost sight of over the years of increased responsibility and pressure.

Ramat's comm link quickly brought him back to reality.

"Sir, I think I got something. I'm going to break off and see what it is," Riley broke the silence. Ramat looked down at his screens but saw nothing. Riley's computer may not have transferred the data yet, or Riley was acting on a hunch. Ramat trusted his hunch, so let him be.

"Copy, standing by for a report."

After a few moments, four red dots showed up right on their flight path.

"Sir, looks like there are four fighters, they know I spotted them, looks like they're maneuvering now."

This brought up multiple problems. The shuttles weren't armed and had very little in the way of defenses. They also hadn't fully exited the atmosphere, so the maneuvering capabilities were next to nothing. If they wanted, they could return to land, but then they'd be even more vulnerable. They had to maintain this trajectory or it wouldn't make it to orbit. Riley had to handle this.

"Rip, they're making their way to us," Ramat said back to Riley after studying the trajectory change of the four fighters.

"I read you sir," Riley responded, "Moving to intercept."

Ramat could see Riley moving to intercept before he even called him about the threats. This kid has it together, Ramat thought to himself.

Ramat called up to the pilots in the front, "We have four incoming, stay on course."

"Sir, we might need to turn back. We're sitting ducks here," One of the pilots interjected.

"We'll be even worse off if we try to reenter and land. The safest place is on the Redemption. Our escort can handle them," Ramat responded, hoping his confidence made it through the radio.

Ramat tried to follow along on his personal display. He wished he had his command center right now; it was much easier to get a better picture of what was going on in three-dimensional space. Actually, he wished he had his fighter to help. *Not now, Trap*. He mentally kicked himself. *Focus on what you can control.*

He went back to his display. Riley had already fired four missiles, two missiles for each of the two closest fighters. Something they learned during their last engagement which drastically improved their chances of impact. He had already closed the gap and would engage them long before they could engage the shuttle. *Good tactics* Ramat thought to himself. Get them to focus on the fighter, distract them.

Ramat saw two red dots disappear from his screen. *Splash two*. He thought again. Riley already swiveled his Gatling gun to engage another enemy fighter as streaks from his last missiles, and the subsequent explosions blotted the void. Ramat could only tell by the way Riley maneuvered, and also the lack of missile signatures. He made quick work of the next one as the smaller and more maneuverable enemy fighter had not nearly enough armor to protect it from hundreds of depleted-uranium armor-piercing slugs. The fourth and final fighter had maneuvered behind Riley by this time.

This made Ramat smile. If there is one lesson to learn from fighting an enemy, it is to learn your lesson. This enemy had not learned its lesson. The AIMS and the pilot inside did not care which way they traveled to engage an enemy. Ramat could just imagine what Riley did with the fighter at this point.

Riley would tilt the engines in one direction and swing the fuselage to face the enemy. Now they were going the same direction as the enemy, trying to follow Riley, but Riley's close-range weapon was facing directly at the enemy's face. The enemy fighter must have looked shocked just before Riley blew it to bits. The pieces of debris would burn up in the atmosphere long before they reached the surface of the planet.

"Looks like that's all of them for now. I'm going to continue to patrol your route," Riley said over the comm link to Ramat.

"Copy that, good hunting," Ramat responded. He would continue to scan for threats and keep up with the battlespace. They had a brief trip to get to the fleet, and he wanted no more surprises.

CHAPTER 21

Riley–Advanced Individual Maneuvering Shuttle–Razuud Orbit

Riley continued his patrol along the shuttle route. He focused on the mission, but he couldn't stop thinking about the occupants on the shuttle, particularly one occupant, and the last words she said to him. The moment replayed in his mind, just once more, he allowed. He couldn't afford to focus on it now.

As he progressed his sweeps, sector by sector, this nagging feeling kept making its way into his mind. Those fighters were headed directly toward them. How did they know? The Tartins could have been taking an educated guess that the shuttle was important and wanted to stop it. They could have gotten lucky. Or, they could have been a target of opportunity.

There could also be one more reason. A diversion. Something to draw his attention away from something more important to them. After all, he did eliminate them with relative ease. He then thought about when he first arrived in the system during this trip. The fighters he stumbled upon, sitting out in some kind of stealth.

Riley changed a couple of settings on his instrument panel, kicking himself for not thinking of it sooner. The screen lit up almost instantly with three more blips that hadn't been there before. Because he had been out of place after chasing the other fighters, this new threat stood between him and the shuttle. The shuttle rapidly approached the threat position.

"Trap, three enemies right in your path. They're in stealth right now. Break toward my direction," Riley burst into Ramat's comm link.

"Understood, stand by," Ramat responded.

Riley hoped Ramat trusted him by this point and that the pilots listened. He tried to buy as much time as he could. He needed their ship to intercept him before the enemy got within range of the shuttle.

The enemy fighters must have realized their detection and immediately went active. Their signatures were much easier to detect and the shuttle and Riley were being targeted. Riley locked on to one of them and fired off two missiles. Two missiles streaked out, the traditional combustion engines accelerated it to unimaginable speeds. Even though he was at the edge of his missile's range, he had to take a chance, or at the very least, distract them. As he put the throttle into max, the pulse engine kicked into high gear, his cockpit absorbed in the goo, shifting and rotating within the fuselage to keep him from blacking out. He kept focus. This fight would be him or them, and it sure as hell wouldn't be him.

The first missile he fired missed, but the second missile impacted. He didn't detect a secondary explosion, so the ship may not have been destroyed. For now, Riley counted it out of the fight even though he didn't want to. He had to focus on the active threats. Riley focused his attention on the other two, already locking on to both and firing his remaining three missiles. He didn't have a full load out on this trip, something he regretted now.

The first set hit its target, followed by a massive fireball that was quickly replaced with the vacuum of space as all the oxygen burned up. Debris flew off in every direction. He was close enough now that he could feel his fighter's energy shield absorb some of the debris and register it as a shield degradation. Some of the pieces didn't burn up enough before impacted his outer armor, but nothing that caused any real damage.

The third missile missed the last active fighter. He continued to pursue, closing fast with his Gatling gun ready. His ship's gun snapped back and forth, trying to maintain a lock and lead the enemy fighter's unpredictable movements. He ran low on ammo. His shots needed to count.

He checked the connection with his fighter's AI and made sure they were perfectly synced. After a short confirmation, he concentrated hard, waited for an indication that he had a very high likelihood of a hit and pulled the trigger.

A brief burst of shots left the chamber, and the gun ran dry. His anguish at being out of ammo, and next to useless now, turned into relief as he saw another enormous explosion, once again replaced with the cold hard vacuum.

"Looks like it's all clear. I got two for sure, one looks damaged, could be done. I'm all dry," Riley called out over to Ramat.

"Copy that," Ramat responded.

No tone in his response. Had he been upset with him or relieved?

As Riley contemplated what likely had been nothing, he heard a chirp in his ear. He checked his screen. Riley's heart skipped a beat. Someone had locked onto the shuttle, and Riley saw an incoming missile. The fighter was not fully disabled after all. It wasn't moving but could still fire missiles.

Or maybe just the one. Moments after the first missile left and arced toward the shuttle, the enemy fighter completely exploded. Nothing else had blown it up, so it must have finally succumbed to the injuries Riley inflicted.

None of that mattered right now. A missile burned hard and fast toward the shuttle and Riley had to deal with it. The shuttle didn't stand a chance against that missile and it would be totally destroyed if it reached them.

Riley didn't hesitate. He input the destination into his computer and told the AI to take over, overriding the safety inhibits that would keep him conscience. After a few quick clicks to confirm he wanted to do that, the AIMS banked hard and accelerated even harder. So abruptly, in fact, that none of the safeties and technology could keep him awake during the banking and acceleration. When he came to, he took stock of his options.

He only had one. "Sir, I'm going to try and intercept that missile," Riley said, straining from the high g-force load he felt from the acceleration.

"Copy, what do you have to intercept with?" Ramat asked, almost hopeful sounding.

After a brief pause, Riley responded. "I just have my ship, sir. Unless you have any better ideas?"

"Riley, you can't do that," Ramat said, the realization dawning on him.

"There's no other way. You have to make it back to the fleet. You have to get Jenn to safety."

Riley set the computer to intercept the missile. He had to save them. He had to save Jenn. He couldn't do anything else. Or could he? After that, everything happened too fast.

CHAPTER 22

Jennifer–Space Force Shuttle–Razuud Orbit

Jenn had been trying to follow along the action by looking over Ramat's shoulder. He wasn't stopping her, so she wasn't stopping. They sat in the forward cargo section of the shuttle. The ride had been bumpy so far, but she hadn't noticed many turns. The bumps made it difficult to follow along on Ramat's screen. While she had been on the SFG Redemption, she figured out how to tap into the ship's comm networks. She received a little help from Mark to piggyback on his network and from Captain Parrent, or P, to unofficially gain access.

With access to the communication channels, at least the ones that were local to her current location, she could fill in some gaps when she had to steady herself during turbulence and maneuvers. She could listen in to the pilots' channels who were constantly talking with the SFG Redemption control tower. They occasionally spoke with Riley, pointing out potential danger or corrections for new headings. Jenn could only imagine what type of dangerous situations Riley guided them away from. She was decidedly not up to date on military lingo. The speed at which they spoke and the abbreviated phrases made it impossible for her to follow along fully.

She realized in that moment that she both thrived in this environment and didn't belong. This was war, on a distant, alien planet. What was she doing here? That quickly turned to a sense of belonging, of purpose. She had written stories about many things, but compared to this, compared to people putting their lives at risk for a greater cause, she couldn't think of anywhere else she would rather be. She couldn't think of a more noble story to tell. Not about Riley or the humans, but about friendship and loyalty in the face of evil and death.

Riley, however, took her attention back. The channel she had most focused on linked Ramat to Riley. She listened intently.

"Rip, check your six, hard to tell if there's any more out there," Ramat said.

"Copy. Pulsing behind me." Then after a second. "Looks clear in the short range. I'm headed back your way to clear the path."

"We're linked to your ship and tracking your scans. We'll keep an eye on your sensors."

Ramat guided him but gave him space to make the decisions he needed at that time. The lack of Ramat correcting Riley made Jenn believe Riley was doing all the right things. She could sense the trust between them. The unspoken communication sounded louder and more clear than the communication link. They were in sync.

She heard him speak, saw him move in his craft while following along on the display. The course made little sense to her. She had never seen him in action in his fighter before. She had seen him in the shuttle back at Earth while maneuvering around to rescue stranded sailors. Though, everything about it said something else entirely. If it weren't for the danger that currently surrounded them, she would have a lot of different feelings about what she witnessed.

After she saw him take out the last wave of fighters, a sudden sense of relief washed over her. Her shoulders rested down. Her eyes, presently glued to Ramat's screen, peeled away and scanned the shuttle bay. She looked over at the people inside, most scared. Fear was present on their faces. Some crying. Some praying. She attempted to brighten her mood, willing her expression to change. Hoping the passengers would share her newfound optimism and because of that, relax some. They approached the fleet and the SFG Redemption, their security blanket.

She glanced back at the screen and saw another pair of human fighters closing the distance to them. Riley would get backup soon.

She scanned the room again. Either she had impacted the mood of the room or her own feelings observed the room in a different light because everyone seemed more upbeat. The flight felt more like a normal trip. They were just taking a normal shuttle from the surface of a planet back to their ship. Much better, she thought to herself.

Jenn turned back around to look at Ramat, who continued to stare intently at his screen. She saw his face go pale. She looked at the screen. That feeling of relief and safety quickly turned around when she saw what Ramat had seen. A new blip on the screen coupled with audible alarms inside her shuttle.

Without warning, the shuttle violently maneuvered from side to side.

The pilots came over the intercom system. "All passengers, get secured in your seats. Seal your suits. Brace for impact." Jenn knew what everyone else didn't, save Ramat. A missile, somehow from somewhere, had found them. She knew from the conversations between Ramat and Riley that he had no ammunition left, nothing he could use to defeat that missile.

She looked closer at the screen, trying to figure out where Riley had gone. It wasn't where she expected, on the path she last saw it. He changed course and made a much more direct path toward them. He flew fast, faster than she thought his ship could go with him still alive inside.

That's when she realized Riley's intent. She tried to will him to stop, to save himself, but it was no use. She switched back to the channel with Riley and Ramat and overheard their conversation, kicking herself for not staying on it to begin with. Like she could have changed his mind if only she had been listening earlier.

"There's no other way. You have to make it back to the fleet. You have to get Jenn to safety." She heard Riley say.

"NO!" Jenn screamed on the channel. This startled Ramat, who didn't realize she had been listening in.

It didn't matter. Ramat couldn't do anything about it now. Jenn couldn't do anything about it either.

The shuttle shook violently, knocking the screen out of Ramat's hands, sending it slamming into the wall before becoming a missile through the cabin. A crew member toward the side of the wall reached up and managed to grab it before it flew to the back of the shuttle as they accelerated even faster. The force pushed them back into their seats, and they both braced their armrests.

Jenn didn't know what had just happened. But she could feel it. Her stomach tensed up at the thought. The ship still shook. Since they were no longer in the atmosphere, it could only mean explosions and impacts with other objects were to blame. Her heart, just moments ago filled with such relief, sank to the lowest of lows. The next jolt from the shuttle's maneuvering jump-started her heart back to life. She felt pieces of debris hitting the shuttle. She could only imagine it had been pieces of Riley's fighter. They were flying through Riley.

Jenn didn't know what to do. She turned to Ramat and put her arms around him. She cried. Her tears turned to sobs. She felt Ramat put his hand on her back and gently pat it. His other hand had pulled out his personal device. She didn't care what for. She could hear him saying something into his mic, but couldn't make it all out.

"Riley?" That is all she could hear him say. She started calling out his name, too. As if it would make him alive again.

Jenn could only listen in horror at what she could only assume happened outside. She felt the jostling and maneuvering of the shuttle.

The motion took her back to a time when Riley, Star, and she were witnessing the original attack and were going to rescue survivors. That time, Riley commanded the shuttle. This time, Riley acted as the protector. She trusted him then, and they all trusted him now. He just gave up his life for them. For her. But now what? He sacrificed himself for them. She attempted to regain her composure as they closed the remaining distance back to the ship. Back to the safety that would have saved Riley.

CHAPTER 23

Darnwich–Battleship Gracium–Unknown System

Darnwich paced the floor, furious about the way the Tartins had treated him. He drew strange looks from the others sitting on their beds in the room with him. None of them dared say anything, or stare too long. He then realized that they may be spies, watching his actions. Not knowing what they were looking for, he decided that sitting and giving off the appearance of someone in control would make for a better impression.

Sitting still didn't last long, though. He stood to pace the room again, determined to trace every inch in there in a show of defiance. Darnwich's mind raced while he sat and now paced. After a few moments, the door slid open. He hadn't noticed anyone approaching from the outside, or perhaps he hadn't heard them. His thoughts explored all the possible scenarios. He walked toward the door as if he had been expecting the someone. He finally landed on what he would say to General Tragdor to convince him that he had a use to the Tartins. Anything to extend his life and increase standing.

But when the door opened, it wasn't General Tragdor who walked in as he had expected and hoped. Instead, the one that stood silently next to the general when he first boarded their ship. Darnwich only recognized him by the style of uniform. It had differed from the others. This person's position next to General Tragdor and the different uniform style led him to believe he had to be the general's deputy, or his aide. It didn't matter much. Darnwich would only make progress with the general. He could only use whoever this was as a means to get to the general.

Being caught off guard and not wanting to waste his pleas on this person, Darnwich took another angle. A familiar one. Deputies in his forces typically cared for all the background work, including intelligence. He would then feed that information to the commander to make the tactical decisions. He assumed that the Tartins still had a similar construct, so he pleaded his case on having intelligence that nobody else could.

"Can I finally share my report on the humans or are you going to wait until it's too late?" That would show him who's in charge, Darnwich thought.

The deputy's expression didn't change. Darnwich recognized the look of being unamused. He had given it many times himself.

"Darnwich, is it? I'm to show you around the ship. Your, intel, as you say, can wait."

Darnwich withdrew ever so slightly. He wondered if he was blindly following his executioner. He had used this very same tactic. Lure an unsuspecting victim out under the guise of friendship and then take care of them. They always went much easier that way. He regained his confidence and stepped toward the deputy. Darnwich couldn't pinpoint if the deputy's response had been that of anger for getting this assignment, or jealousy that General Tragdor trusted Darnwich on the ship.

Perhaps angry that Darnwich may take over his position. Darnwich knew he could, or should be, in the second position. He had enough to offer and experience with his people and the humans. He had rare traits.

"After you." Darnwich finally responded and gestured toward the door. Darnwich had to get past this deputy, who he knew must be acting as a gatekeeper to the general. His mind raced, trying to come up with something, anything, that he hadn't already said that might get through to this deputy. But he couldn't. For once in his life, he had no play, no anything.

As they walked, Darnwich thought. What if the general didn't want him there? What if he is just biding his time for something else? He might as well be stuck. The general dismissed him as an afterthought, focusing on more important matters. Nobody realized his potential. The frustration built.

Like the flip of a switch, in normal Darnwich fashion, he began making plans to make them pay for their lapse of judgment. But it appeared at the moment that it would be some time before that would come to fruition.

The deputy didn't budge at his gesture, so Darnwich stepped out the door and decided to walk in whatever direction he wanted. He turned down the hall and kept walking. As he turned to leave, the deputy rushed to catch up to him.

"General Tragdor wants me to show you around the ship. You may be here for some time if you end up remaining with us," The deputy said, a brief hiss in his voice. Darnwich got the feeling, or the realization, that this man was not jealous or angry but had disdain in his voice. The question of whether or not he planned to stay with the Tartins was not something that was in Darnwich's control, he suddenly realized. What the deputy meant by 'remaining with us' had been, if he remains alive. If he cooperated enough to remain alive. This deal looked a lot worse than spending the rest of his life in a Razuud jail. They would siphon him dry of knowledge and discard him with the rest of the workers.

This realization showed on his face. It took him by surprise. He also couldn't keep it from emanating through his body. His glands released a scent that confirmed his feelings.

"Ah, you're starting to understand. You're alive because we let you live. Every minute is a gift. We don't need the information you have. We don't even need you. The idea of you is what we want. A traitor to the Razuud goes a long way to bolster Tartin resolve," The deputy said with a smile, trying to get under Darnwich's skin. Skin which did not have enough years to get thick enough for the situation he currently found himself in. This response further confirmed the deep shit Darnwich stepped in, "Please, let me show you around the ship. You must be starving? We'll start at the kitchen."

Darnwich could not speak just then. He decided, or his body decided for him, to remain silent. The deputy showed him to the kitchen and a few other areas. He was seemingly limited to just those locations. None of them were important. Not the command center where the general would be sitting. No crew quarters, nothing. There were guards that followed them everywhere they went. Darnwich continued to look back at them. This caught the attention of the deputy.

"Don't mind them. They'll be with you while you're on board this ship. They are there to keep you safe," The deputy said after yet another glance.

"They aren't there to keep you safe?" Darnwich asked, hoping to gain the upper hand in what had so far been a one-sided battle of words and dominance. It was time Darnwich showed his ability as the leader he once was. He needed to strike fear in them if talking would not work. After all, that was the Tartin way. Ruling with an iron fist.

The deputy gave off a slight laugh that trailed into a hiss. "Don't be silly, you don't have the combat experience to pose a threat to me."

Darnwich expected that response. He narrowed his eyes and clenched his teeth while giving off a startling growl. His scent matched his intentions. This seemed to catch the deputy off guard. The deputy shot a glance at the guards, possibly second-guessing their real purpose.

Darnwich decided he won this round and relaxed. The atmosphere noticeably changing. "Shall we continue the tour?" Darnwich asked, feeling he had the upper hand now.

After a few more stops at unimportant locations on the ship, they returned to his room. The guards waited outside. The others in his room hadn't even moved. He could not tell what they did on the ship. They were part of the crew, but were they the paid crew or the forced crew? He remembered his father telling stories of a time when serving on a ship was a punishment. Punishment for either doing something stupid or just having the wrong name and heritage.

These Tartins continued to ignore him completely. Someone ordered them not to talk to him because of his identity, or they just didn't want to. Either way, Darnwich preferred the silence. They didn't seem important, anyway.

He sat on the side of his bed, his legs bouncing from anticipation. He couldn't just sit in his room with everything going on out there. Did he have a choice? They didn't say he couldn't leave.

Also, nagging in the back of his mind, the image of the human kept creeping up. He felt he needed to see her again. That thought, the vision of seeing her when he boarded, stuck with him and he wasn't able to stop thinking about it. If General Tragdor spoke the truth and her execution loomed near, then he may not get another chance to see her, maybe even speak to her.

He decided he would try. Darnwich stopped the bouncing in his legs and stood with a quick motion. He strode to the door and pushed the button to open it. He sighed in relief as the door slid open, knowing then that he wasn't locked in. Stepping out into the hall, he faced one guard. "That human, where is she being held?" He didn't expect any response, or something about how he wasn't allowed to know.

But the first guard responded without hesitation, "Down this hall, not too far away. Would you like to see her, Leader Darnwich?"

That took Darnwich aback. He even used his title. Maybe some of his work on Razuud had made its way here, and they respected him. Maybe the deputy was the odd one out. He could be jealous, after all. Maybe the guard was happy to do something other than sit next to a door guarding someone who was supposedly not a threat. It didn't matter either way, he would get his wish after all. Anticipation filled his brain as his heart raced.

Darnwich realized he had not responded when he saw the two guards exchanging glances. They must have thought he was crazy. He abruptly responded, "Why, yes, of course. I've seen them up close before, but not where they belong, in a cage. It would be excellent to study one without worrying about how they feel."

"Of course. This way," The second guard responded. He pivoted and began walking down the cramped hall. Darnwich followed, trailed only by the first guard.

After only a couple of turns and a few doors, the lead guard slowed to a stop in front of an unassuming door. It hadn't been where Darnwich thought he saw the female human earlier. The guard looked over his shoulder and looked at the other guard. "Should we show him that too." Nodding to the door that they stopped in front of. Darnwich did not know what they were talking about, so he just glanced between the two of them quizzically.

"A quick peek wouldn't hurt." The rear guard said while he stepped forward and reached for the door. When he opened it, flashing lights and sparks flew throughout the chamber. In the back corner, under the spotlight, Darnwich saw what he recognized as a human fighter torn to pieces. But the sleek design was unmistakable. Darnwich just confirmed how the Tartins obtained a human. They must have captured her on the ship. The other possibilities were far less likely.

Darnwich spent considerable effort maintaining the expression he had before they opened the door. He didn't want to let on any surprise or shock. The guards appeared disappointed by his reaction. They must have hoped for some type of excitement when they showed him.

Not wanting to disappoint them, but also not wanting to let on that he knew anything, he came up with a response. "Yes, I have seen many of these on Razuud, how did you come by this one?" He thought he played it off well. He wanted to gauge if they bought his answer.

"We captured it in the first battle, where you teamed up with them to tip the scales, your kind, I mean. The Razuuds or the humans won't have that opportunity this next time. I believe this one is called…"

"an AIMS." Darnwich said, cutting him off. "This is their small and nimble craft. Only holds one person. They call it a fighter. What happened to that one?"

Darnwich sensed that these guards maybe knew a little more than he initially expected. He pressed them to see just what they knew. Every piece of information would be useful. The Tartins maybe didn't want to admit it yet, but he knew information that would help them in future conflicts. The more he knew about the Tartins and their plan or capabilities, the better he could put the pieces together. He felt the leverage of his future coming back.

"Tell me, what happened to the ship? Did you find it that way, or did you take it apart?" Darnwich asked.

"It was in one piece mostly when we brought it in. We cut it open to get the human out," One guard answered.

"Then we made some new weapons that melt the skin like it wasn't there," The other guard said.

Darnwich had to concentrate on not letting his mouth hang open. He stood there, stunned at how easily they divulged that information. Darnwich didn't have to pry hard at all. He noticed they looked a little nervous. The other guard was giving a look that said, 'time to shut up'.

"Yes, certain energy weapons have a pleasant effect on those ships. They don't have the energy shields we do to protect them," Darnwich replied. He wanted to keep them relaxed, to speak more. Darnwich played it off as if he already knew what they told him. He saw them relax once again.

"And what of the pilot? Is she still in one piece or did she turn out like her ship?"

"She's locked up in the back. Doesn't talk much," One of them said.

"But she sure can kick your ass," The other interjected.

"I was taking it easy on the weak human," He responded with a scowl. The other returned it and they both took a more aggressive stance toward each other. They both released a scent that told Darnwich they were about to get into another fight, but with each other this time. As much as he would love for them to kill each other right there, he needed to know how to get into her cell.

Before they took their petty squabble to the next level, he

chimed in. "Maybe we should see her now?" Darnwich asked, pointing down the hall with an open palm as he led the way. Intentionally asserting himself as the leader in this small group.

They both let their guard back down and grinned at each other.

On the walk over, though, he could overhear them talking. They weren't talking to each other, but on the radio. They must have had it turned up loud, because he could hear both sides of the conversation, but just barely. He acted as if he couldn't hear anything.

He forced his ears to the rear ever so slightly, not wanting to give away that he eavesdropped on their radio conversations.

"We're walking with him now, sir," The guard said.

"Good. Bring him and the human to the command center. We are moving ahead with our scheduled executions." The distant tone of the radio rang clear in his head.

It was time for the executions. The plurality of the word stuck in his mind. The hiss of the trailing s hung in the air for a moment before being seared into his mind. He only saw one human. His confusion cleared up by the next message. "It's time to show the humans and the Razuuds that none are welcome here. It's time to take back our world."

He just now realized he was about to die. Would pleading his case help at all? He didn't think so. Reacting to the news wouldn't change anything, either. It may make it worse. He didn't want to get restrained during his last moments. He didn't want these to be his last moments.

Darnwich didn't have time to regret his decision to come here. But maybe coming here could still serve a purpose. He didn't get his reputation on Razuud by only sending others to do his dirty work. He did plenty on his own. The time came to take action like he had done many times before. At this point, he had already assessed both guards, determining they lacked the training for hand-to-hand combat against him, even as a pair. They didn't have the experience that he had.

As they continued to walk toward the human's room, other Tartins exited into the halls and ran about the ship. This would be much harder in the halls. No, he couldn't do anything here. He could only handle them in an enclosed space. Ideally, in the room with the human. Maybe she would leave him alone long enough to do his work.

He wanted the Tartins to pay for what they were trying to do to him. They were going to pay.

CHAPTER 24

Maggie–Unknown

Maggie paced back and forth in her cell. She heard a lot of commotion outside. Well, a lot more than the normal of no traffic at all. She usually only heard this much movement in the moments leading up to and just after a transition to faster-than-light speed. She did not know what that meant in terms of where they were currently. But because of the alarm bells sounding, she thought it could only mean they were on Earth or back at Razuud, the alien home world.

If they were at Earth, that meant the aliens took the fight home. She knew that wouldn't be good, as Earth had sent a sizable portion of her fleet to support the Razuuds, leaving Earth wide open to attack. Things didn't look good when she got knocked out of the fight. If they were at Razuud, at least that meant Earth and humans were still OK. For the time being, anyway.

She didn't let herself think that for long, though. There was no way humans wouldn't fight to the end and win, she told herself. Repeatedly. But truth be told, she did not know what this enemy was capable of. She didn't want to stick around to find out. She didn't think they would keep her around much longer. They would either take her back to their home world and show her around and then probably kill her. Or just kill her. She hoped for the latter. Well, she hoped to be long gone before either of those options came to fruition.

She thought she heard some voices outside. Although faint, she could usually only make out voices through the walls if they were very near her door. Only just before they entered. She assumed it was them game planning just how they would avoid getting beat up this time. At least that thought put a smile on her face. The sounds of someone manipulating the lock outside with a key didn't disappoint her. This time, she stood ready. Standing by the door, she was ready to pounce and knock them inside. Once they were inside, she would exit and lock them in. Unless they were watching some video feed, or someone was relaying to them where she was, she could get the upper hand and jump them.

This time, the goal wasn't to beat them up. She needed to get out and lock them in and retain her energy. Then she could find a ship. She took a deep breath to try to calm her nerves. Her breathing slowed, and she focused her mind.

Maggie heard the door slide open. She shifted her weight to her back foot in anticipation of lunging forward to take out the second guard. She had to time it just right. Maggie had to begin her attack right when she saw the first guard enter the room or else they may spot her and be able to react.

She saw the head of the first guard burst through the plane of the now open door. Something was off. His head was much lower than it should be. It was also the top of his head instead of his face, with a body below it. Before she could react, she realized he was flying through the air headfirst. This was enough to give her pause and not attack.

The second guard followed suit and crashed onto the first guard with a thud and guttural grunt. A third Razuud rushed in after with the door closing behind him. That's when the next unexpected thing happened. He pulled a blade from underneath his cloak and quickly brought it down onto each of the guards' necks. Fresh, deep red blood flowed freely out onto the floor. The assailant was careful not to get any of his clothes. The blood did not spray like it probably would have for a human. It flowed freely, like a small stream until it collected into a puddle in the room's corner. A small drain she hadn't noticed before bubbled as blood replaced the air in the small opening. The aliens' squirms and gurgling were short-lived. There was a precision with the strikes and movement that said this alien knew what it was doing.

"Attack him while his back is turned." Face said, trying to maintain the upper hand.

Wait, something is off. Why would he kill the guards? Maggie said, hoping this meant the new alien was on her side. He looked different, too. Not in complexion or features, but in size. His legs and core were much stronger looking. Maggie had a decision to make. Attack this thing that had a weapon and continue her plan or wait and see what he did next. If she attacked this alien, he had a weapon and knew how to use it. If she won the fight, she would now be stuck in her cell with three dead aliens. There's no way that would work out in her favor. This thing didn't like the guards. Was his qualm with the guards themselves and he didn't care about her? Or was he there to help her? He could also be there to hurt her.

This all flashed through her mind in a fraction of a second. The internal struggle raged in her mind. Attack or wait. Just when she had made up her mind, it spoke. Even stranger, it spoke in English. Broken English but English nonetheless.

"Do you want out of here?" He managed to ask.

Maggie couldn't think of anything to say. Of course, she didn't want to be locked up and be a prisoner to these assholes. But she was still stunned by what she had just witnessed and heard. Up to this point, as far as she knew, none of the aliens knew her language. They certainly seemed pissed trying to communicate with her. So why suddenly do they have someone that speaks her language, and pretty well at that?

"I am leader Darnwich. Was leader. In Razuud," Darnwich said. After a brief pause, he continued, "If you want to go home, you must leave now. You must fly yourself. My shuttle is ready. We are in the Razuud system."

She wanted to know why he was doing this. She wanted to know what was going on. But the thought of getting out of here, and having some help to do it, overwhelmed her and took priority. She didn't want to soil the opportunity with questions. So instead, she just asked, "Which way do I go?"

Leader Darnwich explained the situation. What was going on outside of the ship, how to get to his ship, and how to get his shuttle moving. He would help her get the ship out of the airlock, but she would be on her own after that. When he told her about her ship and the weapons they created to defeat them, she assumed he knew she was a pilot. That was why he didn't go into any more details about how to fly his shuttle. Because he was from the allies of the humans, she now learned, he must have figured out that their flight controls were similar enough for hers to grasp.

He also did his best to explain that she was to be executed, along with him, in a system-wide broadcast to the humans and Razuud planet. And he couldn't let that happen.

After the brief explanation, Darnwich continued, "We must be quick. Please, tell them what I did here. I have screwed up many times, but I hope my last efforts atone for my behavior."

"You're not going with me?" Maggie probed. She was half hoping he would, but knew from his tone that he was going to stay.

"No. That is not my path. I have unfinished business to do on this ship. Please, follow me."

Darnwich pushed the door open, which hadn't been fully closed and locked and held onto Face's arm. She tried to shrug away, feeling briefly that this was some kind of trap.

"Please, if anyone sees us, they must think you're still a prisoner."

Face understood and remembered an old Earth movie her dad had shown her as a child. A tradition passed down through the generations. Some futuristic space saga that managed to get some of the science right, as it turned out.

They worked their way through the hallways. Acting as normal as one could in this situation. She tensed as they passed several crew members. But nobody seemed to even notice or acknowledge her. That didn't stop her from keeping her guard up. They finally stopped at the door.

Darnwich pulled a key out of his pocket. It looked to be the guard's keys. The door opened, and they stepped through. The small hangar was dimly lit. But sitting in the middle, all alone, was a Razuud shuttle. There were no guards or crew in the room, to their surprise and delight. Darnwich lowered the ramp, and they stepped on board. He began the startup sequence, then stood from the seat.

"It's all yours. I'll go open the door. When you get out to space, you will see your fleet. Your best bet is to make your way to them and hope they can protect you. The radios are set for our fleets."

Maggie nodded back. Then said, "Thank you. Thank you for doing this. I'll tell everyone what you did here."

"I believe a term I have heard you humans say is, good

luck," Darnwich responded. He then walked down the ramp and Maggie lost sight of him.

He closed the ramp, and she strapped into the seat as best she could. She couldn't fit comfortably, but it was good enough that she wouldn't get thrown around when she tried to maneuver. She heard some loud noises that sounded like decompression. He must be opening the door. That conclusion was confirmed when she saw the exterior door to the hangar open.

As soon as the opening appeared sufficiently large, she increased the throttle and gently nudged the craft forward by adjusting the console controls. Or what she thought was forward. She instead started moving backward. This reminded her of another classic movie her father made her watch every year. The nostalgia, combined with a lack of human contact, made these two situations seem funnier than they were. She couldn't help but crack a smile before she corrected her input and moved the shuttle out into the vacuum of space.

She didn't quite understand the displays and what they showed her, but she could decipher the chaotic scene that unfolded in front of her. Ships were everywhere. She could tell that there was one large group of ships near her and another large group in front of her.

"That must be where we need to get to. Without getting blown up." Maggie said to herself, but out loud this time, not caring if anyone could hear her talking with herself. The freedom felt better than she expected.

"Better get a move on, don't want to be late to the party," Face said.

Maggie knew they needed to go as fast as they could before anyone figured out what was going on, or before the real action started and she got destroyed in a crossfire.

"I'm going to take a straight approach to our fleet, to my fleet," Maggie corrected herself.

"And if someone shows up to take you out," Face said, sounding like the voice of reason.

"I'll deal with that if it happens. I'm hoping they're too preoccupied to notice us. But if there's one thing I know I'm good at, it's flying. They'll have to be better than me to take me out, even in this thing."

Maggie pushed the throttle to the max, and she sped away from the enemy fleet. She just realized she never got the name of the other aliens, if it was even different, since they looked the same. None of that mattered now.

She studied the screens, trying to make sense of what they told her. As she moved farther away from the fleet she left, it became clear where she was in relation to everything else, and just how far she had to go. Maggie needed to hold out just a little longer. She closed the distance to the human fleet faster than she expected to. Slowly letting the tension out of her neck and arms, she relaxed her grip on the controls. She didn't realize how hard she had been gripping them.

"Now's not the time to relax, looks like we have incoming."

Maggie looked at the screen and saw several blips breaking off and heading in her direction.

They were closing the distance rapidly. Then several smaller blips shot out of the ones chasing her, closing the distance even faster. She recognized those as missiles. She hoped they weren't the laser missiles. This shuttle couldn't take much from those. She also didn't know what kind of automatic, evasive maneuvering capability this shuttle had.

"Time to improvise," Maggie said. She pulled the shuttle tightly in one direction, then back in another, testing how well it maneuvered. Spinning and rolling, she tried to get the missiles to lose track of her. Maggie couldn't feel or hear anything, but knew the lasers were firing because one screen showed a picture of her shuttle lighting up in a section.

Intuitively, this looked like a section of the energy shield absorbing a laser hit. She spun the shuttle to distribute the energy over the whole shuttle, hoping it wasn't just slicing through the whole thing. She didn't see any warnings of damage.

"There's more incoming, from our side," Face said.

Maggie just needed to hold out long enough. Warning bells went off in the cabin, different parts of the ship on the display lit up red. One screen caught her attention. It lit up red for a moment before going completely blank. Remembering one of the screens Darnwich had shown her, she knew her comms just went out.

"Shit looks like comms are down. We can't take this much longer." Maggie looked at the screen to judge how much longer it would take before the humans could intercept. Too long. "We're not going to make it."

"Keep fighting. We're not out of this yet," Face encouraged.

Maggie continued to spin and jink and turn as best she could. She glanced at the screen one more time. More blips suddenly appeared between her and the enemy fighters. She knew what had just happened. Human fighters did a quick transition to intercept and cut down on the time it took them to get there. She heard about the capability being developed and improved on before she got taken out. They must have figured it out.

The warning alarms stopped. The enemy fighters seemed to focus on the new threat. She kept pushing hard to the human side.

"How are they going to know you're not the enemy?" Face interjected, *"They'll blow us both up."*

Maggie thought about it for a hard second, but that's all she needed. A big smile overcame her. Something she hadn't done out of joy in quite some time.

CHAPTER 25

Ramat–Space Force Guard Ship Redemption–Razuud System

Ramat pulled himself into the command chair and fastened the straps. The command section, buried deep within the SFG Redemptions hull, gave the leadership teams the best chance at survival during attacks. It also made for a claustrophobic experience. It felt more like he was in a submarine, which was probably true, but Ramat resigned himself to adapting to the new ways. He had just started his normal duty shift, rotating with Colonel Jennifer Mentle, the ship's captain.

"There's nothing significant to report, sir. Same as last shift. They're waiting for something, or just trying to piss us off," Colonel Mentle reported to Ramat.

Besides the enemy fleet hanging out in relative space with them, things were pretty calm. They were far enough away still they could react to any movements they could make, but so far there had only been what Ramat thought to be a few attempts to bait them into attacking. The humans appeared to have the advantage with their close-range light transitions. The Razuuds inadvertently revealed that their ships could only transition to light speeds over much longer distances, not within a local battle space like the humans demonstrated to great effect. While Ramat knew the Razuuds were eager to learn that technique, he also knew that the Tartins likely still had similar capabilities as the Razuuds.

Both sides were situated in a shared orbit where Earth's fleets were, a Lagrange point that kept them in orbit with the local star but hovering over the Razuud home world. Following the initial arrival of the enemy fleet the Tartins had sent just a few ships out, which all got destroyed.

"Still silence on the comms traffic?" Ramat asked. Assuming she would have told him otherwise.

"Still nothing. We pick up fragments of directed laser traffic but can't get enough to decipher still."

Ramat remained constrained by his acting orders of not instigating any conflicts with the Tartins. While they arrived a bit aggressive, the orbital bombardment had turned out to be something less. The Razuuds fired far more missiles from the ground than were targeted at the planet by the Tartins. None of the Tartin missiles hit their targets, getting intercepted before making contact. Then their attacks stopped, besides the attempt on his shuttle. As soon as additional fighters were scrambled from the human ships, the Tartin fighters and ships pulled back. With all of that, he did not interpret their actions as going on an offensive.

Ramat conferred with his Razuud counterparts, who agreed that this activity was unusual and suspected they may be here for peace talks. The initial minor attacks could have been the work of fighters who disagreed with their leaders' plans and decided to restart the conflict themselves.

Ramat had a different idea about their behavior, one he only shared with Colonel Mentle so far.

"I believe they are gearing up for something. Not peace

talks. I think the idea of individual fighters going off on their own doesn't fit with what we know about the Tartins. They would never break away. They are either buying time or trying to bait us into attacking. They want us close for some reason," Ramat said after Colonel Mentle finished the shift change briefing.

"I agree. They aren't exactly the type to make friends. Especially after the history between the two. It doesn't make sense for them to go into peace talks," Colonel Mentle responded.

"They also don't seem like the type that has any tolerance for disobedience. The only reason would be to make us let our guard down. They want nothing to do with how both of our people operate. They stand completely opposed to it," Ramat said, continuing to ponder the issue. "I think it's time we go on a bit of an offensive ourselves. I want to work up a plan where we get some of our fighters in close and back out quickly. Get what information we can and see if we can't see what they are up to." Ramat paused for a moment to think. "Or get them to act before they are ready. Might as well plant some drones and maybe leave behind some presents for future use if we can."

"I can get Barker on it," Colonel Mentle responded, referring to Lieutenant Colonel Marry Ann Barker, her deputy. They kept the same roles as the previous mission. Partly to keep things similar to the last expedition for familiarity between the Razuuds, but more importantly, because they were the best at their jobs. Only the best went on this expedition.

"Good. We could be able to execute something within the next couple of hours."

"Copy," Ramat acknowledged. Colonel Mentle pushed off to the door. Ramat knew she needed to get some rest but still had some work to do before that. If they were going to execute this mission, things could get interesting quickly, which would require all hands on deck.

"Thanks Jennifer. Get some rest, we'll see you next shift."

"If not sooner sir, we might be stirring up the hornets' nest with this next one," She said with a smile and pushed herself out of the room and down the corridor.

Ramat nodded back, but mostly to himself. They were ready for an offensive. They had continuous patrols with reserves of fighters. He spaced them so that they could react to threats from any direction. Ramat always had to make sure his plans were confident, but not cocky. He couldn't stop wondering what the Tartins were up to. Waiting to find out could prove deadly.

As he contemplated that and waited for the tasking plan for sending a small fighter contingent out for recon, he continued checking over the ship systems and shift change reports. He tried to find any pattern in the enemy's movements. Something they were trying to conceal, anything that stood out from previous shifts. So far, nothing stood out as dangerous. Just his orders to sit and wait and not make new enemies.

The reports were pretty bland internally to the ship as well. A battery bank needed to come offline for maintenance. Someone twisted their ankle avoiding a maintenance cart. The Tartins had small contingents of fighters sticking close to their larger ships. Occasionally they would venture close to the human and Razuud fleets but wouldn't do anything. They would make their way back and continue in this way. The list of activities and issues on the ship went on like that.

After the assassination attempt and bombing during the ceremony on the planet, Mark DeCanus had been in talks non-stop with the Razuuds trying to move past it all. The events that almost left the leader of the Razuuds dead. Many others were dead or wounded. On Razuud, teams worked to understand the events, and whether the assassination attempt and the Tartin fleet's arrival were connected.

The consensus so far was that it was not entirely intentional. There had to be some Tartin spies on the planet, spies that caught wind of something. Even just the ceremony could be enough to draw the Tartins in. Ramat decided that when the Tartin fleet caught wind of that, they showed up to see if they could cause chaos or capitalize on it. It mattered little now; the Tartins were here and Mark remained busy cleaning up the mess between the two sides. Maybe, just maybe, the Tartins just wanted to show that they had more ships in reserves, then they would be on their way. Ramat seriously doubted that though.

As long as he didn't get complacent, the calm before the storm could be a good thing, he kept reminding himself. Battle in space wasn't an ideal situation. While he felt prepared, any battle, no matter how small, always carried a toll. It wasn't like the old days of fighting in the atmosphere. In space, if you got a small hole in your ship and the emergency systems couldn't handle it, you were dead. The enemy didn't even have to shoot at you. The dangers of space could kill you all on its own. Still, though, humans have adapted well to it.

As Ramat continued to scan the report, finally making it to the end, one account caught his eye. It hadn't been significant, but he wondered when he would see it. And what happened? "Oh, interesting," Ramat said out loud as he looked at the details. Some heads turned to him, but quickly went back to their workstations when he didn't continue. Someone finally brought Riley's ship back.

Just then, his comm device rang. Lieutenant Colonel Barker's name showed up. He pushed the accept button.

"Trap here," Ramat said, using his callsign out of habit.

"Sir, I just sent the operational order to probe the Tartin fleet," She said.

"I see it now, step me through it," Ramat responded. With time being of the essence, he didn't want to have any back and forth. He preferred to hash out any issues and details live.

"Yes, sir. We'll send two fighters outside of the normal patrol. They'll be outfitted with the newer light gates. We'll find a path to get them in the middle of the Tartin fleet. They'll drop off relay drones and some tactical nukes. Once those are away they'll use some additional light gates to make their way back to behind the fleet."

"Do we have a lane clear for them?" Ramat interjected. Making sure they didn't have to work hard to find a path to get back behind friendly lines.

"Yes, we'll make sure they have several paths clear, depending on how the Tartins fleet shifts. We'll also have a squadron of fighters on standby in case they run into any issues," Colonel Barker added.

"What unit do you have on this?" Ramat asked, more curious than anything. He would trust any of the squadrons to do any job he asked. But one unit meant a little more to him.

"The Luckys, sir. They're next up in the rotation. They also have the most experience with things like this," She responded. Always ready with an answer. Ramat respected the hell out of Colonel Barker and couldn't wait to see her commanding her own ship someday.

"Agreed," Ramat said. Then followed up with another question. He wouldn't normally do this in the lead-up to a battle, but he needed to know. "Did we find anything on Lieutenant McCovee? How's the unit taking it?"

Colonel Barker didn't respond right away.

"Colonel?" Ramat prompted.

"Sir, did you not hear?" She asked.

Ramat sat in his chair, confused. "Hear what?" He couldn't think of what more there was to know about the situation. Riley died. He was right there when it happened. He had at least hoped they recovered his body from the wreckage. That's what he was asking for.

"Riley's fine, sir. I'm sending you a detailed report from him. That kid's something else."

Ramat didn't know what to say. A tear welled up in his eye. The sudden joy of learning one of your own, like a son, was in fact not dead but alive and well. Nothing could stop that emotion from showing through. He hadn't realized he had been holding back anything until then.

Ramat opened the report and tried to read it through blurred eyes. He wiped them away. Now wasn't the time to lose focus.

"Well I'll be damned," Ramat said after reading the summary.

"Yes sir. That was some damn good flying, and quick thinking. He saved his ship, and yours."

"Yes it was. And he did. I don't know that I would have thought to use my light gates as a fly swatter in the heat of battle."

"We're already talking about some plans to weaponize them, if the situation is right. He timed the light gate explosion perfectly to intercept that last missile. Riley was just too close to the explosion and it knocked his ship offline. He's ok, Ramat."

She used his first name. Not normal for their different rank, but this wasn't a work conversation, this was personal. "Thank you Marry Ann. We got lucky on that one. Learned some good lessons, fortunately not the hard way." Ramat paused again. "Alright. These look good. I'm approving them now and sending them to Wisp."

"Copy that, sir. Wisp is already on standby and ready to execute. They'll be able to launch within the hour."

The line dropped. Ramat marked the order as approved and sent it to Lieutenant Colonel Charlie 'Wisp' Broadway. Charlie had continued to lead the Luckys following Ramat's transition to fleet commander. Secretly proud of how Charlie had grown into that role, Ramat couldn't help but think about how Charlie had always been his grumpy, hard-nosed, but fair second in command. He now led one of the best space fighter squadrons in history and earned everyone's respect for the job he did.

Ramat received confirmation that the flight accepted the orders. Now all he needed to do was wait. *Great, more waiting,* he thought to himself.

He didn't have to wait long. Charlie already had his squadron outside, waiting for the orders to go through. He followed the sensor data as two AIMS broke off from their normal formation to create some separation between them and the human fleet. Then, in an instant, they were gone. He waited patiently, or as patiently as he could. Because of the distances between the two opposing fleets, the AIMS would return before they would even register on the other side of the Tartin fleet on Ramat's sensor screen.

They shouldn't be gone for more than thirty seconds.

It wasn't until the AIMS returned that Trap realized he had been holding his breath the whole time. Ramat looked at the reports the AIMS posted upon their return. Everything looked as though it went according to plan. Seconds after their indicators showed up in his sensor feed out with the Tartin fleet, they disappeared again. Then, after that, his view of the Tartin fleet sharpened. The drones they dropped off began feeding much more detailed information to the human fleet.

They would continue doing so until the Tartins discovered them.

He studied the new sensor data, along with the sensor crew on the ship. That's when he noticed some flashing on his screens. Because of how negligible amount of activity was going on prior to this, he had his screens to show him every anomaly, not just major ones. This blip sat somewhere in between normal and interesting.

"What is that activity going on over there? Did we spook them?" Trap said into the command center, highlighting an area of the battlespace where he saw the new target. He thought aloud but wanted confirmation that the recent activity had been tracked and analyzed.

One of the sensor operators spoke up. "There seemed to be a ship, not a fighter, alone, headed in our direction. It's breaking away from the Tartin fleet."

"What type of ship is it?" Ramat asked.

"It looks like a Razuud shuttle, but it's hard to get a clear picture."

"Razuud or Tartin?"

"It's hard to tell, but we think Razuud," Came the response.

"What the hell is a Razuud shuttle doing all the way out here?" Ramat asked the rhetorical question.

"Sir, there's also some new fighter activity. It looks like some Tartin fighters are breaking off and heading toward the shuttle. They're all heading our direction."

Then more information about the ship started coming in. The commotion in the command center picked up. All the return sensor data confirmed it as a Razuud shuttle.

"Sir," The sensor operator said to Ramat, getting his full attention. "it's confirmed, that ship is a Razuud shuttle. It matches the one that left Rutaun shortly after the attack at the banquet."

"How certain are you?" Trap asked in response. Being the same shuttle could mean many things. It could be a trap, or whoever originally escaped had a change of heart. He wasn't sure he wanted to be the one to find out, though.

"We're working on it, Sir. But right now it's over ninety percent sure," The sensor operator responded. Then continued, "Sir, the beacon just turned on. It's the same ship. No comms yet."

"Good. Keep trying to contact that ship." Ramat said. He also knew he needed to act on this situation, not just sit back and wait. "Scramble a flight of fighters, intercept, see if we can get a closer look before those Tartin fighters take it out. Protect it for now," Ramat ordered.

"Yes sir, Luckys are going out," The operations officer said, coordinating the flight activity in the battle space.

Ramat smiled inwardly; glad they were the ones on call. He could count on all his troops, but he had a special tie with the Luckys.

"Are they responding to comms yet?" Ramat asked again. Knowing that it hadn't been that long since he last asked. All of this felt wrong.

"Nothing sir. It could be damaged or out of range still. The Tartins also seem to be jamming everything over there," The comms officer replied, sounding frustrated that he couldn't do more.

"Keep working on it, let me know as soon as you have something."

"Yes, sir."

Ramat sat still, closely monitoring the flight of fighters headed out to intercept. He checked on the flight crew. Lieutenant Colonel Charlie 'Wisp' Broadway, Lieutenant Riley 'Ripcord' McCovee, Lieutenant Jade 'Star' Starilla, and Captain

James 'P' Parrant. A smile spread across his face, ear to ear. Those enemy Tartins were in for one hell of a surprise. As he watched them separate from the main ships, they vanished in a telltale flash of a light gate transition. Good, he thought to himself. We can't afford to waste any time.

CHAPTER 26

Riley—Advanced Individual Maneuvering Shuttle—Razuud System

Riley flew number two in the flight, acting as Wisp's wingman, the commander. With P leading Star, the flight of four set off to intercept, and protect, an unknown shuttle. Their flight, call sign Victor, would put Riley in an all too familiar and recent situation.

"All Victors, this is Victor One. We have the assignment we've been waiting for. Everyone link up and prepare to transition," Wisp said over the comm unit. There were four of them, the rest of the squadron and other fighters sat in reserves to prepare for the potential of a much larger battle.

"Victor One, Victor Two copies, I'm synched," Riley said in response.

"Victors Three and Four copy, we're synched," Captain 'P' Parrant responded, answering for both him and Lieutenant Jade 'Star' Starilla.

"Stand by for transition. This is going to be a fast one," Wisp said, a countdown timer showing up on all of their screens. This indication meant that all fighters were in fact synched and could make their transitions precisely together and reenter normal speeds together. This allowed them to make a bigger impact on the battlespace instantly.

Riley looked at his screen, then at his radar scope that showed the image of the shuttle, and the incoming Tartin fighters. Because of the close distance of this transition, it would be difficult to return to an exact normal-speed re-entry location. They would need to act and adjust in real time to the situation. They wanted to appear somewhere in between the two groups, but it was anyone's guess where they would end up.

The countdown timer reached zero. Within seconds, Riley and the rest of the fighters transitioned to near-light speed and back to relative speeds. But now they were close to the shuttle and enemy fighters. When they emerged from the transition, they quickly determined that they were short of their mark. They had to flip and burn hard to avoid the shuttle flying right by them. They also didn't want to be sitting ducks for the Tartin fighters.

The precise timing of the practiced maneuvers paid off. The two sets of ships split their trajectories just enough that they created a book end on either side of the outermost Tartin fighters. Their plan was to squeeze the Tartin fighters to either stop their pursuit of the shuttle and engage with their AIMS or force them to turn tail and run. Both options got them what they wanted; the shuttle to be left alone. Their plan partially worked. Two fighters pursued their fighters while three others continued their pursuit of the shuttle.

The two sets of fighters coordinated their attack, choosing to split up, using their AIMS superiority to their advantage. Riley acquired the closest fighter and locked on his missiles. As soon as he locked on, a targeting alert from the enemy sounded. Clearly the Tartins had no intention of fleeing.

"Rip, you and I take the two closest to us. P, Star, you two take the three that are still following the shuttle. Don't let them intercept," Wisp ordered. His voice was crisp and level. His intentions were unmistakable; let nothing happen to that shuttle.

Riley wondered why they all didn't go after the three that were still going after the shuttle. If they wanted to ensure the shuttle's safety, why didn't all of their fighters intercept anything close? As the picture unfolded, Riley understood why. If they had all converged on the shuttle, they would have been stuck playing defense and brought all the Tartin fighters back toward the shuttle. They were in offensive fighters. That would have put them at a disadvantage. He also got the impression that Wisp wanted to pursue the leader of this flight.

Riley's last large-scale engagement taught him that taking out the leader cripples the others' ability to operate effectively. Wisp used this to their advantage. It put pressure on the other three while taking out the leader. Don't concentrate all forces on that shuttle. The chances of an accident or the shuttle getting taken out would have gone up drastically if Victor flight merged around the shuttle.

Riley understood now, and he acted. He loosed two of his missiles, following the new standard operating procedures they learned the last time they fought the Tartins. He wanted to send three just to be sure but wasn't sure how long they would be out here and if they were going to encounter any more resistance. The chances were good that Riley and the rest of Victor flight had just hit the beehive.

Wisp did the same with his missiles, and both sent a volley toward the Tartins fighters. They continued to perform evasive maneuvers, trying to get into a better position. Energy management was just as important with the AIMS as it had been with the atmosphere-based fighters. The added element of no air resistance or gravity made the balance much different. Every action had to be countered with a follow-up action. The reaction thrusters were firing constantly to keep the AIMS pointed in the direction it needed to go. His engines pivoted and swung to keep the ship going in the direction it needed to go or stop speed and change course. The cockpit sitting inside the gel cavity rotated and slid within the ship's hull to give the pilot the best chance of staying conscious and operating the craft.

Fortunately, the AIMS flight computer handled all of this automatically. This gave Riley time to focus on the fighters and adjust to what they were doing. He could do this through his heads-up display that showed the exterior view of his ship, with all the instrumentation he needed just within view. That's when his shield gauge went from the normal green status to yellow, then red almost instantly. Before he could react, his ship spun in a rotisserie motion to dissipate the energy from the laser weapon that the Tartins fired at him.

"Wisp, they're hitting us with lasers. Much stronger than before, it went right through my shields and started working through my armor before I could even react," Riley called out over the Victor flight channel. He wanted to make sure everyone got the message. Riley checked the status of Wisp and saw him making the same maneuvers. They must have targeted him, too.

"Copy," Wisp responded, followed by "splash four on our missiles. Looks like they made some upgrades to their offense and defense. It's time to change things up. Let's get in their personal space."

"Right behind you," Riley responded with a grin.

They both aborted their more circling trajectory that had them spiral closer to the Tartin fighters and pivoted to an almost direct approach. They had their fighters set to jink and maneuver in random patterns, with the hull rotating around them in an effort to dissipate any laser energy that hit their ships, despite the movement. All it would take is one lucky shot.

"Get your Gatlin synced to mine, where going to get them in a crossfire," Wisp ordered.

Riley knew what to do. He split a little farther as he set the command for his Gatling gun to synch to Wisps. This would effectively allow Wisp to take control, although not complete control, of his gun. It allowed them to work together to eliminate the fighters, one at a time. Riley could still lock on and fire more missiles, which he worked on doing. He wanted to hold off until they were within Gatlin range though, so they could act as a distraction, without wasting the shot. Something had to make its way through.

"Get ready. Almost in range," Wisp said over the comms channel. After a few seconds, they closed the distance just enough. Wisp followed up with "Fire!"

Wisp let loose a volley of hundreds of high-density armor-piercing rounds. The ship's flight computer guided the rounds into the Tartin fighter and walked them up the center of the hull, each penetration producing sparks and atmosphere shooting out into space. They found their mark.

At the same time, Riley sent two missiles toward the second fighter, counting on it being distracted by the gunfire. A flash of light and fire, swallowed quickly by the vacuum of space, never got old to Riley as he witnessed the second fighter succumb to the same fate as the first. Debris scattered in every direction. The added detonation of the warheads on the missiles combined with the explosion of the ship, made for a more fantastic display.

They both turned their attention to the remaining three, scratch that, two fighters. Riley zoomed in on his radar, making sure the shuttle continued its advance toward the human fleet. It did.

"Riley, break off and protect the shuttle, you have some recent experience with that," Wisp said, with a hint of humor in his voice. "Just try to keep your ship in one piece this time, alright. No guarantees of a speedy rescue."

"No promises, sir," Riley broke off and headed for the shuttle. The memory of his recent escort duties still a vivid one.

"P, Star, continue your attack on the remaining fighters, I'm coming in from behind. Going stealth," Wisp said, activating a mode on the ship, which made it very difficult to detect.

With all the radar energy floating around, Riley wasn't sure how well it would work, but in the confusion, the other Tartin fighters could assume someone had taken out one AIMS. That would be their mistake. Riley continued his approach to the shuttle. Accelerating hard, it wouldn't take him long to catch up. His previous engagement didn't stray far from the original flight path of the shuttle.

As Riley approached, he tried to contact the shuttle. Maybe an issue with the comm system on the shuttle prevented long-range communication. "Unknown shuttle, this is Lieutenant Riley McCovee with the human fleet, identify yourself. I repeat this is Lieutenant Riley McCovee with the human fleet, identify yourself." He allowed for a response. Seemingly out of danger for the moment, the shuttle reduced the maneuvering, making it a little easier for Riley to move alongside the shuttle. There were no exterior windows, at least none he could see into and get a visual. He looked for anything that indicated who or what piloted the shuttle and who could be onboard.

It could be a giant bomb for all they knew, and everything

else was just a show. If a large bomb made it into the hangar bay of the ship, that would spell the end of that ship. Riley had to figure out how to communicate with it.

The ship rocked side to side. At first quick, then slow. Then quick again. It repeated. The wings rocked back and forth rapidly. Then slowly, then rapidly again. It did it one more time. At first, Riley thought maybe there had been an issue with the flight controls and the shuttle became hard to pilot. Then, he noticed a pattern within the movements. He could just be imagining it, but he had nothing else to go on at the moment.

The shuttle rocked exactly three times rapidly, then three times slowly, then three more times rapidly. He recognized that pattern, or at least he thought he did. He had seen it during his initial flight school. Some old-school atmospheric pilot taught them survival basics. It resembled an old code. But he didn't know what it meant right away.

"Wisp, the shuttle is doing something weird. It's rocking very specifically. Three quick, three long, three quick. I think it's a code but don't remember," Riley said, calling out to his flight, but he sent it back to the main fleet, too. Their response time would be longer. Someone could decipher it if Wisp couldn't.

Riley received a text response from Wisp. "Stand by."

Riley looked at his radar and saw P and Star engaged with the remaining two fighters while Wisp remained in stealth mode. He didn't want a radio transmission to give away his position. A directed laser link with a text message would be far less likely to be detected.

Riley started looking through old files, trying to figure out what they could mean. His ship kept a lot of storage, but not everything. He couldn't do much right now except keep a lookout for more enemies and keep the shuttle safe. The other two fighters were less concerned about the shuttle now and more concerned with the rest of the AIMS fighters, or not dying, because they were nowhere near the shuttle.

Riley thought about going to help, but knew he needed to stay with this shuttle. His orders were explicit, but he couldn't shake the feeling that something felt off about this.

"Victor Two. That code is Morse Code. Your ship now has the translation. First message is Sierra Oscar Sierra. It is an old human distress signal." The communications officer on the Redemption radioed to Riley.

"Copy that," Riley responded. He quickly opened the message and looked at the translator.

Then the shuttle started a new pattern. Two rapid rocks, one long rock, one rapid rock, pause. 'F'. Riley made a note on his lapboard. One rapid rock, one long rock, pause. 'A', he made another note. One long rock, one rapid rock, one long rock, one rapid, pause. 'C'. The picture came together in a wave of emotions and disbelief. No way. One rapid rock, pause. 'E'.

"Face? FACE!" Riley first said confused, then repeated excitedly.

"Repeat your last," Wisp said over the comms.

Riley, so focused on the shuttle and message that he lost track of the battle, which was now apparently over. The three AIMS were closing in with him and the shuttle, and no Tartin fighters showed up on the radar. He assumed the Tartin fighters had been eliminated.

"The shuttle, it just spelled F, A, C, E. Face. In an old American code. There's no way the enemy knows that code, and no way they know Maggie's call sign. It's got to be her," Riley responded, the feeling of hope but also dread of everything she must have gone through. Then the regret of letting her get captured. The feelings of being responsible suddenly crept back in. He thought he had locked those feelings up for good.

There would be time for that later.

"Copy," That is all Wisp said. All business as usual. Riley knew he was secretly excited or trying not to get his hopes up. Either way, Riley believed Maggie piloted that shuttle. It had to be her.

Just then, Riley's sensors screamed at him. The Tartin fleet erupted in chaos on his scope.

"We have a massive force incoming. The whole Tartin fleet is moving toward us. Time to get home," Wisp said. They had to get back the long way. They couldn't leave the shuttle behind which meant no transitions.

"Victor flight, RTB quickest speed. Tartin fleet incoming," The comms officer reported to the flight. They already knew that. They also heard battle station claxons blaring in the background. The real battle would begin soon.

CHAPTER 27

Maggie–Space Force Guard Ship Redemption–Razuud System

Maggie wanted to go out with everyone. She wanted to be part of the team again. Anything to feel useful.

"But sir, I can still fly. I can help. I need to help!" Maggie insisted to Lieutenant Colonel Charlie 'Wisp' Broadway.

Wisp stared intently at Maggie for a few moments. He looked to be carefully considering the situation.

"Don't let them sideline you, Maggie. You need to get back out there," Face interjected. Maggie almost lost control. She wasn't on that ship anymore. She wasn't being held captive.

"Captain Lorrent," Charlie said, sternly at first. But then changing to a softer, more fatherly tone. "Maggie. Back in my first deployment we were stationed in Europe. We were responsible for patrolling North Africa to deter threats from the SHUR. It was pretty slow at the time. We had run-ins with flights of two or three. We'd lock on, they'd break off and RTB. Nothing much came of it."

Maggie knew he had started off in atmospheric fighters, but wasn't sure where this was going, or how it applied to her situation now. Her frustration showed on her face. She focused solely on her situation and getting back out there.

"Get him to the point or I will!" Face demanded.

No, he's a friend. Maggie said back in her head. This conversation must have been clear on her face.

Wisp held up his hands. "Just hold on, I'm getting to the point," Charlie said with a half-smile. He recognized the distress she felt, but also seemed to experience some of his own.

Charlie continued, "One day after a sortie, we were unwinding with some SF guys at the base. Rangers or something like that. Rugby was the sport of choice over there. Well, I got laid out pretty good. Ran into this guy that made me look like a rag doll. I got a concussion. But I hid it. I played it off like everything was fine, just got the wind knocked out of me." Then after a long pause. "But I wasn't fine."

Maggie saw where this was going now. She had heard part of this story, but she didn't know the backstory or what happened. She knew he was in a major conflict with the SHUR. Both sides lost planes and pilots.

"So I went out to fly the next day. I figured, it wouldn't be that bad, it never was. Tensions were low at that point. That would give me some time to recover. That's where I was wrong. Twelve fighters from the SHUR went up to meet our flight of four. They didn't just lock on and turn and run. They fired. Right away, no warning, nothing. We scrambled. Spread out, started pairing off and picking them off one by one. We couldn't flee. They were faster in the straight, but we were far more maneuverable and better armed. We just had to hold off until reinforcements got there. And we were doing pretty good too. We had scratched four of them at that point. They were having a hard time targeting us."

Maggie sat intently now. Focused on his every word. This

was a battle that was talked about in every dog fighting course and training she had. But only the tactics, never what was going on behind the scenes. This story briefly transported her away from her current situation. At first she tried to find the meaning in every word. Then she got so caught up in the story, she forgot everything else around her.

"I was fighting the SHUR, but also the biggest headache of my life. My g-force tolerance was no good. I neared blacking out at almost every turn. Until I did. We were working on our fifth SHUR fighter when he banked, we followed, and I blacked out. My ship went straight and level, the enemy's wingman came circling behind my lead and took him out before he even knew I was out of the fight." Wisp was on the verge of breaking down at that point. The pain was evident in his face. The look of guilt curled with the corner of his lips as he held back tears.

"I had no idea," Is all Maggie could say.

"Not many do. It's something I live with," Wisp responded and took a breath. "But the point is, your trauma, your event, needs to be addressed before you go back out there. Because you will not only be living with what you just experienced, but also with the experience if you cause something that goes wrong." He paused again. "I very likely got him killed that day because I couldn't admit I needed help. I won't let you relive my failure."

It made sense, it all made sense. Maggie grasped the reality of her situation and could finally see through her rage to the simple facts. She needed a break; she needed to be safe and heal first.

All she could do was nod to Wisp. She would come back to talk to him about it at another time. She felt bad that she didn't have the willpower to do it now, but there was just so much weighing on her right now, from her own fight.

"Now, I know you want revenge, let us exact that for you. You'll get your chance back in the fighter in due time. But right now, we need your help in another way. General D'Pol has an assignment for you, if you're up for it."

"Understood," Maggie responded, cold sounding. "I understand," She repeated, this time much softer. Letting Wisp know she understood and was contemplating everything he just told her. "What's the assignment?"

"He wants you in the command center with him. There may be valuable intel you can shed on the Tartins in real time," Wisp said, quickly outlining what he expected of her. She thought it was also to keep an eye on her. General D'Pol, or Trap as she knew him, was a close friend and mentor for many years. A father to her, in many ways. This request felt like an extension of that.

"Yes sir. I'll head right over."

"And Face," Wisp said, back to his commander role.

Maggie stopped at the door, the sound of alarms still blaring in the halls. She froze at the name. How did he know Face waited in silence? Did he know? Face wanted to get back out. She didn't want to be sidelined. Maggie struggled to regain control of herself.

"It's great to have you back."

Maggie nodded and continued her way to the command center. It being in the middle of the ship meant she had some time before she got there. She thought about what had just happened, what she just learned. About Wisp and herself. Even with the pending emergency going on, he still took the time to make sure she was OK. He made sure she felt like she was back home. And she did. But Face came with her and she needed to figure out what to do with her.

She raced to the command center and sealed the door behind her. They compartmentalized the ship so that if anything penetrated the outer shields and armor, the entire ship wouldn't lose atmosphere.

When she entered, she made eye contact with Ramat and couldn't hold it anymore. She didn't know why, but she lost it right there. She felt safe, really safe. Finally. Even though they were in the middle of a combat zone and about to be in one of the largest space battles ever, she felt safe seeing him there. She felt like he wouldn't let anything happen to them, or to her.

Trap made his way over to her and pulled her close. No, this wasn't a standard operating procedure or a normal occurrence. But extenuating circumstances sometimes called for a human act. There were no rules or guidelines on how to handle what had happened or what was going on. They were just being human.

He released her, held her back, and looked into her eyes.

"Glad to have you back, Maggie," Trap said.

Maggie smiled back at him, trying to clear the tears from her eyes. Knowing there was a lot going on that needed his attention, she cut right to business. "Happy to be back, Sir. How can I help?"

CHAPTER 28

Ramat–Space Force Guard Ship Redemption–Razuud System

As expected, Ramat needed all hands on deck for this battle. Crew rest regulations were waived, duty limiting conditions waived, every able-bodied person sat at their battle stations ready to support. If they weren't actively working a station, or a weapon, they were assisting in every way they could. Running coffee or food, switching out for bathroom breaks, running messages, cleaning up damage on emergency teams; the list went on. Not to diminish any previous space battle, this was gearing up to be the fight of their lives. If they didn't make it through this, there would be no rescue. There would be no safety or salvation. There would be no more Razuuds and possibly even humans after that. Everyone had to work together to even stand a chance at victory.

Ramat looked out over his crew in the dimly lit command center. He gazed over the console he sat at. He considered the souls that were under his command, on this ship and all the supporting vessels. The Razuud lives hung in the balance of his decisions. The weight felt as though it pushed him tighter into his command seat.

He couldn't ask for a better crew. For all the things that were going on, they were performing admirably. Would it be enough? If it wasn't enough, that would be on him and nobody else. Earth had no more ships to give to the effort. Could he have been in a better defensive position? Should he have gone on the offensive against orders?

All the what-ifs clouded the current situation, and he knew it would get him nowhere. He cleared his mind and once again observed the battlespace.

The three main Tartin battleships were closing with his. They had many other medium-class destroyer ships and countless fighters equipped with their laser missiles. The battlespace became cluttered with enemy ships. The numbers overwhelmed the sensor systems.

"What's the status of the AIMS refit?" Trap asked the operations officer and the ship's deputy, Lieutenant Colonel Marry Ann Barker.

"Almost reloaded and refueled with reactants. Need about five more minutes," She responded. Ramat knew there was a lot more that went into it, but the reactant fuel meant both for the main engines but also for the reaction control system that kept the fighters facing the directions they needed. They also were probably getting a power pack replacement and reloading all the weapons. Light gates took much longer, so they were probably not doing that. Ramat ordered that two AIMS be kept in reserve for emergency use.

"Copy," Ramat said, then turned to Maggie, who sat next to him on the command deck. He didn't want her alone in her room or off somewhere else. She could be an asset, but also didn't need to be alone. She had had enough of that lately.

"Face, what do you know of their weapons on the fighters, it looked like they were more effective in that last engagement?"

Maggie seemed to hesitate at first. Like she felt uncomfortable with her own name. "Yes, sir, they are. They tore my fighter apart and I saw them testing new weapons on it. Melted it like butter. They seem to get through our shields too," She responded.

Then Tobias chimed in. He had been mostly silent, working on a console in the background. "Sir, they aren't necessarily more powerful, but they have tuned the frequency of the lasers so that they better counter our energy shields. Then when they defeat the shields they adjust the frequency again that resonates with the armor and causes it to break down rather rapidly," He said excitedly.

"Is there anything we can do about that?" Ramat asked, trying to coax the answer out of him. He knew Tobias must be working on something, he always was. But he also needed an answer now.

"Yes. I have sent an update to the fighters and to our main battleships. That should help with the initial energy burst and save our energy shields. Not much I can do with the fighter armor. Luckily, the armor on our larger ships comprises a different composite so we should fare better," He responded.

"Let's just hope they don't have any samples of our main battleships," Ramat said.

"What about their targeting? It seems to have improved. We were much better at bouncing around and avoiding direct hits toward the end of our last engagement," Maggie stated. Her face said she was reliving the time when she got hit and her ship disappeared.

"I noticed that as well. I have adjusted the maneuvering sequence of the fighter automatic avoidance system to account for that," Tobias replied.

"Good. What about our weapons on theirs?" Ramat asked,

wanting to know if they could have a better outcome without using nukes. They were going to be so close together that nukes may not work without significant damage to his own ships. They also weren't having any luck getting nukes to hit their ships from a distance. It was shaping up to be an old-fashioned close-up slug fest.

"Too soon to say yet. We have our kinetic weapons and conventional warheads. Those still seem to penetrate their energy fields just fine. We're not sure if they have made any changes to address our main guns yet. Sorry Ramat, we just don't know."

"Thanks Tobias, keep working on it," Ramat said, then turned back to Lieutenant Colonel Barker. "Make sure the fighters know the plan. We're gonna need them to stay in the fight as long as possible."

"Yes, sir," She responded, then turned back to her console to relay the orders.

There had been casualties to his fighter squadrons. He used them to probe the Tartin positions that surrounded them. He had them pull back to the relative safety of his battleships, cruisers, and the carrier after finding no actionable weakness. But that would not do in the long term. He hoped, and trusted, that the live updates were going to make some improvements. He needed them to. The situation looked dire. The enemy outnumbered them in ships, even including the Razuud ships. But the Razuuds took the brunt of the initial fight. Trap received reports from his sensor operator and comms officers.

"Sir, almost all Razuud ships are out of the fight. Some transitioned out of the system. The direction of travel doesn't make sense. Others appeared to go planetside," The sensor operator relayed to Ramat.

"Thank you. They have some underground bases, they must think they are safe there for now. They'll never be able to get back into orbit. Their ships are scattering," Ramat observed out loud.

Then he continued, trying to find something he could use to exploit the situation. "Are any of their forces following? Is there any opening you see for us to fit into?" If the Tartins started splitting up, that might be the opening he was looking for. They could squeeze many weapons into a tight space and overwhelm a target before it reacted. Although they were surrounded, the main contingent of Tartin forces were concentrated in a single area.

"Not that I can see sir. They are focused on this ship," The sensor operator responded.

"They learned from the last engagement." He pondered another scenario. "Based on our best understanding of their laser range, is there a space between those three main ships that don't have overlapping fields of fire?" He asked, trying to find a place they could transition to where they wouldn't get immediately destroyed.

"Standby."

"Ramat," Tobias interjected, "I think I see what you're looking for but we don't have that level of precision. Plus we would need a free line to that location."

"I know, but it might be our only chance. We can't wait," Ramat responded, grasping at a solution.

"We might make it there, but if anything happens that disrupts our transition back, even a small piece of debris, that could spell disaster for the whole ship," Tobias came back.

Tobias acted as the voice of reason right now. But he also didn't have the experience that Ramat had. Experience that said it is possible to defy the odds, to accomplish the impossible.

"They are going to tighten their grip around us. Then we'll be sitting ducks. Our only chance is to take them by surprise, even if it puts us in a worse initial position." He paused again in thought. A plan forming as he spoke.

"What if we transition us and two other battleships into any dead space between their ships' field of fire. Then transition all remaining ships into a picket, englobing them. They could have too many directions to focus on and they'd be even farther spread out. If we jump the smaller ships that can fit between their debris fields we can at least get the fighters on the outside and fight their way back in."

"Englobe?" Colonel Mentle asked, the ship's captain.

"Yes, englobe. I may have just made it up, but in three-dimensional space, we would need to encircle them from every direction, not just a flat plane. The Tartins are clustered enough that we could do that. They would be englobed, with us as the white-hot core right next to their main battleships."

The command center all thought about it. Resigning to their fates. That, of course, wasn't their only option. The humans could collect their ships and try to run. Run back home. Live to fight another day. Leave their allies high and dry.

But there was something about humans, something that didn't allow them to abandon a friend, even if it wasn't theirs. Ramat knew the right move. Because they were so outnumbered and outgunned, a creative option appeared to be the best option. This would catch them off guard, to be sure, but would they be able to respond? Were they ready to respond?

"Draw up some plans, we need to get moving now," Ramat responded. Although he hadn't asked to see if anyone was against the idea, his crew knew they could at any time. This time, everyone remained silent.

Ramat took this as an acknowledgment that they were about to do something that could likely mean the end of the fleet and their lives, but that they also agreed with it. They all contemplated their choices, the future, what got them here. Time was the only thing left, and how much, remained unknown. With the decision made, Ramat laid out the course. All the ships knew their assignment and what to do when things broke down. Things were going to break down. Performing under chaos would decide this battle. That, and luck.

That's when Colonel Mentle floated up next to him. She grabbed a handle and pulled in close, so that only he could hear her words. "Sir, you know I'm with you, and I agree with this path, but it's also my job to question decisions."

"That's right," Ramat responded, respecting her approach and timing.

"What if they know where our home world is? What's to stop them from going there next and taking care of the small fleet and partially built ships right after us? We stand a much better chance as a species if we go home, regroup our forces and stand our ground at home," She stated. The tone she used, Ramat felt like she hated saying those words but he knew she needed to point them out. Nobody liked abandoning an ally, even if it meant having a better chance at saving your own species.

"All good points. But what's to say they do that anyway, or they already are. Going home now wouldn't stop that. If their intentions are to take over Razuud and move on to Earth, our best bet to stop them is right here and now. We could gain strength, but so could they. And based on what they sent here, they have far more ships than what the Razuuds thought. What's to say they don't have even more waiting." Ramat paused in thought. He appreciated the perspective, it just made him more sure he was making the right decision.

"My thoughts exactly, sir," Colonel Mentle said as she

floated away back to the captain's seat.

"Sir!" Barker called out to Ramat, "All fighters are reloaded and out in the open. All ships are in position. We are ready to execute."

"Very well," Ramat responded. He wanted to talk to the fleet, to everyone, to let them know what they were doing and why. Why their sacrifice was so important. Why it was so important they gave it their all. But he knew they already knew that and that they would give their all. He had the best serving under him. Instead, Ramat stayed silent. In addition to knowing they didn't need a pep talk, he didn't want to let the Tartins know of their plan, or that there was even any plan about to happen. The enemy ships were almost in range. Perfect time to set the trap.

"Sync timers and execute starting on my mark, five-second countdown." Ramat waited for the go-ahead that they were ready. Once he received the nod from Barker, he continued, "Let's begin."

CHAPTER 29

Riley—Advanced Individual Maneuvering Shuttle—Razuud System

It had been a long day up to this point for Riley. If it could even be called a day. Riley had been going at it for several days now with almost no sleep. It all started with the assassination attempt and subsequent escort of Jenn and Ramat back to the SFG Redemption. Then it continued to his rescue of Maggie. Now here he sat. The outer picket of the englobement.

The med systems were keeping him awake and alert, but they couldn't do that forever. He had nearly been shot, blown up, shot again, intercepted a Tartin missile with his light gates that also impacted his own fighter, redeployed to intercept Maggie and bring her home, and then redeployed again for what could be his final flight. Not just of the day, but of his life.

His thoughts wandered. They wandered to his parents back home. His mom baking in the kitchen. His dad and grandfather sitting on the front porch. Grandpa Riley. He dreaded not being able to see him again; to tell him he did the right thing, the hard thing. His parents would understand.

They lived that life his whole childhood. Maybe even still.

Then his attention drifted closer. Jenn. Did he say enough to her? Did she know how he felt? He wouldn't get a chance to see where they would go together. The thought made his eyes well up. At first, fear gripped him for what she might experience, at the end. Then sorrow for not being able to see it all through. They had already lost so many.

He knew that their fleet was thinly spread, and that the crews of the remaining ships were exhausted. Just one more push, that's all they needed. Ramat had a plan, and it had to be their best chance to get out of this thing alive. At least for some of them.

His heads-up display beeped with a message. That wasn't unusual. Sometimes they would get sent text or voice messages between the squadron for various reasons. That it came from Jenn had been unusual. Only the command center or someone running ops on the main ship could do that. Jenn wouldn't normally be able to do that. It was direct, just like when they first met. "*I like you, stay in touch.*" It read. The simple note brought him back to a time when everything seemed much simpler, even though it would be the start of something complex. He remembered everything that had happened, all they had done together between now and the time when she gave him that note that said the same thing after they first met. This put a smile on his face. He cleared his eyes and finished preparing his ship and his mind for the battle to come.

Everything would happen quickly. He was aware of only a fraction of the details, but he knew there was a remote chance it would be successful. He could work with that. Riley flew number one in their formation of two. Star flew as his wingman. He called over to her to check on her status.

"Are you clear on the plan, Star?"

"As clear as mud. But I get the gist of it," She replied, a

little more zest than her usual responses.

"Just remember, the main battleships are going to jump into gaps in the middle of their lines. We will 'englobe' them," Riley said, exaggerating the word englobe, both because it was a new term and also because it felt silly to say.

"Then what? We keep everyone in the 'globe' at whatever cost? Or do we press inward?"

"Contain for now. This is going to be a very dynamic mission. We will have to adjust on the fly. You know, like our first mission together," Riley said, recalling the first time he transported Star up into space.

"Does that count as a mission? I'm pretty sure we played that whole thing by ear."

"The good ol' days. Back when there was only a few enemy ships to deal with." This time Riley felt the weight, the seriousness of what was about to happen.

"Ain't that the truth. Nothing like being outnumbered and finding a way through," Star said. Her voice cracked. It wasn't the radio transmission's fault.

Riley didn't want her to linger in that thought or have a negative frame of mind at the onset of the battle. "We've always been outnumbered and we've always made it through. We will this time." He may not have felt what he said, but he portrayed the confidence to Star.

Just then, a countdown timer popped up on their displays. A big five centered on his screens.

Five. This was it. Four. The battle was just around the corner. Three. "Star, no matter what." Two. "We stick together." One. "I won't let anything happen to you."

In a flash of light, they ceased to exist. Before they realized, before anyone realized, they were back, but now they were in their formation. Riley only knew for sure that he and Star were in position. It would take some time before he got confirmation that everyone else had made it. Now they had to get to work.

They patrolled their sector. Looking for anyone trying to escape or attack. They played a sort of zone defense. At first, everything seemed quiet in their zone. He knew that wasn't the case for everyone, and that it wouldn't stay that way for long. Their scopes were blank, still trying to gather new information from the now spread-out fleet. Riley didn't expect to see any action in his sector for quite a while. He figured the Tartins would need to first try to figure out what was going on before they reacted. That's why it surprised him when they spotted their first target so quickly.

"Eyes on targets, hard to say how many. They're in our zone and headed our way. Move to engage," Riley said to Star.

"I see them. I'm on your six," Star replied, indicating she followed right behind Riley, protecting his back.

They both pulled hard to engage. The g-forces forced them into their seats. The cockpits rotated, trying to keep their bodies and minds awake. Their suits squeezed and strained systematically, struggling to assist in the endeavor.

"Zero in on that lead ship. When we get within range of their laser weapons, automate evasion and send a nuke down the edge of the ship," Riley ordered. All of their tactics with the nukes hadn't worked yet. They were all disintegrated with laser weapons before they even came close to impacting.

"Not on a direct path?" Star questioned back.

"No. I want to try something out. What do we have to lose?"

"I'm all ears."

"I noticed that they only engaged the missiles that were headed right at them and were going to impact. There were some that went by close but didn't get intercepted. They also missed. I want to send ours on a course that goes right up next to that ship and have the nukes detonate on proximity. That may get enough of the energy through to do some damage, at the very least disrupt them." Riley wasn't certain of the tactic. But like he said, what did they have to lose?

They lined up their shots, coming in just off the center of the larger ship. They didn't have backup. Everyone else had their own problems to deal with. It was just them out on this picket of the globe. Riley switched his maneuvering to automatic and focused on the targeting system for the nuke. He would have to target and fly it manually. There wasn't a function for it to miss a target purposefully.

"Sit tight, Star, they're almost in range," Riley prepared Star to get thrown around in her ship, even more than they already were.

His AIMS shook violently from the constant maneuvering. The updated evasive maneuvering program that Tobias made felt far more jarring than before. He wasn't going to be able to take this for long before needing to get out of range. He would need to get some relief from the movement.

Bearing down, he focused on the targeting system. He strained to judge the range of the nuke. He did some quick calculations and decided on a time that would be close enough.

"Release." His labored breath said into the comm system.

"Releasing," He heard in response, sensing a similar struggle coming from Star.

"Good track. Keep it going." Riley gazed at the target and guided the small but powerful weapon to its invisible mark in space. He tracked the changing movement of the ship, adjusting the trajectory ever so slightly.

"Almost there." The mental countdown screamed in his head. He would need to guide the missile the rest of the way by feel, and intuition.

"Detonate!" He sent the command. With a bright flash that

propagated and seemed to spread like a virus to the enemy ships shields. The Tartin ships glowed red hot. His and Star's ships continued to maneuver, but they no longer received notifications that the enemy targeted them. Their AIMS only knew that they were in range, not the status of the enemy weapons. Better to be safe than sorry.

The enemy ships stopped maneuvering. Their engines went dark.

"Holy shit, I think that worked!" An excited voice from Star came over the radio, "We need to get the word out. At least some fighters might stand a chance now."

"Let's finish them off first to make sure it worked," Riley said as they positioned their fighters to close with the Tartin ships. As they approached, they released short bursts of explosive-tipped, armor-piercing Gatling gun rounds at the fuel storage compartments of each ship. The Tartin ships didn't even try to move. Minor explosions were followed by large ones. The bright flash quickly swallowed by space. The Gatling gun rounds annihilated all the ships.

"That seemed to do the trick. Sending instructions out now." Riley looked at his screens as he worked a message to send to the fleet and saw more indicators of enemy ships. "Looks like we got more company incoming." He knew in the back of his mind that at this distance, it may arrive too late to make a difference.

"I'm tracking. Should we send some nukes sooner, let them fly right into them?" Star suggested.

Riley was thinking the same thing. "Sounds like a good plan to me." Just then, they saw dozens more ships heading their way. As if that one they just took out kicked the hornets' nest.

"We're in trouble Riley. We can't take all of those," Star's voice betrayed her earlier confidence.

Riley looked at the display. He tried to come up with a

solution. They were getting some help, but would it be enough and in time?

"Release your nukes, let's fall back. We don't need to pursue into the globe, just keep them from getting out. That will buy us some time." Riley felt that might give them a fighting chance. Either way, they were about to be in the thick of it and there was no telling the outcome. If they went into this next engagement head long with an enemy that knew where they were and expected them, Riley shivered at the thought. Don't be stupid, he thought to himself. Now isn't the time. When is it ever?

They both released their nukes and drove them on a path that took them next to some ships in the middle of the new pack. They were hoping to split them up. While they did this, they had their AIMS take them back to the edge of the globe.

Just then, Riley thought of getting an updated status on the core of the globe. Where were his friends, Jenn, Maggie, and Ramat? His jaw dropped when the telemetry came in, showing him the gloomy picture. There was only one ship left transmitting. That meant it still had power, that it could still fight. It was their ship, Jenn's ship.

Debris surrounded them. He also only spotted one main enemy battleship in close proximity. He saw a warning go up above Jenn's ship. It just took another hit. Systems were shutting down. Their shields were down now too. They were leaking atmosphere. Their weapons were reloading or charging, or maybe offline all together. He wasn't sure which. They were sitting ducks.

An overwhelming sense of helplessness came over him as he watched the ship carrying his friends, his family, in distress. It was about to be destroyed.

No, he couldn't stand for that. He knew he had his orders, but they were all screwed if that ship got taken out. No, he had to do something, and he had to do it now. But what?

"Star, do you trust—" Riley started but couldn't even finish his question.

"Rip, whatever it is you have planned, you know I'm with you. What crazy shit are we doing this time?"

CHAPTER 30

Ramat–Space Force Guard Ship Redemption–Razuud System

Chaos overwhelmed the room. Overshadowed only by the palpable gloom they all felt. Warning alarms lit up everyone's screens. Ramat had the team silence the cacophony of alarms. They all knew they were in trouble and didn't need another reminder. With all options exhausted, the fate of the ship and the human race in this battlespace rested on those in this room.

Ramat, Tobias, Maggie, Jenn, and Mark huddled in the command center. The rest of the crew in the room monitored their stations, trying to coordinate the status of the ship and their enemy. They had all been doing everything they could to think of a way out of this situation. They were out of options and time. The batteries continued their slow recharge, grasping to replenish their energy weapons and shields. Humming and clanking in the missile bays told the story of rapid reloading, but not fast enough. A red light above a bay flashed, indicating depleted stores. The fighters were all out on the perimeter, scattered. The only thing left seemed to be hope. But from where they stood, even that was in short supply. The Razuuds were nowhere to be found. A call for help would go unanswered.

Ramat knew they had given the Tartins a beating. They couldn't have much left to give either. Even still, they seemed to have the upper hand. From Ramat's estimation, one more hit for either would be the end for anyone on the receiving end. It appeared the Tartins would get the last blow. Ramat knew—hell, everyone knew—that losing his ship would be the tipping point and the battle would be lost. There would be nowhere for the fighters to go back to. No more defense. Nothing. The lanes would be clear for the Tartins to invade Rutaun, or even Earth. They would certainly figure out where Earth spun if they didn't already know.

Ramat thought of the many decisions, different choices, both in his life, career, and this battle. These all flashed before his eyes. Ramat always thought that he would go down fighting, that it would be in an instant. Where he didn't have time to think about anything. Now he had a moment of reflection in the face of certain death. Ramat knew he couldn't call it anything else. Certain death.

The enemy main ship squared off in a now familiar and dreadful turn that showed its principal weapon toward its target. Them, his ship. His people. Its sights lined up. Ramat's crew got the timing down for how long it took between lining up and then firing. Tobias believed this phase recharged and refocused the beam based on the firing range. It mattered little now. The crew knew it meant death.

Ramat took a deep breath. Maybe his last opportunity.

"Eject the last of the comm drones with as much information as you can. They'll need everything they can get if they ever have to face these ships," Ramat said. He finished with a note to his crew. "Ladies and gentlemen, it's been a pleasure serving alongside you. You must all know that we did our very best out here, and you should be proud of that." A mental countdown for each crew member closed on zero. That was an odd feeling, knowing exactly when and how you were going to die, almost down to the last second, and there was nothing that could be done about it. There was a peace that came with that. Also, a slow-burning rage.

Ramat looked around the room. He looked over to Tobias, to Mark. He looked at Maggie. They gave each other a nod, tears forming in Maggie's eyes, but she remained composed. Ramat's time had finally come. All of theirs had. They all tried to keep busy with their own tasks, mentally ready and waiting for the end.

But then, just when it was supposed to happen, it didn't. It just didn't, and it kept on not happening.

"What's going on?" Ramat asked. "Are they trying to contact us?" He asked again, trying to make sense of his extended life. Or just filling the time between now and when the shot would inevitably come.

"Nothing sir," The comms officer said.

"Nothing from the weapons either," The sensor operator said.

"What's the status of our main weapons?" Ramat asked again. He could find this information himself, but he also wanted the crew to know there still might be hope. They needed to feel useful, important, even at a time like this.

"Thirty more seconds and we can fire," The weapons officer replied.

"Keep your finger on the trigger and pull as soon as they are ready."

"Yes sir," The weapons officer replied.

Ramat continued to look over his screens, including the external live views. That's when he noticed a familiar sign from the cameras outside. It had to be luck, or some other force that pulled him to those screens at that moment. And for the event to happen within view.

"Sensors, are you watching the external views?" Ramat asked excitedly.

"No, sir. I'm working on getting the EM suite to settle down to feed us better data," The sensor operator replied hesitantly.

"Switch to the mid-starboard camera, wide field. I'm pretty sure I just saw a transition." The sensors that could detect those signatures were intermittent, so Ramat was glad that they were working to fix it. But at this range he had seen enough to know what they look like. Just within range of their ships, but below them, he saw something. It flew just under the enemy ship.

"Whatever it was just flew below us. Those cameras are out of view," Ramat added.

"Sir, their weapons are getting hot," The sensor operator said. This was an indication that they were about to fire within seconds.

Ramat didn't respond. The faint glimmer of hope fizzled as he remained fixated on the external view screen. Too little, too late.

But then, a bright flash filled the screen. The combined light from anyone looking at the external views on their monitors illuminated the room as if it were a sunny afternoon on Earth. As quickly as it came, the screens, and all other light sources, went dark. A loud *BOOM* echoed through the ship. It rocked and reverberated in space. Everyone heard new creaks and moans from the ship and crew. Screens showing the external views remained dark. Emergency lights activated and lit the room with a dim green hue. The backup systems came online.

"What the hell was that? Did they miss?" Trap asked. Nothing fit together right now.

"I don't know sir. Sensors are offline. Might have been a glancing blow. I got a radiation spike just before I lost them," The sensor operator said, feverishly, looking through his screens, desperately trying to get the systems back online.

"Are weapons still online?" Trap asked, desperation clear in his voice.

"Yes sir, everything's still online. But targeting is down, I can't see shit sir," The weapons officer replied in frustration. Taking his headset off and slamming it on the console in front of him.

"Keep it together, Mac. We're going to fire blind. Manually correct for our attitude change and fire. We're so close, it may not even matter," Ramat said to the weapons officer, Captain Johnathan Mac.

Captain Mac straightened his uniform and placed the headset back on his head. Part of the earpiece hanging down but still usable. He looked at Ramat.

"Understood sir. Standby."

The crew kept it together remarkably well, given the circumstances. Ramat beamed with pride. "Mac, fire when ready." Ramat resigned to that decision, to all the decisions. The defining moment. The one that made a leader, or got his whole crew killed. He had to make this decision. Even if it killed his whole crew. The enemy must be defeated here and now or else there wouldn't be a tomorrow for everyone else. Everyone else. Ramat wasn't doing this for the crew on board or himself. He did it for the rest of the fleet and for those back home. He knew that their proximity could kill them too, given the amount of damage they had already sustained.

"Energy weapons back online." Mac announced in the command center. Followed shortly by, "missile tubes and defense cannons reloaded."

"Fire everything!" Ramat commanded again. The last thirty seconds were a gift that he would not waste. They unloaded everything the ship could. With none of the sensors online and only manually firing enabled, Ramat knew that all ordinance and energy weapons were loose because of the violent shaking of the ship. With the counteracting thrusters offline, the ship continued to move away from the target while it rotated around. The groaning of the ship reverberated within the frame and along the skin.

They were shaken shortly after that with a much more violent sensation. Either their ship was getting torn apart by the enemy weapons, or their weapons found purchase on the Tartin ship.

The backup lights went dark. Fear swept the room. A panic-inducing claustrophobia soon followed for everyone, even if they were used to it. This situation proved to be a more unique experience than anything seen before. Ramat fought it off as long as he could. Just when he was about to give in to the roller coaster of emotions they had just experienced and resign himself once again to his fate, he heard a soft voice ring out in the room. *Was he already dead?* He thought to himself.

An unmistakable voice pierced the tension, releasing it all like a flood. One of the crew had been in this situation before, and fought through it, coming out the other side seemingly stronger than before.

Maggie called out in a calm and resolved voice. "Everyone stay calm. We're not dead. Keep working the problems. Focus on what you can control," She reassured everyone. She gave the room purpose again. Her own recent experience became evident in that moment.

Ramat knew right then that this was not unfamiliar territory for her. She had mastered the dark, the feeling of being alone and helpless. She used that to her advantage now.

Ramat joined in. "Sensors, Comms, check the status, see if we can get anything working," Ramat said, his eyes adjusting to the darkness. Small lights from personal devices provided some direction and a sense of movement. His eyes used that light to help produce an image within the command center.

"Yes sir," One of the crew rang back. Although he didn't know who spoke, he knew they were all focused on the task.

He went around, just like Maggie, and checked on each person, one by one. After he had checked on the first few people, someone, who he thought he recognized as the comms officer, excitedly broke the now calm of the room.

"Sir, I've tied my handheld into the comm line, I think we're starting to get something. It sounds like a friendly ship."

"What ship is it?" Ramat asked.

"Lucky Five," Came the response.

Lucky Five, go figure it was a Lucky. Five? Ramat didn't recall who had been assigned as Lucky Five on that mission. Why would he? There were hundreds of fighters and ships, he couldn't possibly remember who was who. That mattered little now, though.

"That's Riley!" Jenn yelled, unable to hold back the tears any longer. Until that moment, she hadn't realized she feared his death, again, and wasn't ready to accept it. The tears were from joy that she didn't have to face that, not now. She looked at Maggie, relief clear on both of their faces.

"Go figure," Ramat said, barely able to hold back a grin. "What is he saying? What's going on out there?"

"He's saying we won. He's saying they retreated and we're regrouping."

The lights flickered back on, followed by the screens on each console. They were rebooting. Someone back in the ship must have patched the power.

With the screens up, Ramat could get a genuine sense of what was going on outside.

"We're not out of the woods yet people, but damn nice work," Ramat said to the room. He made the call on his comm unit also for anyone that might hear on the ship, if the system even worked at all.

Nothing but silence filled the room. Ramat wasn't sure what the right response should have been, but this wasn't it. With one more shout, he said. "We made it people!" and let out a triumphant yell. The room followed suit and burst into cheers. He could hear cheers echoing in the halls. That made him smile. They were going to make it after all.

He didn't waste any time. He began issuing orders. They needed to assess the damage, begin repairs, and begin rescue efforts. He needed to take stock of the situation. They needed to return home.

CHAPTER 31

Jennifer–Space Force Guard Ship Redemption–Razuud System

Rescue operations were well underway. Mechanics made enough repairs to the hangars to allow the most damaged but still flyable ships to enter and land for repairs. They docked other ships at external ports. In-space mechanics checked the worst of the ships to begin salvage operations.

They also paid special attention to the disposable light gates. Without those, that ship couldn't go anywhere. The ships didn't need to be in the best shape to transition. The event was very benign to the ship and its occupants. It just needed to be able to get up to a certain speed and be able to slow down again. Even still, not every ship would make it back.

Rescue and recovery teams, dedicated to their craft and mission, continued their tireless search for survivors. Even though the rate of recoveries dwindled rapidly, they didn't give up. Every life mattered.

Jenn worked to make herself useful wherever needed. She ran supplies to various stations. She helped carry the injured crew to the makeshift sick bays. It reminded her of the sheets hung up in the hallways when she boarded the Kennedy after the first alien attack. Back when she and Riley met and grew close. She wanted to help, but she also used it to keep her occupied while she waited for Riley.

She knew he was alive. There was no real confirmation other than his transmission to the command center. But a lot had happened since then. So she kept hope alive. With that hope, she couldn't wait to see him. She couldn't wait to hold him. Jenn knew then that everything would be ok. She just needed to get to that point. She knew his callsign. Lucky Five. That name seared in her head. She couldn't access any systems to see where his ship was at and when it would return. None of the Luckys had returned yet. She kept herself busy to avoid dwelling on it with the added benefit of time going by much quicker.

She ran first aid kits and other medical supplies from the medical bay to the various temporary locations. Ramat consolidated the medical treatment from the surrounding ships to his. As soon as that ship's medical bay got filled, any extras were brought on board the SFG Redemption. They also transported critical patients there, too. This freed up the other ships to continue cleanup and maneuvering without risking their condition worsening. This also freed them to be on the lookout for any follow-on attack and respond if needed. Jenn just hoped they wouldn't need to respond to a follow-on attack. If the Tartins had any remaining ships in reserve, it would spell disaster for the humans and Razuud. The Razuud ships slowly filtered back into local space. Other recovery vessels escaped Razuud gravity to aid in the efforts.

Repair drones floated around, controlled by any crew that had the slightest training in them. Some got on-the-job training right then. It was all hands on deck.

Jenn had just dropped off supplies to a repurposed medical room just outside one of the main hangars, hangar two, when she noticed on the screen that two AIMS were on approach to land. She looked at the viewscreen to that hangar posted outside the door. The image showed two AIMS semi-graciously fall onto the floor, parts falling to the ground as they contacted the landing pad with a thud she felt through the floor. She didn't know what she expected, given the recent conflict outside, but that image sat in stark contrast to every other landing she had witnessed.

There were no landing legs deployed. The collision left the ships mangled and almost unrecognizable. One had a giant piece of metal protruding out; clear it came from another ship. The screen next to the one she looked at listed the hangar manifest and schedule. It had been wrong several times today. Space control towers couldn't read the damaged markings, and the ship's radios and transponders frequently failed.

But this time she read the screen and felt hope. '*Hangar Two: Lucky Five, Lucky Six.*'

A sudden rush of emotions came over her. They hadn't heard from Riley since after his first contact with the command center. Given the amount of wreckage going on outside and the level of damage already sustained by his own ship, she held on to hope that he could limp the ship back into safety. But the longer she went without news, the more her fears took over. That hope surged within her as she read the screen.

The screen resolution made it impossible to make out any physical details of who the pilots were as they crawled out of their ships. The ground crews stood by to assist, prying pieces of the ship away to make room. One pilot came to the aid of the other, reaching a hand down to pull the figure out the last few feet. The lack of gravity made the task more difficult.

When the two finally broke free, they began floating away in an embrace. A ground crew member arrested their movement by grabbing a foot and pulling them back to the ground. The ground crews' magnetic boots secured them in place.

Jenn saw the pair hook up to the guidelines that led to the airlock. The images of them getting out of the ship and hooking up to guidelines to float to the hangar airlock were all that Jenn needed to see. She knew that movement from anywhere. "Riley!" She yelled out loud. Only the busy crew passing by heard her joy. Those close by smiled in a familiar sense of relief. Another one made it back alive. That feeling was overshadowed by the countless crew that never would return.

Her heart skipped a beat. Jenn raced to the airlock entrance, trying to appear calm as she waited for the airlock to cycle, internally her mind and heart raced a mile a minute. She held onto the handle to still her body, but her knuckles turned white as her grip nearly broke it. She wasn't thinking about anything else.

Jenn heard the beep of the door followed by a hiss as the slight pressure difference equalized. She flew into Riley's arms before the door fully opened. The collision took him off guard and drove both of them back to the other door. The masked figure did nothing to stop her and their movement, only to wrap his arms around her. They hit the back airlock with a soft thud. Instead of releasing they squeezed tighter.

A chirp in the airlock signified they needed to exit because it needed to recycle and prepare for the next people to go through. Both pilots slowly took their helmets off. Jenn, being attached to one pilot, made the task a little more difficult.

The smile of the man she loved, the one that saved their lives, revealed itself as she finished lifting the helmet for him. One final confirmation she had clung to the right person.

Jenn's legs wrapped around Riley's waist, easy to do in zero gravity, and they kissed. Her hands on each side of his face, taking in every crease and hair. He pressed his hands to her back, squeezing them tighter together. Neither wanting to release the other. Not bracing onto anything, they floated around the airlock.

Star stood by, trying to avoid looking at them. The small space made that task difficult.

"Ahemm," Star grunted, faking clearing her throat.

Jenn and Riley broke their embrace and looked over at Star then back at each other, realizing for the first time that they were still in the airlock, and not alone.

They all three laughed. Jenn and Riley pulled Star in close. The three friends embraced, a welcome and familiar distraction from the devastation outside and a brief respite from all the work that needed to be done.

They exited the airlock, pulling themselves along the guidelines and out into the hall. The airlock closed behind them and recycled, ready for the next crew. Riley and Star looked up at the screen. This appeared to be second nature for them, they wanted to take stock of how their unit did. After a moment they both looked at each other in stunned silence, eyes wide. The jubilation from moments ago a distant memory, replaced by fear. They both pulled out their personal devices and began typing away.

"What's going on?" Jenn asked, not following what they were working on.

After no response, she asked again. "Hey, what's going on?"

Star looked up. "It's P," Star said. Jenn began getting the picture. "He got hit. His fighter is still intact but his vitals went offline. They're bringing him back now."

"This way, they're taking him to Airlock One," Riley said,

already moving quickly in a new direction. Jenn remembered airlock one. That airlock is where she, Mark, and Tobias flew in Tobias's personal shuttle. It could fit his entire shuttle, and some more.

They got there just in time to see crews working on the shuttle. They cut, pried, and pulled. The ship was almost unrecognizable before they started working on it. Now it was just a heap of metal and exotic material. Looking on from the viewport, they crowded around the small window. Crews converged on a single point, evidently one of them made a breakthrough.

A crew member laid some type of cloth around the opening and then crawled in. They all waited in anticipation. Holding their breath and hoping to see P exit the airlock, instead, a lifeless body emerged from the hole. Crews reached for him and pulled him the rest of the way out. The weightlessness kept his arms and legs outstretched in their last position.

They all looked at each other, fearing the worst again. Jenn and Star began crying, followed closely by Riley. They didn't want to believe it to be true. Jenn looked up and through her tears saw the team placing P on a stretcher, securing him with straps. They placed a mask over his face.

"Look!" Jenn shouted. They all peered through the small window. Instantly realizing that he may still be alive.

The team moved him out of the airlock with a practiced skill, no doubt heading to the medical bay. They all stayed silent.

RILEY

At the sudden relief that P may still make it, Riley's thoughts shifted to Maggie. "Did you see Maggie?" He asked Jenn.

"Yes, she was in the command center last I checked. She was coordinating some of the rescues," Jenn responded. The realization came over her face that Riley hadn't seen her since they found out she was still alive.

Riley hoped Jenn wasn't upset about that. About wanting to know where she was and how she was doing. But he didn't feel like he had time to figure that out, he just wanted to see her. The person he felt like he abandoned to be held hostage and who knows what else at the hands of the enemy. At the same time he wanted to avoid her. He wanted to avoid the guilt and the blame he knew she felt toward him. Riley wasn't one to avoid conflict, so he headed to the command center. They made it to the door just outside. A guard waited to greet them.

"Hold it. We're in lockdown, nobody in right now Lieutenant," The guard said.

"I was just in there," Jenn said, hoping he remembered and would let her back in.

"Only critical personnel are allowed in right now. And they are all in there," He responded.

"That's fine. We'll check back later," Riley said. Partially happy he didn't need to face her right now. He was exhausted and needed some food and sleep. Just as he turned, the door opened. Riley didn't see who it was, he had already turned his back.

But he could hear Star yell. "Maggie!"

Riley turned in time to see the two hugging. They both held each other apart with big smiles. Maggie's gaze turned to Riley. The smile faded. They both stared. Riley didn't know what to do. Should he hug her, shake her hand. *Say something* he told himself. But he couldn't compel himself.

Finally, Maggie spoke, "Good timing, I need your help." She waved for all of them to enter the command center.

Entering the dimly lit room, the previous awkward interaction clung to Riley. He couldn't shake the feeling that all of his negative thoughts about how Maggie must feel about him were confirmed. She must hate him, blame him even. He took it even harder than he had up to this point. He had to put that aside for now though and help where he could.

Ramat looked up. "Riley! Star! Great work out there!" Ramat unbuckled and pushed away from his chair toward the cluster of people. He grabbed onto a rail and stopped short of them. "You really saved us out there. Great thinking. I see the reports coming in. We made it out, and stronger for it," Ramat continued. His energy changed the mood for the better. Riley nodded in silent recognition, not one to take credit for just doing his job.

"What do you need from us, sir?" Riley asked, trying to stay upbeat.

"Help Maggie with the recovery efforts. We sent out messages to everyone everywhere to return, that it's safe. The Razuuds took a beating and scattered. We'll need them back to help repair our ships and get us back home." Then Ramat turned to the rest of the command center. "Listen up, everyone." The room fell silent and they all turned to face him. Then Riley saw Ramat pull something out of his pocket. "Riley, Jade, come on over here."

Riley, confused at what was going on, didn't hesitate and pushed and pulled himself forward so that he was aligned next to Ramat.

"Sir," They both said in unison.

"Riley, Jade, we'll do this in a more formal setting when we get back, but I feel like the time is right now." Ramat paused briefly. "Due to your bravery and decisive action in the face of certain defeat. I am awarding you both the Space Force Cross."

Riley looked down at the medal. The bronze-colored cross with a green wreath. An eagle with wings spread, sat on top. The red, white, and gray ribbon floated in splendid weightlessness. Remembering what he was taught to do next, he reached out and shook Ramat's hand, taking the medal.

"Thank you, sir," Riley couldn't think to say anything else.

The room cheered and erupted with whistles and claps. Ramat struggled to calm them all down. Jenn and other nearby crew members circled them, patting their backs and giving them high-fives. Riley looked through the crowd and saw Maggie. She had a slight smile on her face, looking on. He saw her turn back to a screen and put a headset on, talking to someone on the other end.

Riley knew then that they would be alright. It might take some time, but they would be alright. They were returning home.

EPILOGUE

Rictor–Southern Hemisphere United Republic–Location Unknown

Rictor walked past the front desk of the motel clerk, where he paid in cash. His gaze toward the floor, head down and concealed. The rain dripped off of his hood. He walked briskly, but not too briskly. He didn't want to draw attention to himself. But he had some place to be. Rictor had risked a trip to an internet café in SHUR territory, where until not too long ago he had mostly been welcome. Following the most recent news from the expedition, he was a wanted man by all. Dead or alive.

The underground reports he received from the few who were still willing to speak with him pointed toward the assassin he hired. He supposed she wasn't much of an assassin really, more like a highly motivated and talented individual. Killing hadn't been her strong suit when Rictor hired her, but it didn't need to be. Maybe he should have reconsidered what he looked for in someone for the job he needed performed on that expedition. He assessed that motivation would have been enough. People highly recommended her for her spycraft abilities, but apparently, that's where her talents ended.

Helena seemed to have failed and spilled her guts about him. He didn't know how true those reports were but it didn't matter. He hadn't intended to pay her, anyway; this just gave him the excuse. He scoffed at the notion of her tracking him down and trying to demand payment.

Rictor turned the corner and entered his room, pausing briefly to look around to make sure nobody had followed him. As he entered, he carefully closed the door behind him, looking into the street one last time for a tail. Rictor strode to the corner of the room, where a lamp stood at eye level. He reached up and pulled the chain. The soft glow filled the room and the partially covered window.

He turned on the TV. Rictor didn't intend to watch anything, but the default channel showed his face. He smiled at the thought. *Now you've done it,* he thought, *you've become a wanted man.* All this wanted nonsense mattered little to him. He wouldn't be on Earth much longer. Placing the remote on the bed, he walked to the internal door of the adjacent room. He entered the connecting room that he bought under a different name and disguise.

Not one to be too careful, he closed both doors, locking them behind him and went to the bathroom. After making sure no light could escape, showing someone was in that room, he opened his personal device.

"Rictor, we are interested to make deal. Coordinates are enclosed in this message."

That was it. The broken, but complete, English from the Tartins confirmed that the first phase had succeeded and needed to move on to the next steps. He didn't need to respond. He probably wouldn't be able to the same way, anyway. Sneaking a message onto the human fleet and delivering it undetected to the Tartins was a very complicated process, and difficult to repeat. But this was confirmation that it made it through.

It was time to gather his things and finish planning the next phase. He glanced in his briefcase, documents labeled "*TOP SECRET*" filled with weapons systems, government plans, everything that he knew he could use to barter with the Tartins. He had waited so long that he thought his plan would never come to fruition. Now that it was finally here, finally happening, he couldn't wait any longer. The downfall of humanity still loomed in his mind and made him smile.

For a more in-depth look and visualizations of the characters, ships, and worlds, visit my website at:

www.archergrantbooks.com

For a glossary of terms, visit the website or jump to the end of the book. Be sure not to spoil the ending!

If you would like additional information about upcoming books in the Relativity series, and The Breaker Series, visit the website and join the mailing list. I'd love to go on this journey with you.

GLOSSARY

Advanced Individual Maneuvering Shuttle or **AIMS** are single-seat fighter spacecraft equipped with smaller versions of the engines and weapons systems as the larger ships. They are highly maneuverable and equipped with a subset of artificial intelligence to aid in piloting.

Space Force Platform or **SFP** are large rotating platforms that offer partial "artificial" spin gravity and long central structures for docking larger spacecraft for cargo and personnel delivery.

Space Force Guard Ship or **SFG** are most closely related to battleships. They are well armored and well equipped with multiple weapons systems including centerline rail guns, missile tubes, and close-space-defense rapid-fire machine guns.

Space Force Shuttle or **SFS** are small shuttles used to transport crew and cargo between Earth's surface and into orbit. These are typically not named but are given a numerical identifier.

SFP Kennedy or **The Spin** is the pride and joy of the Northern Hemisphere Nation Space Force. At one point, it was the only space platform that has a strictly military mission.

SFG Catalyst or **The Catalyst** is the flagship guard ship for the NHN Space Force. This ship was in the middle of construction during the attacks on Earth. Following the attacks, the ship's mission and construction were modified to act also as a carrier for several AIMS squadrons instead of the typical single squadron. This ship can bring the fight to anyone, anywhere.

Battleship Ryceen is the flagship of the Razuuds. Its capabilities are unknown but seem to match closely with an SFG class ship.

SFG Redemption is the new flagship guard ship for the NHN Space Force. Built as a sister ship to the SFG Catalyst, it is the same size and has much of the same armament. However, following the events of conflict at Razuud, the SFG Redemption was upgraded even further to better handle the new threat.

Gracium is one of the main battleships of the Tartin fleet. With a size that matches a Space Force Guard ship, the devastating energy weapons and swarm of enemy fighters make it a formidable opponent.

Razuud is the home planet of the Razuuds and is located an unknown amount of light years away from Earth.

Rutaun is the capital city of Razuud and the crown jewel of the above-ground cities. The underground cities are even more impressive.

City Rache is a small Razuud city. It was created out of necessity due to overpopulation on the planet but is not a desirable travel or work destination. It's also on the opposite side of the planet as Rutaun.

Earth Light Gates are a collection of circular gates or tunnels that are used to accelerate outgoing ships to speeds much over the speed of light and receive incoming ships from light gates in the outer solar system to slow them down to relative speeds. They are located at strategic solar orbits or Lagrange Points within reach of Earth.

World Council Delegation Room is what it sounds like. All political happenings are discussed here, but instead of for the world, it is for the NHN.

Southern Hemisphere United Republic or the **SHUR** is the collection of countries and territories, primarily but not exclusively located in the southern hemisphere, that most benefited by the proximity to the newly discovered natural stores of rare Earth and exotic materials.

Northern Hemisphere Nation or the **NHN** is the collection of the countries and territories, primarily but not exclusively located in the northern hemisphere, that did not directly benefit from the discoveries of the natural rare Earth and exotic materials.

ABOUT THE AUTHOR

I grew up with a deep love for flying, space and space exploration. To nobody's surprise, I also had a hatred for reading and writing. While I pursued my love by consuming anything I could on the topic of flying and space, typically in the form of shows and video games, I eventually discovered science fiction books and was hooked. This love led to a Bachelor of Science degree in Aerospace Engineering, and later a Master of Science in Astronautical Engineering. My education was accompanied by a career in the Air Force where I was a developmental engineer on ground, air, and space projects. Following my time in the Air Force, I worked for several space companies working on advancing the human presence in space. With a mind for the technical as well as science fiction, I decided to finally try my hand at telling stories from my mind that merge the two in a fun, but believable way.

CONTACT ARCHER AT:

Website: Archergrantbooks.com
Email: archeragrant@gmail.com